Zach sent her a tired smile and crawled under the wagon to stretch out on his bedroll.

Alex crept in next to him, but he had already fallen asleep. Inexplicably happy, she propped herself on one elbow and watched him. She couldn't help it. He'd laid one arm over his eyes and didn't so much as twitch.

What are you doing, staring at a sleeping man?

Back in Chicago this would be purely scandalous! But out here in this rough, untamed land, no one was watching. And even if they were, she didn't care. She liked looking at Zach Strickland.

She released a long breath and was about to stretch out full length on her own bedroll when his voice stopped her.

"You can build up a powerful hunger in a man lookin' at him that way, Dusty."

Oh, my stars and little chickens, Zach was watching me!

Author Note

I have always admired women who struck out on their own, doing things that were important to them regardless of whether they were "usual" or even accepted by society. That was how we got Marie Curie, Florence Nightingale, George Eliot (Mary Anne Evans), Sojourner Truth, Eleanor Roosevelt, Rosa Parks, Amelia Earhart and many others.

Cattle drives in the Old West were all male. Except for this one.

MISS MURRAY ON THE CATTLE TRAIL

LYNNA BANNING

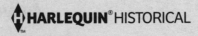

Recycling programs
for this product may
not exist in your area.

ISBN-13: 978-1-335-46767-6

Miss Murray on the Cattle Trail

Printed in U.S.A.

Lynna Banning combined a lifelong love of history and literature into a satisfying career as a writer. Born in Oregon, she graduated from Scripps College and embarked on a career as an editor and technical writer and later as a high school English teacher. She enjoys hearing from her readers. You may write to her directly at PO Box 324, Felton, CA 95018, USA, email her at carowoolston@att.net or visit Lynna's website at lynnabanning.net.

Books by Lynna Banning

Harlequin Historical

The Lone Sheriff
Wild West Christmas
"Christmas in Smoke River"
Dreaming of a Western Christmas
"His Christmas Belle"
Smoke River Family
Western Spring Weddings
"The City Girl and the Rancher"
Printer in Petticoats
Her Sheriff Bodyguard
Baby on the Oregon Trail
Western Christmas Brides
"Miss Christina's Christmas Wish"
The Hired Man
Miss Murray on the Cattle Trail
Marianne's Marriage of Convenience
Western Christmas Homecoming
"Christmas Day Wedding Bells"

Visit the Author Profile page
at Harlequin.com for more titles.

For my dear and admired friend Shirley Marcus.

Chapter One

Smoke River, Oregon, 1871

He knew something was wrong the minute he stepped up onto the front porch. For one thing, Charlie was rocking away in the lawn swing with a big grin on his lined face. And for another, Alice, the ranch owner's wife sitting beside him, wasn't.

"Been waitin' for ya," Charlie drawled.

"Yeah? Not late, am I?" Maybe that was why Alice's heart-shaped face looked so set, but Zach discarded that thought right away. When Alice Kingman was displeased about something, she didn't waste time looking dour; she bared her nails and lit right into your hide.

"All the hands are inside, Zach. And they're damn hungry," Charlie added.

Alice stopped the swing with her foot and rose in such a ladylike motion for a woman climbing up on her forties that it brought a chuckle to Zach's throat. Alice was pure female, and in her blue denim skirt and ruffly red-check blouse she looked good enough to eat.

Charlie slapped him on the back. "Come on, Zach. Consuelo's fried chicken is getting cold."

Alice disappeared through the screen door, and Charlie draped a heavy arm across Zach's shoulders. "Got somethin' I want to show ya."

All Zach's senses went on alert. The last time Charlie had had something to show him, Zach had limped for three days after the boss's new stud horse threw him.

"It's not a horse, is it?"

"Heck, no," Charlie spluttered. "Cain't invite a horse to Sunday dinner, can I?"

So it was a some*one*, not a some*thing* the boss was showing off. Some*ones* got invited to Sunday dinner at the ranch house, along with Zach and the Rocking K ranch hands.

In the dining room, Zach stood between slim, dark-skinned José and Roberto, an older, slightly overweight man with a salt-and-pepper mustache, and waited for Alice to seat herself. He eyed the vacant chair across from him. *Okay, boss, we're here. So where's the some-one?*

He heard the rustle of petticoats behind him and caught a whiff of something that smelled like lilacs. Oh, no, not Alice's Great-Aunt Hortense! Hell's bells, Roberto had put her on the train for San Francisco scarcely a month ago, and...

Zach swallowed hard and the other hands stiffened to attention, waiting for Aunt Hortense's entrance.

But it wasn't Aunt Hortense.

A young woman so pretty it made him swallow hard glided across the room and sat down next to Roberto's nephew, Juan. The young Mexican's blush turned the tips of his ears red.

Everyone dropped onto their chairs like boneless sandbags and Zach slid into his upholstered seat and waited. No one said a word. Finally, Alice signaled Consuelo and the meal got under way.

"Boys," Charlie announced, snagging a drumstick off the platter the cook offered, "say howdy to Miss Murray."

A rumble of respectful male voices rose. Then another long silence fell.

"Miss Murray is visiting from Chicago," Alice said, thin lipped. She split a biscuit with a stab of her knife.

"Welcome, Señorita Murray," Roberto offered. The older man had civilized manners; his nephew also knew what to do, but he was real young and not as polished as Roberto.

"Ees an honor, *señorita*," Juan said with an even deeper blush.

Miss Murray smiled across the table. "Why, thank you, gentlemen."

Charlie took over the introductions. "On your left is Juan Tapia, and to your right is Skip Billings. Across the table is José Moreno, Zach Strickland and Jase Snell. Zach's the trail boss for the cattle drive."

Miss Murray inclined her head. "Gentlemen," she said again.

Man, oh, man, her hair was something else, dark as blackstrap molasses and so soft-looking that Zach curled his fingers into fists.

What was Charlie's game here? He thought it over while platters of mashed potatoes and green beans were handed around the table. A prettier girl he hadn't seen in too many years to count, but Charlie knew Zach wasn't interested in romancing a female ever again, so what did Charlie want to show him?

Before Zach picked up his fork, Charlie dropped a hint.

"You boys still readin' those newspaper stories from back East?"

"Sure, boss," Jase volunteered. "Got 'em all pinned up on the bunkhouse wall."

"Can't hardly wait for the next one," Skip added. "Best da—uh, darn horse-racin' stories I ever read."

Zach drove his fork into the pile of mashed potatoes on his plate. So that was it. This Murray woman was somehow related to A. Davis Murray, the newspaper reporter whose stories the hands devoured each week. His daughter, maybe? Or…his gut tightened…his wife? Who was she, exactly? And what was she doing sitting all pink and white at Sunday dinner at the Rocking K ranch house?

The hands couldn't stop jabbering about A. Davis Murray's horse-racing stories, and Miss Whoever-She-Was Murray looked mighty interested. More than interested. She was hanging on every word and her eyes… Oh, those eyes. Blue as desert lupines. Anyway, they sparkled like they'd been polished.

Zach caught Charlie's eye and quirked one eyebrow.

"More chicken?" Charlie asked, his voice bland.

Zach shot a glance at Alice at the opposite end of the long walnut table and lowered his eyebrows into a frown. Alice looked madder than a wet cat, and that was a real puzzler. Alice never got mad about anything—not Skip's rough table manners or Consuelo's constant nattering about her dwindling supply of coffee beans, not even the time Charlie forgot her birthday.

But for darn sure she was mad today, and Zach figured it had something to do with pretty Miss Murray.

But Charlie always took his own sweet time about things, and this afternoon was no exception. Finally,

finally, the owner of the Rocking K swallowed his last bite of strawberry shortcake, groaned like a contented heifer and rapped on his coffee cup for attention.

"Well, boys, today I've got a surprise for you."

Jase's scraggly blond head came up. "Yeah?"

"What if I told you…" Charlie paused dramatically and Alice rolled her eyes "…that Miss Murray's first name is Alexandra."

"What if ya did, boss?" Jase said. "Fancy name, but it don't ring no bells for me." Jase's grammar stopped at the fourth grade.

"*Doesn't* ring *any* bells," Consuelo hissed as she circled with her coffeepot. "You set a bad example for my José."

José ducked his head.

"I mean," Charlie continued, "what if her name was Alexandra *Davis* Murray?"

"She is marry to the newspaper man?" Juan guessed.

Charlie gulped a swallow of coffee. "Nah. She *is* the newspaperman. Or, rather, newspaperwoman. This here lady is A. Davis Murray."

"Ees not possible," José protested.

Zach stared across the table at Miss Murray. Miss Alexandra Davis Murray. José was dead right, it wasn't possible. Just what kind of game was Charlie playing?

Miss Alexandra Murray sent Zach an apologetic smile. "It's true," she said. "I write newspaper articles for the *Chicago Times*."

Skip gaped at her. "*You* write about all them horse races?"

"I do." She looked around the table at each of the ranch hands in turn until she came to Alice, who was still tight-jawed. "Aunt Alice doesn't approve, obviously. But I like horse races. And I like writing about them."

"Jehoshaphat," Jase breathed.

"Madre mia," José muttered.

Zach wanted to laugh. The thought of this soft, ruffly female tramping around a horse stable made his lips twitch.

Then they were all talking at once. During the hub-bub, Charlie leaned forward and addressed Zach. "I want to talk to you," he intoned. "In private." He heaved his bulky frame out of the chair and led the way to his office across the hallway.

"Whiskey?" he asked when he'd shut the heavy oak door.

"No, thanks. Gotta ride out at first light."

Charlie pushed the cut-glass decanter across his desk toward him anyway. "I'd change my mind if I was you, Zach."

Without another word, he filled two glasses.

"Spit it out, Charlie, what's up?"

His boss touched his glass to Zach's and tossed back the contents. "Kinda hard to come right out and tell you, son."

Uh-oh. Charlie only called him "son" when bad news was coming. Zach swigged down half his whiskey. "Let's have it, Charlie. Like I said, I've got an early get-up tomorrow."

"Well, Zach, it's like this. It's true that Alexandra is a newspaper reporter."

"You already said that. Or somebody did. Anyway, I know that."

"Yeah, well. See, her newspaper, the *Chicago Times*, wants her to do a story about a cattle drive."

Zach slapped his empty glass onto the desk. "No."

"I understand how you feel, Zach, but you see the answer's gotta be yes."

"No, it doesn't."

Charlie just nodded. "Yeah, it does."

"Why?" Zach demanded. "Why does she pick this ranch? Tell her to choose another cattle drive."

"Can't."

"Why can't you?"

"Because." He refilled his glass. "Because not only is Alexandra a newspaper reporter, she is, uh, as you've no doubt realized, my niece. Her mama is Alice's sister."

Zach said nothing for a long minute. "So?" he inquired at last.

"So," Charlie said, "she wants to—"

"No," Zach repeated.

Charlie reached for the whiskey decanter. "You want to keep your job, don'tcha, son?"

Damn, he hated to be threatened, especially by the man who had his financial ass under his boot heel. Zach sighed and refilled his glass.

"Well, hell, Charlie, can she ride?"

Chapter Two

Aunt Alice settled on the edge of Alex's bed. Her aunt hadn't lit the lamp, but the moonlight streaming through the multipaned window illuminated her usually serene face, which at this moment looked pinched.

"Alex, you simply cannot go through with this. Surely you—"

"Stop!" Slowly Alex pushed up on one elbow. "Aunt Alice, you don't understand. My newspaper editor came up with the idea. He is very insistent."

"But a cattle drive! Women just don't go on cattle drives."

"I know. It's a far cry from my stories on horse racing. It's a far cry from anything I thought I'd ever, ever do. But my editor pays my salary, and he is adamant."

"Oh, Alex, why?"

"Back East people are mad for stories about the wild, untamed West."

"I feel responsible for you," her aunt said. "And a cattle drive is dangerous."

"I don't have a choice, Aunt."

Alice snorted. "Of course you have a choice. Just tell your editor no."

"I can't. If I refuse, he'll fire me, and I've worked too hard to risk losing my job. Eight long, grinding years I've spent working my way up from the proofreading desk to being a top reporter. I'm the only woman on the entire staff, and I won't give it up. I can't."

Alex bit her lip and smoothed a crease in the top sheet over and over. *Why,* why *did her job depend on the harebrained idea of a newspaper editor who'd never traveled west of his favorite restaurant?*

Alice sighed. "Your mother would never allow this."

Alex flung back the sheet and sat up. "Aunt Alice, my mother is dead."

"Yes," Alice said quietly. "I know. And you're just like her. Bright. Beautiful. And..." her voice tightened "...bullheaded."

Alex slid her arms about her aunt's rigid form. "Mama always said *you* were the bullheaded one."

"Don't change the subject," Alice snapped.

"Aunt Alice, you can't stop me. You can't keep me from holding on to my career as a newspaper reporter."

"Oh, I know, honey. I just wish you'd—"

"Settle down and get married," Alex finished. "That's what Mama always wanted, too. But I'm twenty-six. On the shelf."

Alice shook her head and blew out a sigh. "You will be careful, won't you? At least *try* to?"

"Of course I will. Uncle Charlie says Zach Strickland's the best trail boss in three states. I'll be in good hands."

Her aunt let out a long sigh and said nothing.

Zach stuffed his thumbs in his front pockets and watched Miss Newspaper Reporter trip down the porch steps ready to go cattle driving. She looked so bright and shiny it made his head hurt. And, Lord love little chickens, what her butt did to a pair of jeans was indecent.

"Good morning!" she sang.

"Mornin'," he growled. "Got a lot of miles to cover today. Sure hope you can ride."

"Why, certainly I can ride." She rested her hands on her shiny new belt buckle.

"Yeah? Where've you ridden?"

"In the city park," she said, her voice frosty. "On the bridle path."

Zach resisted a snort, looked her up and down and unhooked his thumbs. "Those your ridin' boots?"

She glanced down at the stylish, neatly laced leather boots. "Yes. What's wrong with them? I bought them in Chicago and—"

"They won't work."

She propped her hands on her hips and peered more closely at her feet. "Well, if it's not too much trouble, Mister Knows Everything, would you mind telling me what's wrong with them?"

He spit off to one side. "You won't last half an hour in those fancy city leathers. Brand new and probably too tight. Go ask Alice for a pair of her old riding boots."

For a moment, Miss Newspaper Reporter looked like she was going to argue, but he stared her down. Finally, she pivoted, stomped back up the porch steps and slammed through the front door.

Hell's bells, she was a greenhorn. A ladyfied greenhorn, and one with a mouth on her. Charlie had just used up his last favor.

When Miss Fancy-Pants reappeared, she wore a pair of Alice's well-worn riding boots and a sour look. Zach expelled a long breath and tipped his head toward the corral.

"Saddle up."

"Oh, yes, sir, Mister Trail Boss."

His jaw tightened. *Gonna be a damn long day.*

Alex snapped open her leather-bound notebook and jotted half a line before the chuck wagon rolled into position at the head of the muddle of cows and horses and riders. Her horse jolted forward. She stuffed her pencil in her shirt pocket and grabbed the reins, but the horse danced a few paces to the left before it settled down. She'd never before ridden anything but old, gentle, city-trained mares, and this horse was neither old nor gentle. Or a mare, she'd been told. In fact, she'd never been this close to a horse that had been…well, gelded.

At least forty horses milled around in a whinnying clump, and she counted seven, no, eight scruffy-looking cowboys, not including the horse wrangler and His Highness the Trail Boss.

And hundreds and hundreds of cows. Steers, Uncle Charlie said. Surely they couldn't *all* be steers, because some of them had calves tagging along behind.

She flexed her toes in Aunt Alice's boots. Her aunt had said they were well broken in, but they still felt awfully tight. She was glad she was riding and not walking the four hundred miles that stretched ahead of her.

The chuck wagon, a bulky-looking top-heavy box on wheels, rattled and clanked its way on ahead of the roiling mass of animals and men on horseback. She watched Roberto, the driver, stash his whip under the bench, put two fingers to his lips and give a sharp whistle. Right away she decided she liked the white-haired old man. The wagon lumbered off down the trail, drawn by two horses.

Bellowing cattle, yipping men on horseback and the thunder of horses' hooves added to the hubbub. It was deafening. She clapped both hands over her ears and lost control of her mount. A rider swung in close, grabbed her reins and settled the horse. Juan, Roberto's soft-spoken nephew. He laid the leather straps in her gloved hand, touched his hat brim and reined his horse away.

Dust rose in thick clouds. She had just kneed her horse off to one side when Juan dropped back and shouted something. She couldn't hear over the noise, so she tried to read his lips. *"Señorita."* He mouthed something else, but she had no idea what it was.

She shook her head. He pointed at the bandanna covering his mouth and nose. Oh! Of course. But she didn't *have* a bandanna. Oh, well. She smiled at Juan, lifted her chin, and spurred her mount forward.

She was on her way!

It was all fascinating. So this was how people in places like Philadelphia and New York got their meat, a thousand bawling cows lumbering after one old seasoned bull called a "bell steer" because of the clanging bell hung around its neck. They would all end in some rough, dirty railroad town in Nevada with the Indian-sounding name of Winnemucca, where the cowboys would load them up in cattle cars that would end up two thousand miles farther east in slaughterhouses in Chicago.

Just imagine! Right before her eyes were thousands and thousands of thick juicy steaks on the hoof. People back East would be avid for these sights and sounds.

She patted the notepad and pencil in her breast pocket. She knew her readers would gobble up each delicious detail of this adventure.

They were three hours out, and whenever he could manage it, Zach pried his eyes off the herd and glanced back at Miss Murray. She lagged way behind, a good forty yards in back of Skip, who was riding drag, and she was fighting through thick clouds of dust. She'd pulled her wide-brimmed black hat down so far it almost covered her ears, but hell, she couldn't see what was three feet ahead of her.

He winced in spite of himself. Anybody joining a drive for the first time always rode drag behind the herd, the dustiest position there was. She wasn't complaining. Yet. He knew she must be hot and more miserable than she'd ever been in her pampered little life, and a small part of him felt just a tad sorry for her. An even larger part was making bets on how long she'd last before she'd turn tail for the Rocking K and a hot bath.

Maybe he should... Nah. Let her suffer. Teach her a lesson.

Juan trotted up on his sorrel and signaled that he wanted to talk.

"What's up?" Zach yelled over the lowing steers.

"The *señorita*, she has no..." he swept a thumb and forefinger across his face *"...Panuelo."*

Zach nodded, and the slim kid galloped off. So she'd forgotten her bandanna, had she? Where'd she think she was goin', to a party?

"C'mon, Dancer. Let's go." He loped up to the point riders, and when Curly and the new hand, Cassidy, gave him a thumbs-up, he dropped back to the drag position. The air was so thick he could almost chew it.

Skip rode with his chin tucked into his chest, and when Zach fell in beside him, the lanky cowhand didn't look up.

"Go change with Curly," Zach shouted. Skip touched two fingers to his hat and thundered off to the head of the herd. In a few minutes, Curly appeared to ride drag.

"Thanks, boss," he yelled. "Gettin' bored up front."

Zach laughed. Nothing much got the tubby, blond cowhand down, not even riding drag on a scorching, windless day. Even the cottonwood trees were drooping.

He peered ahead to locate Miss Murray. Crazy name, Alexandra. Like some English queen or something. Yep, there she was, off to the side, trailing the swing riders, Juan and Jase, and losing ground.

She wasn't moving fast enough to keep up, he noted. Pretty soon she'd be eating even more dust back here with Curly, and then she'd drop farther and farther behind, and that would slow down the entire outfit. He clenched his jaw and spurred forward.

Chapter Three

Alex scrunched her eyes shut and prayed the horse would keep moving forward alongside the herd even if she wasn't looking. After a minute she cracked open one eyelid. Puffy white clouds floated in the unbelievably blue sky over her head—faces, fantastical cats, even castles—and in the distance rose snow-capped mountains. Oh, how cool they looked!

Her mouth was crunchy with grit and dust, and she could scarcely draw the filthy air in through her nostrils. Tears streamed down her cheeks. She closed her eyes again.

Aunt Alice had been right. It had taken her only half a day on horseback to realize that a girl raised in the city should never, never, *never* go on a cattle drive. She had never been so tired, so filthy, so miserable in her entire life. *And this is only the first day.*

A glimmer of understanding about her mother penetrated her roiling thoughts. Mama had always refused to go outdoors unless it was to tea at the Savoy Hotel. Her mother liked to be warm and clean and dressed in the latest fashion, and she had always arranged her life for

the maximum comfort with a minimum effort. Maybe
Mama had known something Alex didn't.

Something jostled her, and she snapped her lids open.
Zach Strickland's black horse was beside her mount.
He tipped his head to indicate she should pull off to
the side, then reined in and reached over to grasp her
horse's bridle.

She ran her tongue over her gritty teeth and opened
her mouth. "Is something wrong?"

"Maybe." He gave her a look and quickly glanced
away, then poured water from his canteen over a blue
bandanna and pressed it into her hand. "Tie this over
your nose and mouth. Keeps out the dust." He kicked
his horse and trotted off.

"Thank you," she called after him, but he gave no sign
he'd heard. Hurriedly, she tied on the wet bandanna and
drew in a mercifully grit-free breath. *Oh, no.* He would
surely have noticed her tear-streaked face. Darn him!
She hated it when she appeared weak and wishy-washy.

Like her mother.

With a groan she snatched up the reins and urged her
mount forward. She hated Zach Strickland. Anyone who
would revel in her distress was no gentleman.

But he wasn't reveling. Actually, he had done her a
kindness. It was a civilized gesture, she acknowledged.
Well, she'd thanked him, hadn't she? That was all the
good manners she could summon up on this awful,
scorching afternoon.

Oh, Aunt Alice, what have I done?

How many more hours were there before she could
climb down off this animal and rest her aching thighs?
And her bottom. She squinted up at the sun. Almost
straight overhead, which must mean it was nearly noon.

Did that mean lunch? She could endure anything if there was a meal at the end. She kicked her heels into the horse's flanks and jolted forward over an expanse of tiny purple flowers.

But lunchtime came and went, and still the cowhands prodded the bellowing animals forward. She had long since gulped down the last of the lukewarm contents of her canteen, and her growling stomach didn't let her forget for a single sunbaked minute that she was hungry. Desperately so. Right now she'd eat anything, a handful of cracker crumbs, a morsel of desiccated cheese, even a mouthful of the soft leather glove gripping her reins.

This was misery, all right. Aunt Alice hadn't varnished the truth one bit. She thought longingly of the wide, shaded front porch at the Rocking K ranch house, then determinedly shook her thoughts back to reality. There must be shade ahead somewhere; tall trees with blue-green needles bordered their route, and underneath them she glimpsed a mossy green carpet and some sort of green, grassy plant no more than six inches high.

But there was no shade out here. Apparently there was to be no noon meal, either. She bit her lip. The bandanna helped some, but underneath it the hot air felt as if it were suffocating her. At least it kept out the gnats swarming around her head.

Then out of the dust emerged a sweat-streaked sorrel, and Juan, the young boy, was smiling at her.

He reined in close and thrust a hard biscuit into her hand. "Eat!"

"Thank you!" Oh, no, that was wrong, he was Mexican, wasn't he? *"Gracias!"*

He flashed her a grin and galloped off through the

dust. Why hadn't she thought to bring a biscuit, or an apple, or *something*?

Her aunt had suggested packing a clean shirt and an extra pair of underdrawers in the drawstring canvas bag rolled up behind her saddle. She couldn't blame her for forgetting to mention biscuits.

They didn't stop until late afternoon, and by then Alex's throat was so parched she couldn't even spit. Ahead of her stretched lush green grass and a stand of leafy willow trees and…surely she was beginning to hallucinate…the chuck wagon, parked next to a burbling stream.

She blinked hard. She must be dreaming.

She edged her mount close to the rear wagon wheel and dismounted. The instant her boots touched the ground her knees buckled. She grabbed the saddle and hung on.

"Señorita," Roberto said at her shoulder. "You must put horse in corral, not dismount next to cook wagon."

She groaned. "I can't let go, Roberto. I can't walk."

Carefully he pried her fingers off the saddle, grasped her around the waist and settled her on the ground with her back propped against the wheel. "Cherry!" he shouted to the wrangler. "Come get the *señorita's* horse."

Alex leaned forward and dropped her aching head onto her bent knees. Footsteps approached, and the next minute her saddle plopped down beside her and she heard the horse's hooves clop away.

"Thank you!" she called after whoever had taken her mount.

"Ride too long today," Roberto observed. She nodded, her forehead pressed against her jeans.

"Be plenty sore *mañana*. I go get boss."

"No!" She jerked her head up. "Don't get him." She didn't want to appear weak in front of Mister I-Told-You-So Strickland.

Roberto stood surveying her, his hands propped at his waist. A stained homespun apron covered his bulky form. "I think yes, *señorita*. You hurt much, no?"

She sighed. "Yes, Roberto. Much. Very much."

"Ay de mi," the old man murmured. He moved away and Alex concentrated on straightening one leg, then the other. She tried three times before she gave up.

Then Trail Boss Zach Strickland was standing before her, his long legs spread wide and a stony hardness in his green eyes that made her shudder. He was not smiling. "Sore, huh?"

She clamped her teeth together and nodded.

"Not surprised," he said. "We covered ten miles today."

"Ten miles!" *Ten whole miles?* In her entire life she hadn't ridden more than two miles, and that was along a shaded bridle path.

"Do you always ride this many miles in a single day?"

He shook his head, the dark hair streaked with gray dust. "Nope. Usually ride twelve to fifteen miles each day, but today bein' our first day out, the cattle need some trail learning. And you, bein' a tenderfoot, need some trail learning, too. We'll ride more miles tomorrow."

"Where did all these cows come from? Surely Uncle Charlie's ranch is not big enough for—"

"Huh! Charlie's ranch is plenty big, plus we picked up some steers from neighboring ranches." He leaned forward. "Don't call 'm 'cows' on a trail drive unless you wanna get laughed at." He shot her a hard look. "But as for where they came from, Miss City Girl, cows come from other cows. And a bull, of course."

"I see." How could she ever explain about cows and bulls in a city newspaper?

"Got any more dumb questions, Dusty?"

Dusty? She must look a frightful mess for him to call her that. She wiped her sweaty, gritty hands on her shirtfront. "No, no more questions. But…but I, um, I find that I…I cannot walk," she confessed.

"Not surprised," he said again. "Well, let's get it done." He reached down, grasped her under the arms and heaved her to her feet.

"Ouch-ouch-*ouch*!"

"Yeah," he said, his voice dry. "Come on." He swung her aching body up into his arms and strode away from the chuck wagon and past the roped-off horse corral. When he came to the stream, he paced up and down the bank and suddenly halted, stepped forward and dropped her, bottom first, into the cold water.

"What are you doing?" she screeched. She tried to scramble to the bank, but he laid one hand on her shoulder and pressed down. "Stay there," he ordered. "Cold water will help. I'll be back in thirty minutes."

She had no choice. She could barely move.

Chapter Four

Zach tramped away from the stream where he'd dumped Miss Murray, or Dusty, as he now thought of her, and halted at the chuck wagon. "Save her some supper, Roberto."

"*Si*, boss. But she will not be much hungry."

"She'll eat." He left the aging cook chuckling over his pot of beans and settled himself at the campfire next to Juan.

The young man leaned toward him. "The *señorita*, she is okay?"

"She is okay, yes. Mad, but okay."

"*Madre mia*. She will not be smile tomorrow."

"Not much," Zach agreed. Maybe not at all. He kinda felt sorry for her, but kinda *not* sorry at the same time. Damn Charlie for insisting she come along on this drive. It was no place for a woman. A fancy-assed, citified, back-East newspaper reporter woman was about as welcome as a swarm of locusts.

The clang of a steel triangle announced supper, and the hands around the campfire stampeded to the chuck wagon and lined up with tin plates in their hands. Roberto slapped thick slices of beef onto them, ladled on beans and topped the pile with his special warm tortillas.

Zach brought up the rear of the line, ate leisurely and mentally calculated when Dusty's half hour would be up.

"Hey, boss," someone called. "Where's our newspaper lady?"

Zach laid down his fork and shoved to his feet. "Comin' right up."

Footsteps crunched over the sandy stream bank, and Alex clenched her fists as tall, rangy Zach Strickland came toward her.

"I want you to get me out of here!" she sputtered. "Right now!"

"Yes, ma'am!" He splashed into the water, grabbed her shoulders and jerked her upright.

"Ow! Ow, that hurts!"

"Roberto's got some liniment in one of his secret cubbyholes. Might help some."

"Oh, yes, please."

He swung her upright and half dragged, half walked her onto dry ground. "Not so fast," she pleaded.

He propped her against a thick pine trunk and stood surveying her. "Look, Dusty, you shouldn't be out here with us. A cattle drive is rough, even on a seasoned cowhand. For a greenhorn it's suicidal."

She said nothing, just stared at the trail boss she was coming to detest. He had overlong black hair that brushed the tips of his ears and eyes the color of moss. Right now they were narrowed at her.

"Tomorrow you're going back to the Rocking K," he announced. "I'll send Curly with you, and he can catch up with us before we hit the river. Right now, though, supper's on, and you don't want to miss Roberto's beans and tortillas."

"No," she said.

His dark eyebrows went up. "No, what?"

"I'm not going back." She tried to shove away from the tree trunk, but her legs still felt like jelly.

He propped his hands on his hips. "In case you forgot, Miss Murray, I'm the trail boss on this drive. You do what I say."

"No," she repeated. "I don't work for you, Mister Trail Boss. I work for the *Chicago Times*. And that's who I take orders from."

"Nope, don't work that way, Dusty. On the trail you take orders from me."

She raised her chin. "When we're 'on the trail,' I will take orders from you, but that does not include sending me back to the ranch. That is tantamount to firing me, and as I said, I don't work for you."

He stared at her for a long moment with those unnerving gray-green eyes. "I don't fancy nursemaiding you, whining and stumbling over your boots, for the next four hundred miles. Cattle driving is a tough business. You're gonna get river mud up your nose and grasshoppers in your hair. By tomorrow night, you'll have spent another ten or twelve hours in the saddle and we'll just see what tunc you're playin' then."

"Are you a betting man, Mr. Strickland?" She put as much frost in her voice as she could manage. "I will wager you one silver dollar I will be playing my own tune. And that means I will be riding on to Winnemucca with the rest of you."

Zach rolled his eyes. "I never bet with a fool, Dusty, but in your case I'm makin' an exception."

He walked her back to camp and sat her down at the campfire. Roberto brought her a tin plate and a fork and settled it on her lap, then balanced a mug of coffee on a flat rock beside her. "There ees whiskey, *señorita*," he whispered. "You wish?"

"No, thank you, Roberto. I do not drink spirits."

"Long night tonight," he murmured. "Long day *mañana*."

She shook her head. "I will manage." *Somehow.*

Zach looked up. "Roberto, after supper, give her some of that liniment you squirrel away."

"*Si*. Good idea."

"Hey, Miss Murray?" Jase called from across the smoldering fire pit. "You gonna write about us?" Jase was the one with the unruly blond hair. She wondered if he got grasshoppers in it.

"Why, yes, I am."

"Whoo-eee," he exulted. "You hear that, boys? We're gonna be in the newspaper. We're gonna be famous!"

Curly sat bolt upright. "Yeah? How famous?"

Alex studied the rapt faces around the fire. "Well…" She paused for dramatic effect and sneaked a look at Zach Strickland's unreadable countenance. "More than twenty thousand people read the *Chicago Times* every day."

"No funnin'?" Curly asked.

"No funning," Alex assured him. "And I will want to interview each one of you for my articles."

She could scarcely hear herself think over the cheers. Yes, she would most certainly write about them. And she'd also write about the body-breaking punishment of a trail drive. That is, she would if she could get her tortured body over to the chuck wagon to retrieve her notebook and pencil.

She groaned and stared at the plate of cold beans in her lap. She would last until she rode down the streets of Winnemucca with all those cows or she would die trying.

Zach kicked a hot coal back into the fire pit and surveyed the camp. Roberto had long since splashed water on the canvas-wrapped carcass of the calf he'd slaughtered and hung on a hook in the chuck wagon, washed up the supper plates and crawled under the wagon to sleep. All but two of the cowhands had rolled out their bedrolls. Curly and Cassidy, the new man, were nightherding, riding around and around the steers bedded down in the meadow, moving in opposite directions and singing songs to keep them calm. The kind of songs a mother would sing.

He'd always liked night-herding. It gave him a chance to talk to Dancer, reflect on the day's events and plan for tomorrow's, at least as much as anyone driving a thousand head of prime beef *could* plan. Usually, whatever could go wrong, did.

In spite of all the problems, Zach liked this life. When he'd come West as a boy, right away he'd liked the freewheeling, easy existence of a cowboy, and later, when he'd risen to be Charlie Kingman's top hand, he liked the admiration working for the Rocking K brought him. He liked being in charge, doing his job and doing it well. *I'm responsible only to myself, my cattle and my ranch hands.*

A successful drive brought him the gratitude and respect of people he cared about, Charlie and Alice Kingman. And this drive would bring him something else, something he'd dreamed about ever since he was a scrawny kid with no home; it would bring him enough money to buy a spread of his own and start his own ranch.

He sucked in a lungful of sagebrush-scented air and surveyed the camp. Dusty sat as close to the chuck wagon as she could get without nuzzling right up to Roberto. He guessed Dusty didn't trust his cowhands. Zach did, though. Had to, on a long drive like this.

After supper he'd watched her limp off behind the chuck wagon with the bottle of Roberto's liniment clutched in her hand. When she returned, her gait had evened out some and she was walking easier, at least easier enough to let her climb back on her horse tomorrow. He knew she'd be sleeping in wet jeans; by morning they'd still be pretty clammy. That ought to hurry things up a bit for her deciding she ought to hightail it back to the Rocking K.

He'd sure hate to take that silver dollar off her, but he guessed that by tomorrow she'd yell uncle and turn back, and then he'd be a buck richer.

Alex huddled by the campfire, sipping from a mug of coffee Roberto kept refilling from the blackened metal coffeepot and staring into the flames. *What have I gotten myself into?* She could never, never admit it to Mister Know-It-All Strickland, but she was starting to feel just the tiniest bit uneasy. The night was so *dark* out here in the middle of nowhere.

All around the fire pit were sprawled-out cowboys shrouded in their blankets—a lump here, and one over there, and there. They lay without moving, probably too tired to even twitch.

The trail boss was tramping around out there in the dark somewhere, and while she could hear him, she couldn't see anything beyond the circle of dying firelight where she sat.

She pulled out her notebook and began writing.

First she described the camp and the dwindling campfire, the dark shapes of the sleeping cowhands, even how the camp smelled after their supper of tortillas and beans. But she did not write about how frightened she felt at the huge expanse of black, black sky overhead. Or the stinging mosquitos. Or her aching muscles.

Finally she admitted she was exhausted and she needed to sleep. She tiptoed to the chuck wagon, scrabbled around in the back and pulled out her roll of blankets. Just one other unclaimed bedroll remained. Roberto had long since crawled under the wagon to sleep, so this one had to belong to Zach Strickland.

She stood uncertainly near the remains of the campfire, wondering where to spread out her blankets. It would be most improper to curl up next to one of the cowhands, even one who was sound asleep, but out beyond the haphazard sprinkling of bedrolls it was pitch black. Wild animals could be lurking out there. Wolves, even.

Or... She caught her breath. Even wild Indians.

She crept forward to an unoccupied space and spread out her blue wool blanket. The other, a forest green one Aunt Alice said wouldn't show the dirt, she wrapped around her body. Then she lay down on the hard ground and pulled the edges of the blue blanket over herself.

She couldn't close her eyes for a long time, and when she did they popped open at the slightest sound. Never in her life had she realized nighttime could be so noisy!

She listened to the faint hoofbeats of the horses ridden by the two night-herders Mr. Strickland had assigned.

One of them was singing something; she couldn't identify the song, but it was soothing. Which was no doubt
what that herd of cows out there somewhere was feeling. *She*, however, was feeling anything but soothed.

Something made a *whoohing* sound off in the dark.
An owl. She hoped. Indians made wolf calls, didn't they?
Not owl calls. At least that's what she'd read once in a
dime novel she'd found in Uncle Charlie's bookcase.

Something rustled out beyond the fire pit. *Oh, mercy!
What was that?* A… What did they call them? A moun-
tain lion? She tugged her blankets more securely around
her.

Suddenly she became aware of another sound, a
crunching noise. She lay still, listening. Footsteps, that
was it! They came closer, and then she was startled by
a low voice at her back.

"Dusty?"

"Y-yes?"

"Everything all right?"

"N-no. I mean, yes. Everything is just fine."

She heard him chuckle. "I mean, did Roberto's liniment help your sore backsi—your sore muscles?"

"Of course," she answered.

"Good. Just checking whether you're ready to throw
in the towel tomorrow and hightail it back to a hot bath
and a soft bed."

She refused to dignify that remark with an acknowledgment of any kind. Instead, she wrapped her blankets more securely around her and purposefully closed
her eyes.

Before the sun rose the next morning, the hands were
lined up at the chuck wagon for Roberto's thick-sliced

bacon, fried potatoes and sourdough biscuits. Zach studied them as they lounged bleary-eyed around the campfire, warming their behinds and shoveling in their breakfasts. All nine men and one stubborn woman.

He watched Dusty more closely than anyone else. She'd tamed her long, wavy hair into one thick, glossy-looking braid that hung down her back and swung enticingly when she moved. She was wearing a form-fitting blue plaid shirt that hinted at lush breasts beneath the light cotton material, and he swallowed hard.

Didn't help. After her half hour in the stream yesterday, her jeans had shrunk so tight across her butt that watching her move made his mouth go dry.

He couldn't help wondering all kinds of things about her. What made her tick? What made a woman who looked the way she did, all soft and desirable, want to pal around with a hardened bunch of cowboys instead of staying home with a husband and a dozen children? What made Dusty prickly as a desert cactus with a spine stiff as a railroad tie?

She tucked into her fried spuds, crunched up the bacon slices like a hungry kid and carefully slipped two of Roberto's float-off-your-plate biscuits into her shirt pocket. He tried not to smile. Looked like she'd learned something yesterday.

He tossed the dregs of his coffee into the fire and stood up. "Time to roll."

Twenty minutes later, the chuck wagon lumbered off after Wally, the scout, to set up ten or fifteen miles farther on, somewhere with good grass and enough water for the herd. His wrangler, Cherry, followed with the rest of the horses in the remuda, and the two point men, José and Skip, uncovered the bell clapper on the lead steer and set off. A muddle of lowing animals thundered after the clanging bell.

Zach let out a satisfied breath and studied the pinkening sky over the mountains in the distance. God, he loved chasing steers across pretty country with the sunlight coming up and glinting off their horns.

He spurred forward and began calling out orders. "Curly, Juan, cover the flanks. Cassidy, you ride drag."

He guessed stubborn, determined Miss Dusty Murray would tag along somewhere, at least until suppertime. Then he'd pry her off her horse, drop her into another cold stream, collect his silver dollar and send her back to the Rocking K. Kinda made him chuckle.

He had to admit he just plain didn't trust a woman that pretty. Or that sassy. He set his eyes on the trail ahead and kicked his horse into a trot.

A cattle drive, Alex acknowledged as she guided her mount beside the mass of mooing cows, had to be one of the strangest endeavors ever conceived by modern man. No one would believe most of the things that went on, so her task as a newspaper reporter was easy: write about everything and make it interesting.

Today, for instance, she noticed strange little brown birds no bigger than sparrows that rode along on the backs of the steers, pecking insects off their hides. The sparrows weren't the least intimidated by the lumbering animals beneath them, and the steers didn't seem to mind. In a way, it was sort of like Zach Strickland and herself; she survived the best way she could, and Zach paid no attention.

This morning she'd gotten another taste of the strange habits of cowboys on a trail drive. Roberto rose before the moon had set and began to rattle around in the chuck wagon, cutting out biscuit rounds and frying bacon. Before the sun was up, the cowhands dragged themselves out of their bedrolls.

All except the scout, Wally Mortenson. Wally was an older man with laugh lines etched deep in his tanned face, and of all things, he woke up singing. Sometimes it was a hymn; sometimes it was a song so bawdy her ears burned. "Oh, my sweethcart's not true like she should be," he bellowed. "At night she lies close and she—"

His voice would break off and he would swear at whoever had kicked him into silence and start again.

The day started off well. Alex was riding a roan gelding that seemed to like her, his gait was gentle enough that her sore behind didn't hurt too much, and the weather was clear and sunny. She rode for an hour, getting used to the dust clouds and the gnats and the heat, and then spurred her horse to join Juan and Curly, who were riding in the flank position.

All of a sudden the sun that had been blazing down on her only moments before slid behind a cloud. For a brief moment she welcomed the suddenly cooler air, and she lifted her face to the breeze and let it wash over her perspiration-soaked shirt. But when she raked off her wide-brimmed black hat, she felt droplets of water dampen her hair.

"Miss Alex!" Curly pointed to the sky. "Rainstorm."

Very quickly it grew darker and wetter, and then thunder began to rumble overhead. Oh, heavens, a thundershower! She looked around for some shelter, but other than an occasional stand of spindly cottonwood trees, there was nothing to shield her from the rain, and it was now coming down in sheets.

Alex clapped her hat back on, snugged it down and tried to see through the mist enveloping them. The herd kept plodding forward, with Curly and Juan keeping pace with the animals. Good heavens, would they just keep going?

Yes, they would.

She tried to keep up. After another rain-soaked mile, large patches of boggy grass slowed her progress even more, and then there were big, wide puddles and stretches of mud-slicked ground that splattered when she rode over them.

Rain slashed at her face. Her thoroughly wet shirt stuck to her body as if glued on; her jeans felt cold as water soaked through the denim to her thighs. Despite the rain, she worked hard to keep up with Juan and Curly, who were still racing after straggling cows and whooping it up, as they always did.

She was thoroughly miserable, wet and cold, her clothes sodden and her hat dripping water onto her jeans. She had never felt so cold and clammy, so disheveled or so disheartened.

They rode on, pushing the herd along, for another hour, and then, as suddenly as it had started, the rain stopped and the sun burst through a cloud. Curly and Juan kept the herd moving as the puddles began to dry up, and her wet shirt and jeans began to steam in the sunshine. Now she felt *hot* and clammy.

By dusk, the moving mass of cows and riders slowed and finally dribbled to a stop near the chuck wagon. The tired cowhands drove the herd to a broad green meadow and bedded them down for the night.

Alex rode straight for the rope corral where the wrangler, Cherry, had gathered the remuda. She left her roan in his care and made a beeline for the chuck wagon. Her boots squished. All she wanted to do was peel off her sticky garments and put on dry clothes.

But Roberto had an iron Dutch oven bubbling over a blazing fire and he clanged his spoon around and around in an iron triangle to announce that supper was ready. One by one, the hands straggled in, dismounted and handed their reins to the wrangler. Then they stumbled tiredly toward the fire and the tin plates the cook was loading up with beef stew and hot biscuits.

She had lived through her first thunderstorm on the trail, and she wanted to record the details right away, while they were still fresh in her mind. Her notebook was damp, but the words were still legible. She nibbled on her pencil and started to write.

"Ain'tcha gonna eat supper, Miss Alex?" Curly inquired.

"Yeah," Skip echoed. "Good thing we had that thunderstorm today, huh?"

"You crazy?" Curly snapped. "Wet is wet and miserable, and steers don't need washin'."

"Aw, wise up, Curly. The boss couldn't send Miss Alex back to the Rocking K during a thunderstorm. That's good, ain't it?"

Oh, yes, Alex thought. This rainstorm had come at a most fortuitous time. Being wet and miserable for a few hours was a small price to pay for continuing on this adventure.

Suddenly she found she was ravenously hungry.

After another bone-crunching day, Alex spied the chuck wagon pulled up in a grassy meadow overlooking a river. She was half dead with exhaustion and so hungry her stomach hurt, and she felt hot and grubby and short-tempered. She sent a longing glance at the serene blue-green river behind the wagon and immediately started to plan how she could indulge in a private, cooling bath with nine cowboys and a cook in the vicinity.

She'd think of something, anything, that would allow her to sponge away the sweat and the faint smell of Roberto's liniment that still clung to her skin. She might not be a seasoned trail rider, but she was not without wiles. Her chance came after supper that evening when the hands were gathered around the fire.

"Gentlemen," she began. "I have a proposition for you."

Jase jerked upright, knocking over his mug of coffee. "Uh, what kind of proposition?"

"Not the kind you're thinkin'," Zach snapped. "Mind your manners, boys."

Aha, she had certainly captured *someone's* attention. "Very well," she said in her best businesslike manner, "I will explain. In exchange for one hour of privacy, *complete* privacy, I will conduct my first interview with one of you for my newspaper column."

"Which one of us?" Jase asked.

"You gentlemen will decide which one it will be," she answered. "You will draw straws. The short straw wins."

"Quick, Cherry," Jase said. "Go get us some sticks!"

"Yeah," Skip echoed. "Short ones."

Alex turned her gaze on Zach, who was sitting across the fire pit from her. "Mr. Strickland, may I rely on you to supervise the drawing?"

"Maybe."

She blinked. "*Maybe?* You do want it to be fair and square, do you not?"

"Sure." He sent her a long look. "For a price."

"Oh." Her heartbeat faltered. "What price would you ask?"

"I don't want to be included in your drawing. Don't want you writin' about me."

"You don't want to be interviewed? I cannot write a story if I have no, um, factual information."

"I said I don't want to be interviewed," he repeated, his voice sharp. "That's my price. Take it or leave it."

She blinked again. What on earth ailed this man? Did he not want—oh, of course. He did not want her to write any newspaper stories at all. He wanted, he *planned*, to send her back to the Rocking K. Well, she would show him.

"Very well, I accept your condition." She suppressed a grin of triumph. "On one condition of my own."

One dark eyebrow went up. "Yeah? What condition?"

"Yeah," came a chorus of male voices. "What condition?"

"That I am granted my hour of privacy *first*, before you all draw your straws. All except Mr. Strickland, that is." She waited half a heartbeat. "And…" she caught a glimmer of something in Zach's eyes "…that Mr. Strickland is the one who stands guard while I am, um, being private."

"Fair enough," Jase said. "Whaddya say, boss?"

He didn't answer for so long Alex thought he hadn't heard her proposal.

"Boss?" Jase prompted.

"Mr. Strickland?" she said, her voice as sweet as she could make it. "What is your decision?"

He stood and tossed the rest of his coffee into the fire. "Come on, Miss Murray. Let's get your 'privacy' over with so the hands can draw their straws and turn in. Night's half over."

She shot to her feet. "Cherry, please gather your sticks. I will return in one hour."

She walked downstream, away from the camp, looking for a sandy beach and a pool suitable for bathing. Zach walked five paces behind her, whistling through his teeth. Suddenly she stopped short. There it was, the perfect spot, a deep pool screened by willow trees.

"Here," she announced. His whistling ceased, and she waited until he caught up with her.

"Right." He tipped his head toward the copse of trees. "I'll be over there."

"Standing guard," she reminded him.

"Yeah." He strode off and disappeared. "Your hour starts now," he called from somewhere behind the greenery.

Quickly she stripped off her shirt, boots and jeans, listening for telltale signs that he was creeping up to spy on her. He wouldn't do that, would he? Well, he might, she acknowledged. On second thought, no, he wouldn't. Zach Strickland was the most maddening man she'd ever come across, but something told her he was a man of his word.

She stripped off her camisole and underdrawers. Then she took three quick steps across the sandy creek bank and dived headfirst into the most blissful, cool bath she could imagine.

She swam and splashed, unwound her braid and washed the grit out of her hair, then floated on her back and gazed up at the purpling sky overhead. Dusk was beautiful out here, soft with tones of lavender and violet, and the air so sweet it was like wine.

"You've got ten minutes," came Zach's voice from somewhere.

She paddled to shore, dragged herself up on the narrow beach and stood shivering while a million crickets yammered at her. Drat! She had no way to get dry except to just stand still and let the water evaporate.

"Four minutes," he called.

Double drat. Not enough time to air-dry. She grabbed her camisole to use as a towel. But when she'd blotted up all the water, the garment was too sodden to wear, so she wadded it up, stuffed it in the back pocket of her jeans and pulled on her drawers, followed by her shirt and trousers. Her wet hair dripped all over her shirt, but it couldn't be helped. At least it was clean.

She heard Zach stalking toward her through the brush. "Time's up. You ready?"

Well, no, she wasn't, but at least she'd washed off the trail dust. "Look," she teased when he appeared. She flipped her wet hair at him. "No grasshoppers!"

Unexpectedly he laughed out loud.

"Tomorrow night when I bathe—"

"Hold on a minute," he interrupted her. "The hands don't take a bath every night, and neither will you."

"But we'll all smell…well, funny after riding in the sun all day, won't we?"

"Yeah. Get used to it. We don't take baths unless there's a river or a stream handy, and that isn't too often. We sleep in our duds, too."

"Oh." That was another snippet of information she could put in her newspaper column, but it wouldn't help her sense of smell for the next few weeks.

"So," he continued, "when you're close to anybody

on a trail drive, just don't breathe too deep. Or maybe hold your nose."

"Oh," she said again.

Back in camp the men sat around the fire, eyeing the fistful of twigs Cherry held in one roughened hand.

"All set, miss?" the graying wrangler inquired. The man was bent from years on the trail, she guessed, but there was something about him she liked. For one thing, he moved so gracefully and deliberately it was like watching a man do a slow sort of dance. And for another, he was the only one of the men who didn't watch everything she did.

"All set," she answered. "You may proceed with the drawing."

The cowhands hunched forward, and one by one each of them drew a stick from Cherry's gnarled fingers. Zach stood on the other side of the campfire, watching.

"Aw, my stick's longer'n a steer's horn," Skip grumbled.

"Mine, too," José said.

Some of the men held their sticks close to their chest. Others, disappointed, snapped theirs in two and tossed the pieces into the flames. At last a chortle rose from Curly, who leaped up and capered around the fire. "It's me! I got the short stick! She's gonna interview me first."

"And we're all gonna listen," Cassidy drawled. "Ain't we, boys?"

"This is okay with you, *señorita*?" José inquired politely.

"More important," came Zach's commanding voice, "is it okay with Curly? He might not want you hearin' all his secrets."

Jase snorted. "Heck, boss, twenty thousand people back East are gonna read all about 'm. After that, Curly won't *have* any secrets!"

Curly settled his work-hardened frame next to Alex and sent her a shy smile. "Guess I'm ready, Miss Murray. Fire away."

Quietly, Roberto set a brimming mug of coffee at her elbow. She took a sip, fished her notebook and pencil out of her shirt pocket and began.

"Your name is Curly, is that right?"

"Yeah. My real name's Garner, miss. Thaddeus Garner."

"Then why are you called Curly? I notice your hair is straight as a licorice whip." The men guffawed.

"Dunno, ma'am. I've always been Curly, ever since I kin remember."

"Very well, Curly. Now, tell me all about yourself, where you were born, where you grew up, how you came to be on this cattle drive."

"Well, lessee, now. I was born in Broken Finger, Idaho. That is, I think I was. My momma could never remember. Some days she said it was Mule Heaven and other days she said it was Broken Finger. Pa died before I could ask him."

"And did you grow up in Broken Finger? Or Mule Heaven?"

"Guess so, miss. Leastways Ma never moved whilst I was growin' up. Went to school for a while, but I never seemed to learn much."

Jase snorted. "Didn't learn nuthin', ya mean."

"Didn't learn *anything*," Skip corrected with a grin.

"You neither, huh?" Jase shot back.

Alex tapped her pencil against the notepad. "Gentlemen, please. Let Curly finish his story."

Curly talked and talked while Alex jotted down pages of notes. The man talked for so long that the other hands began to drift off and retrieve their bedrolls from the chuck wagon, lay them out around the fire and nod off to sleep. And still Curly talked.

Alex's hand began to cramp, but she kept writing. Finally Curly ran out of steam. She thanked him profusely and he blushed like a schoolgirl.

Her fingers ached, but it was a small price to pay for a long, cooling bath. And the notes for an excellent newspaper story.

Chapter Five

After Curly's interview, Zach sent him off to night-herd with José, listened to his wrangler's report about the remuda and grudgingly admitted that Miss Alexandra Murray—Dusty—had more sand than he'd thought. Today she'd ridden a full twelve hours across miles of sunbaked sagebrush and bunch grass without once complaining, or crying, or doing any of a dozen other things most women would under the circumstances. And she could still sit up and talk past suppertime.

Not only that, he'd learned more about Curly tonight than he'd gleaned in the seven years he'd known the man. Dusty had a way of asking questions that sort of drew forth information. And secrets. He'd never known before that Curly had once had a wife. Or that his newborn son had died at birth, along with the baby's mother.

But he knew one thing for certain—he'd never let Dusty within twenty yards of himself with her pencil and that notepad in her hand. The woman was downright dangerous. He had secrets, too, things he'd never told a living soul.

He heard Roberto's wheezy breathing from under the

chuck wagon. Between his cook's snoring and the scrape of crickets, the night seemed to close in around him in an unsettling net. Something was bothering him, but he couldn't figure out what it was. Curly's dead wife? Juan's polite but pointed remark about the river they'd have to ford soon? Swollen, the kid said. "And the current *muy* swift, Señor Boss."

Or was it the way his new hand, Cassidy, kept staring at Dusty and edging closer and closer to her while she sat talking with Curly?

Last night she'd rolled out her pallet as close to the chuck wagon and Roberto as she could get without scaring the cook out of a night's sleep. Zach noted that tonight she'd done the same thing.

Cassidy always seemed to be there beside her around the campfire. Not good. And when Dusty climbed into her bedroll, there was Cassidy, throwing his blankets down right next to her.

Zach moved quietly to where she lay, her dark head poking out from her top blanket. Cassidy was sound asleep. Zach laid one hand on her shoulder.

"I'm not asleep," she murmured.

"Get up and come with me," he said. She slipped out of her bedroll, and he rolled the blankets up under his arm and tipped his head toward the opposite side of the fire pit. She nodded, picked up her boots and quietly followed him.

He positioned her bedroll parallel to the dying coals and motioned for her to crawl in. Then he rolled out his own pallet next to hers. Now no one could reach her without first stepping over him or wading through hot coals.

"Understand?" he whispered.

"Yes. That man, Cassidy, makes me uneasy."

"Yeah. Me, too." He laid his revolver under the saddle he used for a pillow, positioned his hat over his face and closed his eyes.

"Thank you, Zach," she murmured.

"Yeah," he said.

"And I'm still here," she breathed. "You owe me a silver dollar."

"Yeah," he said again. He hated to admit it, but he was halfway glad. Dusty was fun to watch.

He tried like the devil to go to sleep, and he would have succeeded if it hadn't been for the quiet breathing of the woman beside him. He was so aware of her his toes itched.

He damn well didn't want to be aware of her. He didn't want to notice her or find himself watching her or listening for her voice. A female could be a dangerous thing. And a female on a cattle drive, a female he couldn't help admiring, made him sweat bullets.

The next morning, an incident occurred that brought him up short. It wasn't what happened, exactly; it was his puzzling anger about it. He never lost his temper. He'd learned long before he came out West, before he'd learned to ride or shoot a rifle or sweet-talk a girl, how to stuff down rage. So his reaction surprised him.

At first light he saw Cassidy snatch up Dusty's white camisole where it hung drying on the chuck wagon towel rack and caper around camp, twirling the garment over his head. It made Zach see red.

He grabbed the lacy thing out of Cassidy's hand and laid him flat with one punch. Then he stuffed the garment inside his vest and stalked out of camp to cool off down at the creek bank. When he returned, the men were sitting around the fire, sleepily shoveling down bacon and biscuits, and he sent Cassidy out to relieve one of the night-herders.

Dusty sat between Juan and Curly, calmly sipping a mug of coffee. Zach couldn't stop staring at her chest. Without her camisole, he knew her bare nipples were pressing against that thin blue shirt, and it was doing funny things to his insides. His outsides, too.

He slipped the bit of cotton and lace out of his vest and without a word knelt beside her, pressed it into her hand and folded her fingers over it. She gave a little squeak, and he bit back a chuckle.

She leaped up, marched over to the horse Cherry had brought up for her today and pulled herself up into the saddle. Lordy, he'd have to work hard to keep his eyes off that all-too-female body of hers this morning.

It wasn't easy.

Sometime around noon they entered a stretch of red-brown rocks interspersed with clumps of tall mustard, blazing bright yellow in the hot sun. Pretty stuff in the wild. In the summertime, Consuelo used armloads of it to make a kind of spicy-hot spread for venison or baked ham. He watched Dusty slow her mount to admire a patch of the weed. Probably gonna draw a picture of it in her notebook.

She looked up and bit her lip. "How will I ever learn everything there is to know about a cattle drive?" she asked.

"Everything? You don't need to know 'everything,' Dusty. You just need to know enough to stay alive."

"But my newspaper…the readers are simply fascinated by the West. How will I ever report enough to keep them entertained?"

Entertained! Hell's bells, this drive means life or death for me, and all she wants to do is entertain?

"Well, I'll tell ya." He sent her a look from under the brim of his hat. "Do what Charlie told me when I first came to work for him."

"And what would that be?"

"Keep your eyes and ears open, and your mouth shut."

She gave him a sharp look, her lupine-colored eyes widening.

"Got it?" he snapped.

"Yes, sir, I have most certainly 'got it.' In order to keep my readers riveted to their morning newspapers, I thank the Lord I can scribble my notebook full of interesting facts while joggling along on the back of a horse. Nothing will escape me." Her voice was so frosty it made him wince. "I do keep my eyes and ears open," she continued. "And that includes noticing your…your insufferable rudeness. You will not hear another question out of me."

He laughed out loud. "I'll believe that when steers can fly."

She sent him a smoldering look and gigged her mount away from him.

Sure hope you remember the "mouth shut" part, Dusty.

He reined away, but her horse started acting funny, and that caught his attention. She urged it closer to the rocks and all at once the animal shied and danced sideways. What the— Then the sorrel arched its back and bucked her out of the saddle.

She landed flat on her back. By the time he reached

her, the horse had skittered off a ways, and out of the corner of his eye he saw what had startled it. Rattlesnake.

Dusty laid without moving. Zach pulled out his gun, shot the snake, then dropped out of the saddle and raced over to her. Her eyes were open, but she wasn't breathing. Had the wind knocked out of her, he guessed. When he knelt beside her, she grabbed for his arm. Her face was white as flour and she was struggling to draw in a breath.

"You're okay," he barked. "You're winded. Just lie easy."

She tried to sit up, then sucked in a huge breath and started to cough, gasping for breath at the same time. "C-can't breathe!" she choked out.

Zach rocked back on his heels. "Not surprising since you got thrown. Your horse shied at a rattler."

Her eyes widened. "A s-snake?"

"Yeah. Horses are afraid of snakes."

"P-people, t-too," she said. "Oh, my s-stars, a snake!" She shuddered visibly.

Now that she was breathing better, he found himself mad as hell. "Dusty, there's a whole lotta things out here that'll spook a pilgrim like you. It's time you turned tail and—"

She jerked upright and jabbed her forefinger into his chest. "Pilgrim! I am not a 'pilgrim' by any stretch of your minuscule imagination, Mr. Strickland."

Hell, she sure had plenty of breath now. He caught her chest-poking hand and held it out to one side. "Damn right you're a pilgrim. You're a real beginner out here in the West. Oughtta know better than to ride close to the rocks on sunny days. And that's another reason why—"

"I am most certainly not going back!" she hissed. "I can learn about snakes and rocks and…and other things.

I intend to complete this cattle drive, and my newspaper assignment, so you can just stop yammering and let me get on with it!"

He stared at her.

She jerked her hand out of his grasp. "Did you hear me?"

"I heard you, all right. You're more stubborn than a whole passel of mules, Dusty, but I'm the trail boss of this outfit, and I say you're just too much damn trouble out here. I say you're going back to the Rocking K."

Before she could speak, Juan cantered up on his bay. "Is *problema*?"

"No!" Dusty yelled up at him.

"I'll say," Zach contradicted. "Horse threw her."

"It wasn't my fault," she protested. "It…it was the snake!"

"Si," Juan acknowledged with a sidelong glance at Zach. "The snake. And the horse, he did not like, so…" He made an eloquent somersaulting motion with his hand.

"Exactly," Dusty said. She got to her feet, dusted off her jeans and advanced on her horse. Juan walked his mount forward, leaned over to grab the reins and laid them in her hand.

With a nod of thanks, she stuffed her boot into the stirrup and clawed her way up into the saddle. Then she tossed her head, stuck her nose in the air and kicked the horse into a gallop.

Juan and Zach looked at each other. *"Mucho* woman," the young man breathed.

Zach shook his head. *"Mucho* trouble, you mean."

"Si, maybe so. But ees ver' pretty trouble, no? Like I

say, Señor Boss, *mucho* woman." Chuckling, he kicked his gelding and rode off.

Zach stomped over to remount, but instead stood looking after Dusty. *Mucho* problem. Very *mucho*.

Long days followed long days, one after the other, with nothing happening except endless hot, boring hours plodding after a herd of noisy cows, and listening to the thunder of hooves and the yipping of cowhands trying to keep them moving forward. Sometimes she wondered what the cowhands thought about during the interminable hours on horseback with nobody to talk to and nothing to do but chase after wandering animals.

They all smelled sweaty at the end of a day on the trail. When they could, the men bathed in creeks and rivers, and on Sundays, if Zach held the drive over for a day, they'd grab a cake of yellow lye soap and wash out their filthy garments. Like everyone else, she had only one pair of jeans plus an extra shirt and another pair of drawers, so every day she prayed for a camp beside a creek.

Did people in Chicago or Philadelphia or New York have any inkling what whole days lived like this were really like? She knew her readers would want to "see" what happened on a cattle drive, so part of the hours she spent on horseback she planned how she would write about it.

I'll start out by describing the meadows full of red and yellow wildflowers that get trampled by thousands of animal hooves, and how the sky looks in the morning when the sun comes up, all pinky-orange, and how hot it gets at noon, and how the dust smells after it rains. And then I'll...

* * *

A day later Zach's frustration reached the boiling point. He told himself he was just tired, worried about getting a thousand head of prime beef to market, concerned about Cassidy and his over-interest in Dusty and just plain disgusted about nursemaiding a city girl who had no business on his cattle drive. He'd taken to watching her struggle to keep up with the herd as it lumbered along. Kinda enjoyed it, if he was honest about it.

She was green as grass on a horse, stiff in the saddle and inconsistent with the reins. Often the poor animal couldn't read her contradictory signals and stopped dead in the middle of a meadow. Dusty had assured him she knew how to ride, but when he watched her, he sure doubted it. She probably rode on tame, city park bridle paths, ambling along with some poor dude she'd roped into an outing.

This afternoon was no different. There she was, trotting parallel to the herd through a meadow dotted with dandelions and patches of bright yellow mustard, pulling so hard on the reins he winced at what the bit was doing to the poor horse's mouth. He spurred Dancer away and came up on the other side of the herd so he wouldn't have to watch it.

Juan and Jase were riding flank, working hard because the herd seemed restless today. Probably the weather—part sun, part clouds and lots of wind. Juan tipped his hat. Jase started to say something, then broke off to chase a wandering steer.

Zach reined up and waited for the herd to pass, planning to relieve Curly, who was riding drag. The last animal lumbered past, and through the haze of dust behind them he glimpsed Dusty's roan standing stock-still in the middle of a patch of grass. Riderless.

Guess the horse had had enough.

He trotted closer and sure enough, there was Dusty, in a heap on the ground. "You okay?" he shouted as he rode up.

"Yes, I think so. I fell off my horse."

Zach snorted. Got bucked off, more likely. He dismounted and stood beside her. "Want a hand?"

"Yes, thank—" She started to reach up and gave a yelp of pain. "My arm hurts! And my shoulder."

He knelt at her elbow. "Probably bruised it. Let me see." He rolled back her shirt-sleeve to see if her arm was broken.

"Just sprained." But when he touched her shoulder she cried out again.

"That hurt?"

"It most certainly does hurt," she said through clenched teeth. "And I can't move my arm."

Oh, hell.

"Okay, let's get you back on your horse."

She sucked in a breath. "I—I don't think I can ride. I'm right-handed and I won't be able to hold the reins."

"Gotta get you on your feet," he said in a resigned tone. "You hold on to your hurt arm with your left hand." He slid his hands around her waist and lifted her upright. "Ouch!" she cried. "That hurts!"

He walked the roan over and lifted her into the saddle as carefully as he could while she grabbed her injured arm and gave little groans of distress. Then he had to pry her left hand away from her right arm, which she was clutching, and lay the reins in her hand.

"Wait! I told you I'm right-handed, so how—"

"Any good cowhand can ride with the reins in either hand. So do it. And don't jerk on the lines. Tossing you out of the saddle is the horse's way of telling you that you're not doing it right."

"Oh." Her voice sounded funny. "All right, I'll try."

Good girl. She might be green, but she had guts.

She urged the horse forward, and after the animal took a few halting steps, Zach strode over to where he'd left Dancer and hauled himself into the saddle. It was going to be a long, achy day for her. Part of him felt okay about that. Might teach her a lesson. The rest of him felt halfway sorry for her. He'd bruised a few shoulders in his time. Hurt like hell.

Hours later they came upon the chuck wagon and Cherry's remuda on a rise overlooking a long valley. The herd plodded to a halt and the hands began turning their horses over to Cherry and washing up for supper. Almost against his will, Zach kept his eye on Dusty.

Curly lifted her out of the saddle, and she moved very slowly toward the wash bucket. Roberto stopped her.

"Señorita Alex, let me fix your arm."

She followed him to the chuck wagon, where he pulled a clean dishtowel from one of his drawers and expertly fashioned it into a sling. Then he pressed the bottle of liniment into her hand.

"Tonight you must use this again. Make better."

"Thank you, Roberto. I'm sorry I won't be able to help you wash up the plates tonight."

"No *problema*, *señorita*. I get José to help." He spooned a big dollop of beans onto a tin plate and added a chunk of corn bread, then folded her left hand around the edge.

Zach watched her thank the old man again and settle herself on a log by the fire pit. The hands dug into their suppers, and Zach took his plate and a fork and went to stand outside the circle of firelight.

But Dusty just sat there, staring down at her plate.

Roberto noticed. "What is wrong, Señorita Alex? No hungry for my chili beans?"

"I…I can't eat with my left hand. I can't control the fork."

The cook frowned. "I give you a spoon, okay?"

But after she dribbled beans down the front of her shirt it was clear she couldn't manage the spoon, either.

Suddenly Zach couldn't stand it one more minute. "Move over," he ordered, settling himself next to her. He grabbed her spoon and loaded it up with beans. "You're a lot of trouble, you know that? Open your mouth."

Obediently she did so, and he shoveled some beans past her lips. She swallowed them down and looked up at him.

"Thank you, Zach."

He gritted his teeth, broke off a bit of the corn bread and motioned for her to open her mouth again.

"Just like feeding a baby bird," he muttered when the corn bread disappeared. Then he wished he hadn't said it because her cheeks got pink, and when she glanced up there was real pain in her eyes.

Blue eyes, he noted again. Dark blue, like the morning glories Alice grew on the Rocking K porch trellis.

He bit his lip and loaded up her spoon again.

Chapter Six

The day started out like all the others, but after breakfast Cherry told Zach the remuda was worrying him. "Been awful hot and dry the last few days, boss. Mebbe they smell somethin' on the wind."

Zach patted the old man's shoulder. "You'll figure it out, Cherry. Maybe they're just thirsty." He reined away and rode toward the herd. He'd assigned Dusty to ride drag, and he sure didn't envy her on a scorcher like today. But the damn little fool insisted she wanted to do "her fair share" of the work just like the other hands, so he gave in. Riding drag might teach her a lesson.

Still, he'd keep an eye on her. And he might as well start now. There she was, twenty yards in back of the lumbering herd, the blue bandanna he'd given her pulled up over her nose and mouth, trotting along and yipping like any seasoned cowhand. Guess her arm felt better.

He fell in beside her horse without speaking, and she gave him the barest of nods to acknowledge his presence. It was so hot and still she probably didn't have the energy to talk, so she didn't. She wasn't quiet that often, and he had to smile.

They rode in silence for a mile or so and then she glanced up to the sky. "Oh, look, we're in for a thunderstorm!" She pointed at a huge cloud that was moving toward them. It looked dark and menacing, and it had an odd yellow-brown tinge to it.

Oh, my God. He wheeled his horse forward toward the herd.

"Skip! Cherry!" By the time he clattered up, the hands were already staring at the cloud overhead.

"Turn the herd," Zach yelled. "Get them down. Hurry!" He pointed at the cloud bearing down on them, and they jolted into action, spurring hard to round up the steers.

He couldn't leave Dusty alone back there, so he turned and kicked his mount into a gallop.

"What's wrong?" she shouted when he reached her. "Is a thunderstorm coming?"

"Not a thunderstorm," he shouted. "It's a dust storm." She pulled her horse to a halt and sat staring up at the advancing cloud.

The sky darkened to a dirty brown. Zach dismounted, then reached up and pulled her off the gelding. He positioned Dancer next to her mount. "Stand between the horses," he ordered.

"What? But—"

"Don't argue, just do it!"

"Not until you explain—"

"Dusty, shut up and move! Now!" He shoved her toward the animals. Then he grabbed both bridles and pulled her forward.

"Zach, I don't understand. Why—"

"You will," he said shortly. He grabbed her arm, dragged her next to him and pushed her against Dancer's neck. Then he jockeyed the horses closer together to serve as buffers.

"They'll squash us!" she protested.

"No, they won't." He moved in back of her and pressed her body hard into Dancer's quivering form. "A dust storm is dangerous. Can't see. Can't breathe. It's important not to panic."

She started to say something, but at that moment the first gusts of wind hit. "Tie your hat on," he ordered. "Use your bandanna."

When she fumbled, he reached over and pulled the square of cotton tight over her Stetson and knotted it under her chin.

Dirt and sand pelted them, and the air filled with swirling grit. He snugged his own hat down as tight as he could, lifted his arms and positioned them around her head. Then he stepped in close and pressed his chest against her back.

"Breathe through your mouth," he yelled.

He felt her head dip in a nod, and then the storm hit.

The air grew so thick it was hard to see. To Alex it felt as if night was falling, and a bolt of panic stabbed through her. She jerked, and Zach pushed her hat down to shield her face and tightened his arms over her head.

"Don't panic," he said, his voice calm. "It'll get dark but it will pass. Just hang on, okay?"

She tipped her head up and down and felt his warm breath against the back of her neck. In the next minute, the air grew so gritty she couldn't keep her eyes open, and then all at once she was suffocating.

Choking, she reared back and heard Zach's voice against her ear. "Keep breathing," he ordered. "It's thick and dirty, but it's air. Just breathe."

How was *he* able to breathe? she wondered. He was sheltering her with his body, but the air was just as thick and dirty for him.

The wind screamed around them with a strange, eerie cry, and suddenly she was more frightened than she had ever been in her life. She began to tremble and felt his hard body press more tightly against her back.

"You're all right, Dusty. Just hang on." He brought his mouth closer to her ear. "Hang on."

"But I can't breathe!" She felt as if she was drowning. *Could a person drown on dry land?*

"Dusty, take real slow breaths. Don't hurry it."

She wanted to scream, but that would take precious air. She opened her mouth wide to gulp in air, and shut her eyes.

Zach's breath rasped in and out at her back, wafting against her cheek every time he exhaled. Could people choke to death in dust storms?

Don't think about it. As long as she could feel him breathing she would be all right, wouldn't she?

"Dusty, stay quiet. Stop thinking."

How could he know that I'm thinking?

She wanted to ask him how long this would last.

She wanted to thank him for protecting her.

She wanted to stay alive!

Zach could feel her shaking, sending little tremors against his chest, but instead of making him feel protective it made him mad. Damn mad. She was scared? She shouldn't be out here in the first place. Newspaper reporter or not, she had no business on a cattle drive. It put his men at risk. It put his cattle at risk. And, goddammit, it put *him* at risk!

Well, now, Strickland, just how do you figure it puts you at risk?

He tried to shut his mind down and concentrate instead on the wind. And the dust. And the...

Oh, hell and damn, it was hard not to think about Dusty when he could feel every little hitch in her breathing and every shudder traveling along her spine.

He had to admit she didn't complain. She didn't cry. She didn't shirk her share of the work. She didn't ask for special treatment because she was female. Dusty was maddeningly agreeable. He hated to admit it, but she was good company.

And, oh, God, she smelled good.

He could feel grit and sand sifting through his shirt and into his jeans, making his sticky skin itch. He heard the wind pick up. A dust storm could blow for half a day or longer, and this one showed no sign of letting up.

One of the horses tossed its head, but it didn't move. He tried to keep his mind on the animal, but his thoughts kept coming back to Dusty. What was it about her that he found so maddening?

And how much longer can you stand here with her trim little butt snugged into your groin?

Guess he had a bad case of Dusty getting under his skin.

Suddenly she pulled away from the horse she was leaning against and with a half sob turned into his arms.

"Zach, I'm scared."

Well, maybe she did cry sometimes. He pressed her head against his neck and wrapped his arm around her.

"H-how long will this last?"

"Don't know. Sometimes an hour. Sometimes a day."

She gave a little jerk. "A day? A whole day?"

"Sometimes. Forget about the dust storm. Just standing here in one spot for twenty-four hours will probably kill us."

"Oh, but— It couldn't really go on for a whole day, could it? What if I have to, um, relieve myself?"

That made him laugh out loud. He pressed her face back against his neck. "Dusty, stop talking. It takes air."

He let ten minutes go by while the wind screamed across the plain and threw dirt in their faces. After another ten minutes she raised her head and wasted some more air.

"I can't wait to write down some notes about this windstorm!"

Zach just shook his head. She was either crazy or she was a great newspaper reporter. Maybe both.

The storm finally moved off to the north, and Zach heaved a sigh of relief. Their ordeal was over. He took a step away from her, and she moved out of his arms and began brushing dirt off her clothes. Yeah, he was relieved it was over, but maybe *he* was the crazy one, because part of him was sorry.

Everyone gathered around, and they decided to set up camp for the night. Dusty immediately began scribbling away in her notebook and Zach took stock of the damage. The storm had left his hands gritty but uninjured and his herd of cattle was still intact. Cherry assured him the remuda was restless but untouched, and he was already brushing the animals down.

The men were all filthy and the chuck wagon was gritty with sand and dirt. Roberto was beside himself.

"Señor Boss, I cannot cook with dirt in pans, and the wagon—*ay de mi*—it must be scrubbed before supper."

Dusty looked up from her writing. Her face was dirty,

and when she stood up, grit sifted from her jeans. "Roberto, give me a bucket of water and a scrub brush. I'll help you clean up."

Zach grinned all the way out to check on the herd, and when he'd ridden twice around the subdued steers, he was still smiling.

She might be green and scared and a little bit crazy, but maybe she was worth riding the trail with.

That night Alex interviewed the scout, Wally. He told her some of his adventures over his considerable years "on the drover's trail," as he termed it.

"Kinda hard to get used to it at first, scoutin' for a cattle outfit. Gotta ride ahead of ever'body, and it kin get mighty lonesome with nobody to talk to 'cept my horse. Got to be purty good friends with my horse after a while, but…aw, heck, Miss Alex, you don't want to hear about this stuff."

"But I do, Wally. Honestly I do. And just think, thousands of readers back East will want to hear about 'all this stuff,' too. You'll be famous!"

"Aw, heck, Miss Alex. I don't want to be famous. Somebody might come after me for money I owed in a poker game somewhere. Golly, I remember one time down in Texas…" And he was off again.

When Wally stopped regaling her with his wild tales, the hands began to spin their own yarns. Nothing was too outlandish or unbelievable. Skip recalled one cattle drive when they ate "nothin' but oatmeal and bugs" for four days straight. Curly told about riding two days on a spring roundup with a broken foot; it had happened when his horse stepped on his boot, but he'd wanted to stick it out because one of the riders was "a pretty little filly" from a neighboring ranch.

"Aw, that's nuthin'," Jase challenged. "One time I was night-herdin' during a blizzard and my fingers froze up. Had to chop 'em off myself the next morning. Had to, or they'd a got the gangrene."

Alex didn't know whether to believe him or not, but when she noticed his middle two fingers on one hand were missing, she decided he was telling the truth. She dug out her notepad again. This was wonderful human-interest material about the type of people who worked these cattle drives. She could see a whole series of pieces about the men on the trail; maybe she should get to know them better.

After an hour of after-supper talk, she acknowledged she was certainly getting a good education about life on a cattle drive. And it wasn't just about the men. Cherry was constantly instructing her about the horses in his remuda.

"Don't never walk up to a hoss what's pullin' yer rope tight, Miss Alex. Good way to git stomped. Why, I remember one time…" And, like Wally, the wrangler talked nonstop for half an hour.

Chapter Seven

Night after night she watched the men around the camp-fire, how they teased one another and played practical jokes and sang and told stories about other cattle drives they had been on. Somctimes one of them would start to talk about a girl "back home," or a woman of question-able reputation, and then Alex noticed the men would tip their heads in her direction and quickly shush the speaker. She guessed they didn't want to offend her.

But how they did love to talk! "Spin yarns," as they put it. The tales they told were often excruciatingly funny. The listeners would slap their sides and guffaw, and then the next speaker would try to top that story with another tale even funnier or more outlandish, and they would all poke fun and try not to swear too loudly in front of her.

All in all, it was entertaining, funny and heartbreak-ing at the same time. Alex tried to surreptitiously scrib-ble down as many of their outlandish stories as she could in the flickering light from the campfire, and she tried to avoid drawing too much attention to what she was doing for fear they would clam up. These rough, bawdy tales would make rich reading for Easterners starved for pictures of life in the West.

* * *

Juan was right about the river, Zach acknowledged. Rain had brought the level up, and the rushing current looked wicked. It wouldn't be easy getting a thousand head of cattle across that expanse of roiling brown water.

Roberto parked the chuck wagon just close enough to the water to make them all nervous. Cherry had the remuda snugged behind, in his makeshift corral, and as fast as the hands rode in and grabbed off their saddles, the savvy wrangler had their mounts rubbed down and turned into the roped-off enclosure to graze. Good man, Cherry. Zach hoped he'd be as spry when he was that age.

The herd lumbered up to the riverbank behind the lead steer and milled around uncertainly while the two point riders and all the flank men shouted and swore until the cattle moved into a sloppy circle and then discovered the water in the river. They forgot trying to break for freedom and spread out along the bank to drink.

Cassidy looked like a walking dust cloud from riding drag half the day. He pulled his bandanna off his sweaty face and threw himself down next to the chuck wagon. Zach trotted his bay over close to him. "Get up."

"Aw, boss. After six hours behind them steers, I'm plumb tuckered."

"I said get up." Something in his voice must have alerted the big-bellied cowhand because he sat up and then jolted to his feet.

"Yessir. Guess I miscalc'lated some 'bout suppertime."

"Then pay attention," Zach snapped. "If you want any supper around here you'll put in a full day's work."

He rode off to circle the herd. Where was Dusty? Last he'd seen her she was keeping up all right, so she should have reached them by now.

"Hey, Juan? You see Miss Murray on the trail?"

"Si." The young man tipped his dark head over his shoulder. "Back maybe a mile."

Dammit, that'd leave her out on the prairie alone. He craned his neck looking for a telltale puff of dust. Nothing. Maybe she'd dropped back or slowed down some to...to what? She could nibble biscuits while riding. She could tend to personal necessities just by pulling up behind a thicket of rabbit brush, and that'd take five minutes, at most. So where the hell was she?

He waited. He rode in ever-widening circles around the herd, then went back to camp and waited some more.

"Hey, boss," Cherry shouted. "Gonna set there on yer horse all night or gonna let me rub him down?"

"Gonna set," Zach muttered. Before he knew it, he was riding out of camp, retracing their route and trying not to let his temper boil over. Four miles back he spotted her on foot, and leading her horse through a patch of wild buckwheat. What the—

He rode a wide circle around her to avoid kicking up too much dust, and when he walked Dancer in close, he saw she was trying hard not to cry.

"You hurt?"

"No."

"Horse hurt?"

"Yes. I think he's lost a horseshoe."

"Horses don't wear shoes on a drive, Dusty."

She peered up at him, shading her eyes with one hand. "Well, his gait is uneven, so I know something is wrong.

I surmised that I shouldn't ride him, so I thought I'd walk."

That was smarter than she realized. Riding the gelding with a sore foot would make it worse, maybe even cause permanent damage. She plodded past him and Zach studied her sorrel.

"Left leg's swollen," he called out. He fished in his saddlebag for a length of rope and tossed it down to her. "Tie him on behind my horse. We'll ride double."

"Oh, no, I can't—"

"Do as you're told," he snapped. "Unless you fancy draggin' into camp long past supper and gettin' Cherry out of the sack in a bad temper to doctor your mount."

"Yes, sir, Mister Trail Boss, sir," she said, her voice crisp. He could tell her teeth were clenched, but he didn't care. First the rattlesnake, then gettin' bucked off and now a horse with a swollen leg. She was bad news. And he sure didn't have time to coddle a stubborn female.

After two tries she managed to link up the two animals. "Sure hope you tied a square knot," he called.

She propped both hands on her hips and frowned up at him. "What's a square knot?"

Instantly he dismounted and came back to check the rope. Well, hell, nice and tight and square as you please. He remounted, settled her in front of him and kicked Dancer's flank. The horse jolted ahead and she jerked backward against his chest.

Dusty's body was hot and sweaty, but her hair smelled like some kind of spicy soap. The single thick braid that hung down her back was trapped between her spine and his rib cage. She kept jostling her body up and down, trying to get comfortable, he guessed, but that sure kept reminding him she was female. After ten minutes she calmed down some.

"I am sorry to cause you all this trouble," she ventured.

"Not half as sorry as I am."

"Why, how ungracious! I really am sorry. What makes you think—"

"Because you *don't* think, Dusty. You're a damn hazard on a drive like this. Now shut up or we'll both miss supper."

Stung, Alex bit her lip and gripped the saddle horn so hard her knuckles ached. Odious man. Arrogant, bossy and...bossy. She tried to think how she would describe him in her newspaper. Rude, she decided. And all the other negative adjectives she could come up with.

But if she wanted another bath after supper, she'd better hold her tongue. At least he was no longer threatening to send her back to the Rocking K.

They rode in tensc silence until he drew rein in front of the rope corral. "Swollen leg," he said to Cherry.

The wrangler peered up at him. "Bad?"

"Could be worse," Zach said, his voice flat. Cherry helped Dusty climb down, waited for Zach to dismount, then led hcr beautiful sorrel away.

"Will she be all right?" she called.

"He," Cherry said over his shoulder. "Gelding, remember?"

Embarrassed, Alex nodded. How could she forget? Almost every living creature on this drive was male. And *some* of them needed to improve their manners. One of them in particular.

She sat quietly all through Roberto's tasty supper of beans and bacon and tortillas, and when they all gathered around the campfire, she told Zach she was going to go take a bath.

She expected Zach to guard her privacy from behind some trees, as he had before, but tonight he annoyed her by insisting on a much closer vantage point.

"Current's swift," he said at the river's edge. "Might be dangerous to swim."

"Oh?" She eyed the roiling water. He was right. It looked a bit muddy, too.

"I'll bring a bucket of warm water from Roberto's stove." He strode off, returning in a few minutes lugging a tin pail of sloshing water. He plunked it down in front of her and stepped back.

"Where are you going to be?" she asked.

"Close by."

She shot a quick look at him. "How close?"

He chuckled. "Close enough," he said drily.

"And far enough away," she said. "I do not wish for an audience, Mr. Strickland."

"Trust me."

Gracious heavens, she'd be a fool to do that! But, she reasoned, she really had no choice. Very well, she would take the fastest bath of her life.

She heard his footsteps moving back and forth just behind the only tree in sight, a wind-twisted juniper. They didn't stop, or slow down, or pause, and she prayed his eyes were glued on his boots and not her.

She stripped, sponged off with the washcloth Roberto had thoughtfully included, dried herself off and donned her clothes again in four minutes flat. "All done," she called.

He stepped from behind the tree so quickly it gave her pause. *Had* he been watching her?

"Find any grasshoppers in your hair?" His voice held a hint of laughter.

"What? Oh, I have no idea!" She shivered at the thought. "There wasn't enough water to wash my hair."

"Too bad," he said.

"I beg your pardon?" She spun to face him and would swear a flush tinged his cheeks, but in the dim light of dusk she couldn't be sure.

Without looking at her, he grabbed the bucket and started back to camp. She wished he *would* look at her. She liked his eyes. They were the most startling shade of green, and his eyebrows were dark, almost black. She also liked his hands, the fingers long and purposeful-looking, and tanned brown as his exposed forearms.

She watched his long legs eat up the distance back to the chuck wagon. And had a disconcerting thought.

She liked some things about Zach Strickland. But was there anything, *anything at all*, that Zach Strickland liked about *her*?

Chapter Eight

When Cherry came barreling toward him the next evening, waving his once-reputable brown Stetson, Zach knew something was wrong. "Boss! Come quick! Ya got a big problem."

Zach leaned down. "Yeah? What problem?" Probably something about Dusty. That girl could get into trouble just by looking at it.

"It's Roberto," his wrangler shouted. "He done clonked hisself in the head with a piece of wood an' he's out colder'n a witch's—" He broke off and cleared his throat. Zach ran toward the chuck wagon with Cherry at his heels.

He found Roberto down on his hands and knees, shaking his head back and forth. "Roberto!" He squatted next to the dazed man.

Roberto ran one hand over his forehead. "Señor Boss," he said, his voice unsteady. "Was bringing wood for fire, but maybe I stumble."

"Lordy no, ya didn't stumble!" Cherry exclaimed. "A big hunk of pine done smacked yer head."

Zach helped the man stand up, but the cook was so unsteady on his feet he walked him over to the fire pit and sat him down. "Cherry, get that bottle of whiskey Roberto keeps in the chuck wagon." When the wrangler thrust it into his hand, Zach pried out the cork and held the bottle to Roberto's lips.

"I no need this, Señor Boss. Must cook supper."

"You do need this, Roberto. Forget about supper."

The cook swallowed a big mouthful of whiskey, coughed and again tried to stand up. His legs wouldn't support him. Cowhands began to gather in a circle around them, surprised into silence by the sight of their cook with a whiskey bottle in his hand.

"Is he drunk?" Curly asked.

"He got hit in the head," Cherry explained. "He's okay, just woozy."

"Supper ready?"

Jase jabbed Curly's arm. "God, all you think about is your belly. The man is hurting!"

"But he's got a point, boss," Cherry said. "Somebody's gotta finish cookin' supper."

At that moment Dusty rode up and dismounted. Cherry walked over to take the reins. "Miss Alex, can ya cook?"

Zach almost laughed at the expression on her face.

"Me? My gracious, no. I can boil water for tea, but…"

"Roberto's hurt. He hit his head," he explained. "And supper's not started."

"Hurt?" Instantly she spun and knelt at the cook's side. "Roberto, what happened?"

"Ees nothing, Señorita Alex. Head ache just a leetle."

Her gaze landed on the whiskey bottle. "Spirits! No wonder your head aches. Don't you carry any powdered willow bark in your medicine kit?"

"*Si*, but—"

Before he could finish Curly was rummaging through

the drawers in the chuck wagon. He found the bottle of willow bark powder and shook a dose into his palm. Before Zach could stop him, Roberto washed it down with a big gulp of whiskey.

Curly stuck both hands in his back pockets. "So, who's gonna cook supper?"

"Not me," Jase said quickly. "How 'bout you, Curly?"

"Huh! Me, neither. What about you, Skip?"

"Not on yer life!" Skip yelled. "Last thing I ever wanna do is pick up a fryin' pan."

For a long minute the hands looked at each other in silence. And then Dusty stepped forward.

"*I* will cook supper," she announced.

Zach stared at her. "Thought you said you didn't know how to cook, Dusty."

She bit her lip. "Well, I don't know how. But Roberto can tell me what to do."

"*Si*, I can do," the cook said.

Dusty smiled. "However, I will need an assistant." She looked straight at Zach and waited.

Zach looked right back at her.

She tipped her head and grinned at him. "Mr. Strickland?"

And that was how Zach ended up with a dishtowel apron tied around his waist, chopping up onions and carrots for the stew pot.

The hands drifted off to tend the fire; Cherry returned to his roped-off corral to tend the horses, and Roberto called out instructions to Dusty from the chuck wagon. She began snapping out rapid-fire orders so fast Zach couldn't keep up. "Dump all those onions in the Dutch oven. Now, stir them around. No, not like that, Zach! Gently!"

"I feel like saluting," he grumbled.

"And I feel like a trail boss!" she retorted with obvious delight.

Zach said nothing. He didn't know what he was doing, and he was certain that she didn't, either. Tonight's supper was gonna be one big gamble. He figured there was nothing he didn't know about driving a herd of cattle to a railhead, but maybe he'd figured wrong. He didn't know how to make supper. That had always been Roberto's mysterious kingdom, and wearing a damn apron had never crossed Zach's mind.

But the real surprise was realizing that he actually liked working alongside Dusty.

Roberto's instructions were clear, and little by little the mixture in the vessel hanging on the iron tripod over the fire began to bubble away and smell like stew.

"And now," Roberto called, "make biscuits."

"Biscuits!" Dusty leaned close to Zach. "Do you know how to make biscuits?" she asked under her breath.

"Haven't a clue," he murmured. "They're round. I know that much."

"I've seen Roberto cut them out with an empty tin can."

"Starter in big jar in wagon," they heard Roberto say.

Dusty blinked. "Starter? What on earth is starter?"

"Make biscuits rise," Roberto called. "Flour in barrel. Bacon grease, too. Starter in big crock."

Zach dumped flour into a big bowl until it was half full, then scooped out a glop of the starter. Dusty dribbled in some bacon grease and smashed it all together with a fork. When it looked about right she dumped it out onto the fold-down tabletop.

José frowned and shook his head, and when Zach stared down at the sticky mess, he realized why. "I think we should have tossed some flour onto the table first."

"Oh." She worried her bottom lip between her teeth, scraped the dough back into the mixing bowl and waited while he dusted the table surface with a handful of flour. Once more she upended the bowl.

"Maybe we should pat it down flat?" he suggested.

"No. I've seen Roberto knead it some and then flatten it out." She pushed the heel of her hand down onto the dough. "More flour," she instructed.

He was beginning to sweat. Stew was just water and stuff boiled up in a pot, but biscuits were one of God's great mysteries. She nudged him, and he sprinkled another fistful of flour over the mess on the table. Accidentally, he got it all over her, as well. She sent him an exasperated look and began punching the doughy mixture to press it out flat.

"Zach, find that empty tin can so I can cut these out," she ordered.

"Yes, General!" he shot back. That earned him a thin-lipped smile. He located the tin can in one of Roberto's secret cubbyholes, and when Dusty pointed at the flattened dough, she stepped back and he began cutting out rounds.

"What do we bake them in?" she called to Roberto.

"Dutch oven," the cook replied. "Rake coals out of fire and set on top."

Zach laid two dozen perfect rounds in the iron pot, nestled it on a bed of coals, and heaped more coals on top of the lid. "How do we know when they're baked, Roberto?"

"When they are brown, *señor*," the cook answered. Zach thought the old man must be feeling better because he was chuckling.

Every five minutes he and Dusty took turns scraping the hot coals off the lid to peer at the biscuits, then heaping them back on top. Finally Zach thought the biscuits looked done. At least they looked kinda tan. He sent Dusty a questioning look.

She nodded and then held up crossed fingers on both hands. "I want to ring that triangle to announce supper," she said. She grabbed a big spoon and rattled it around and around inside the iron triangle until Zach thought his ears would fall off. She sent him a triumphant grin, and his heart gave an odd kick. She looked flushed and happy, like a pretty girl at her first square dance.

Well, she was a pretty girl, he admitted. The fact that her nose had a smudge of flour on it didn't matter.

Long past midnight Zach rolled over and stared up at the stars winking overhead, trying to brush an annoying thought out of his head. It didn't matter that he and Dusty had forgotten to add salt to the stew or that the biscuits had been hard as horseshoes or that the brown cloth sack of Arbuckle's coffee was wet where he'd spilled a kettle of water on it.

For some reason, that didn't matter at all.

At the end of another long day, Alex nibbled the end of her pencil and studied the grizzled older man seated next to her. "Your name is Cherry, is that right?"

"In a way, yes, ma'am. Short for Cherokee."

"Are you an Indian? A Cherokee?"

"In a way," the graying wrangler said again. "Real name's Rising Hawk. My momma's Cherokee. My daddy was white."

The only time she saw the wrangler upset was when

one of his animals was mistreated. She loved to watch
Cherry catch mounts for the men in the morning; all he
had to do was hold out a hand and the horse he wanted
would trot right over. If Cherry was half Indian, the
other half was horse.

Each morning before breakfast she snuggled under
the blanket and listened to the bird songs; there must
be hundreds of them, even though trees were becoming few and far between. Cherry, of course, was up long
before the birds.

"All right, Cherry…um, Rising Hawk, tell me about
yourself."

"Gosh, Miss Alex, that's gonna be kinda hard. Never
talked much 'bout myself before."

Alex reached to pat his gnarled hand. "Take your
time, Cherry. We have all night."

"Don't know I've got that much to say, miss." He
scratched his graying whiskers. "My young years was
mighty ordinary for a Cherokee. And an Indian. But
things got interesting later."

He stopped and gazed off toward the hills. Alex
waited.

"Guess you could say folks in towns, they don't much
like Indians. Storekeepers don't like 'em. Schoolteach-
ers don't like 'em. We ain't even welcome in saloons."

Alex bit her lip but said nothing.

"Well, anyway, I guess I growed up not knowin'
where someone like me belonged. Started workin' as
a cowboy when I was 'bout thirteen, I guess. Never
knowed 'xactly how old I am, see. Anyway, I could ride
real good, so they showed me the ropes and then I found
I was real good at breakin' horses and takin' care of 'em.
I like horses, see. They don't beat up on ya unless you

don't treat 'em right. A horse won't ever lie to you or say a mean thing, that's why I like 'em."

"Is that how you became a horse wrangler, Cherry?"

"Guess it is, miss. Knowin' about horses comes natural to most Indians. Kinda grew up in tune with 'em. Cows, too. Even some humans." He gave a dry chuckle. "But not too many."

"Oh?" She waited a heartbeat and he took the bait.

"Well, there's them like Zach Strickland. And then there's others."

Alex laughed out loud and saw Zach look up from across the campfire. So the men respected their boss, did they? She could understand that, she guessed. Sort of. In her view, Zach Strickland was short-spoken to a fault. Rude. Unfeeling, even. He rode his cowhands hard, but the only one she'd heard complain out loud was Cassidy.

And Cassidy…well, she preferred not to think about Cassidy.

"Cherry, tell me some more about your life. About being a wrangler."

The old man blew out a long breath. "Well, see, Mr. Kingman, yer uncle, he hired me on as a horse wrangler, and he took a real chance doin' it cuz none of the cowhands liked Indians much. But Mr. Kingman, he was always real fair. Missus Kingman, too. Real nice lady."

"Did you ever have a family of your own?"

Cherry jerked as if she'd punched him. "Started to once, yes ma'am, I did. Her name was Honey, and she worked for Missus Kingman for a while doin' laundry and suchlike. Then she——" He broke off and cleared his throat.

"Then she…what, Cherry?"

"Then…" His mouth worked. "Then I guess she decided she'd rather be white and not Indian, and she run off with one of them travelin' gents sellin' snake oil and fancy aprons."

"Oh, Cherry, that is sad."

"Aw, I dunno," he said, his voice hoarse. "She never liked horses anyway."

Alex didn't know whether to laugh or cry.

"Till you came, Miss Alex, I never talked much 'bout myself. Didn't think anybody much cared."

Tears stung into her eyes and she swallowed hard.

He patted her hand. "Thanks fer listenin', Miss Alex. Thanks a lot."

Cherry talked on, and Alex wrote until the campfire died down and most of the hands had crawled into their bedrolls. When the campfire burned down to coals and Cherry went off to check on his horses, she rolled herself into her blankets and crawled under the wagon next to Roberto. Zach was sleeping somewhere nearby, so she felt safe.

But she found she couldn't sleep. Instead, she listened to the coyotes yip and call back and forth. Their forlorn cries sent chills up her spine.

Immediately after Roberto served a breakfast of Dutch oven biscuits and leftover stew, he packed the chuck wagon up, drove down the gravelly river bank and floated it across the expanse of swirling, muddy water. Cherry and the remuda followed. After that, it took hours for the cowhands to prod the bawling cattle into the turbulent water and swim them across until they staggered up the brush-swathed bank on the opposite side and lumbered on following the bell steer.

It took from dawn until almost suppertime to push the

entire herd across the rain-swollen river. Zach rode back and forth, shouting orders and galloping after stragglers, but all the time he kept half an eye on Dusty, trotting at the back of the herd on her favorite sorrel. Its left hind leg showed no ill effects after Cherry's ministrations, but wisely she kept her pace moderate and her nose and mouth covered by her blue bandanna.

When the last of the steers stumbled down the muddy bank and into the river, Zach watched Dusty tentatively turn her gelding toward the water to follow them. He knew Dusty's sorrel would swim; what he didn't know was how steady its rider's nerves would be. A river crossing could be dangerous. More drovers died from drowning in rain-swollen rivers than from gunfire.

He was halfway across, Dancer swimming strongly in the roiling water, when Dusty's gelding waded in up to its hocks and struck out for the opposite bank. She clung to the saddle horn with both hands, but a sudden surge of current swept her off the animal and dumped her into the river.

"Grab his tail!" Zach yelled. He watched her flail after the horse and lunge for its bushy tail. She held on for a scant minute, then lost her grip. With a strangled cry she went under.

He plunged toward her, but the raging current was sweeping her downstream. "Hold on!" he yelled. He grabbed his lariat, spun it out and dropped it over her head and shoulders.

She made a desperate grab for the rope, and when her hands closed on it he swam Dancer to the sandy bank, dallied the rope around his saddlehorn and began reeling her in, hand over hand, while she thrashed in the icy water. She clung to the lifeline until her feet scrabbled on the river bottom and she staggered up the bank.

Zach dismounted. Holding the rope taut, he pulled her in like a hooked fish. When she reached him he stepped toward her, slipped the lariat off over her shoulders and tossed it aside. She stumbled forward and he snaked out an arm and pulled her against him.

Damn, she was cold! She shook uncontrollably and her teeth were chattering. He put his thumb and forefinger to his lips and gave a piercing whistle. A mile ahead Juan peeled away from the herd and galloped back.

"Get a blanket!" Zach shouted. "And some whiskey. In my saddlebag."

Five minutes later he wrapped the rough wool blanket around her and held the whiskey bottle to her lips. "Swallow," he ordered. She coughed and sputtered and tears came to her eyes. "Again," he barked. Her teeth chattered against the rim of the bottle, but she took another big gulp.

Juan was already building a fire, feeding it with dry brush and tumbleweeds until the flames began to crackle. Then he looked up.

"Ride on ahead and tell Roberto to save us some supper."

"*Si*, boss. Is stew and corn bread tonight."

Dusty was still shaking like an aspen tree in a high wind, and he snugged the blanket around her as he watched Juan clatter off. The minute he was out of sight, Zach set her trembling body away from him.

"Strip," he ordered.

Mute, she stared up at him. "Strip," he repeated. "Get out of those wet duds. Most cowhands die of pneumonia." He dropped to his knees and snagged off her waterlogged boots.

She didn't move.

"Did you hear me?" he yelled. "Get your clothes off!"

She scrabbled ineffectually at her leather belt, but it was plain as pudding her fingers weren't working. He stood up and did the job for her, tugged her jeans over her hips and when she stepped out of them he tossed them aside.

She fumbled at her shirt buttons until he took over. She was shaking so violently he could scarcely force the buttons through the buttonholes. Finally the garment opened all the way down the front and he snaked it off her shoulders, trying hard not to look at her.

Now he was down to her soaked camisole and drawers. He sucked in his breath, let the blanket drop, and pulled her arms up over her head. She made little moaning sounds when he stripped off the upper garment and instantly clasped her arms across her bare breasts. He steeled himself to keep his eyes on the ground, grabbed up the blanket and wrapped it around her shoulders. Then he blew out all the air in his lungs and slid her drawers down over her hips. Lordy, her skin was frigid. And, oh, God, it felt smooth under his fingers.

He pulled the lower part of the blanket closed over her hips and turned away to wring out the garments and lay them out on the flat rocks Juan had gathered around the fire. He nudged her forward and pressed her down onto the largest stone.

She dropped her head to her knees but said nothing. Juan galloped up and thrust a canteen into Zach's hand. "*Café*. Roberto sends."

Zach grinned. *"Gracias, amigo."*

"The *señorita*, she will be all right?"

"Yeah. She will be, in a little bit."

Juan touched his hat brim and reined away. Zach glanced over at Dusty. "You gettin' warm?"

She snugged the blanket tighter about her body and gave a jerky nod, so he uncapped the canteen and held it out. "Hot coffee." She took a sip, and he screwed the cap back on and folded her hands around the warm metal. Her fingers felt like icicles.

For the next half hour he piled dry branches onto the fire and tried not to look at her. Knowing that she was buck naked under that blanket didn't help much. He tried not to think about her satiny skin and her… He tried hard not to think about her at all. Instead, he watched her wet clothes steam away on the rocks. The small, light items dried almost immediately, but he knew by the time everything else got dry, their supper in camp some distance ahead of them would be stone cold.

He stood up, shrugged out of his vest, then unbuttoned his red plaid shirt and tossed it to her.

"Put this on. I'll turn my back."

Her burble of laughter made him blink. "What f-for? You already t-took off all my clothes!" She didn't sound mad, exactly. Just tired and cold and maybe beginning to feel human again. A good sign.

"I didn't look," he said evenly. "I wanted to, but there were more important things."

He risked a glance at her face, expecting… He didn't know what he expected. But even though her lips were still almost blue, she was trying to smile. She downed another swig of coffee and held the canteen out to share with him.

Something in his chest tightened at the gesture. He

waved it off and turned away, and when he looked back, she'd donned his shirt and was eyeing her still-steaming jeans.

"It'll be a tight fit," he said, keeping his voice neutral. "They're still wet."

"I c-could wrap this blanket around my waist, c-couldn't I? Then we could ride on and get some supper."

"You need trousers," he said flatly. He walked off a few yards, found a dry juniper branch and whittled some pointed sticks. He poked four into the ground close to the fire and draped her jeans over them. About twenty more minutes, he figured. Then he scanned the horizon for the chuck wagon. He knew it would be about two miles ahead, but he couldn't see it.

Her jeans were only half dry when she stood up. "I'm g-getting hungry," she announced. "I'm going to get dressed. Turn your back, please."

Her voice had gone all shy and ladyfied. Okay, he'd be a gentleman and turn his back, but he sure couldn't turn off his imagination. Juan was right—Dusty was *mucho* woman. Her skin, where he accidentally brushed against it, felt like silk, smooth and inviting. And…inviting. He clenched his fists so hard his nails bit into his palm.

God forgive him, he wanted to touch her, run his fingers down her bare spine to her…

Don't go there, Strickland. Keep your mind on the business at hand.

But the business at hand was a naked Dusty, who was sitting three feet away from him. Not close enough to touch, but close enough to think about it. Close enough to want to. Oh, hell, he had to admit he wanted to run his tongue over her nipples. In fact, if he was honest with himself, he wanted to touch her all over, in places he'd wager no man had ever touched her. He wanted to be the first.

But there wasn't time to be honest with himself. He had to get her back to camp before he forgot the should and oughts, and when he got her back to camp, what he would give to be able to take a long, cold bath.

He turned away, but it was harder than he thought. He fought not to watch. And he tried like hell to ignore the picture that rose in his mind of her covering that trim little butt with white cotton and pulling that lacy camisole over her breasts. God, as cold as he was, he was beginning to sweat.

After a long ten minutes he heard her tentative voice.

"I—I can only get my jeans halfway up. They're still awfully damp."

His heart turned a big fat somersault inside his chest. "Want some help?"

"N-no." Another long pause. "Well, yes, I guess I do."

He walked around in back of her, keeping his eyes averted as best he could, grabbed the waistband of her jeans and gave a good hard tug. She kind of shimmied her behind back and forth until the jeans fit while Zach gritted his teeth and tried not to notice.

Then he sank down in front of her and pulled her wet leather boots on over first one foot and then the other while she steadied herself with one hand on his shoulder.

He liked that, her touching him. Shouldn't, maybe, but he did.

Finally he stood up. "Think you can ride?"

She nodded. "After s-surviving a cold swim in the river, I c-can do anything. That water was much colder than the other night when I took a bath."

"Different river," Zach said. He kicked dirt over the

fire, walked Dancer over close to her, and boosted her up into the saddle. Her butt was cold and damp, but the fit of her jeans was so snug he had to look away.

"Come on, then." He walked for half a mile or so, leading the horse, then swung up behind her and snugged the blanket around her shoulders. Halfway back to camp he could still feel her trembling with cold, and he snaked one arm around her waist and pulled her back against his chest. Her head fit just under his chin. Her hair smelled of violets.

To his surprise she didn't say a word all the way to camp, just snuggled back against him like a scared kitten. Made him feel funny inside.

When they arrived, she slipped off the horse and stood uncertainly. Zach dismounted and walked her over to the fire pit.

Six cowhands leaped to their feet, but not one of them commented on his red plaid shirt, which she wore with the sleeves rolled up around her wrists. All of them offered to fetch her a plate of supper.

Zach knew better than to acknowledge the eyebrows the men raised at the bare skin of his chest, which they could see plain as day under his leather vest. He also knew better than to drape her still-damp shirt where the hands could see it. He took the rolled-up garment over to Roberto, who accepted it without a word and offered him a dry shirt.

"Tuviste mucha suerte!" Juan said when he sat down at the campfire. "God is good."

"Yeah, she was very lucky," Zach said shortly. He wasn't sure about the God part.

He watched her across the campfire for over an hour before he figured out what was bothering him. Sure, she'd had the starch pretty well knocked out of her britches, but he'd bet half his herd there was more to it than that icy dunking in the river.

But what? She sure wasn't eating very much. Or paying any attention to the cowhands sitting around the fire pit. Her eyes were focused on something beyond the flames. In fact, even though she was staring straight at it, he'd swear she wasn't seeing the fire at all.

She was a puzzle, all right. And he noticed something else. Cassidy positioned himself next to her on the log she was perched on. Every time the man stood up to toss another chunk of wood on the fire, he managed to sit back down a few inches closer to her. She kept scooting away, and he kept on crowding her.

She stared into the fire like she was a million miles away on some different planet. Maybe thinking about Chicago and that newspaper she wrote for, what was the name, the *Chicago Times*? He'd bet another silver dollar she wished she'd never stepped off Alice's front porch to go haring off on a damn cattle drive. Especially after her unplanned swim this afternoon.

Cassidy got up again and once more resettled himself way too close to her. This time when she edged away, he edged right after her. That did it.

"Cassidy," he barked.

"Yeah?"

"Go relieve Skip on night-herding."

"Aw, boss, do I have—"

"Now." He kept his voice quiet, but suddenly everyone stopped talking. Sparks cracked out of the fire pit.

Cassidy stomped off to saddle his horse, and José went to the chuck wagon for his guitar. He strummed idly through some Spanish-sounding tune until Cherry dug his harmonica out of his vest pocket and joined him with a mournful wail.

Zach moved around the fire pit to claim the space Cassidy had vacated. He waited until a song got going before he spoke.

"What's wrong, Dusty?"

"What? Oh, nothing."

"I don't buy that. You're rolling something around in your head, and if it's not too private, I'd like to know what it is. Something about what happened today, maybe?"

She didn't answer for so long he thought she was going to ignore the question. He leaned toward her and lowered his voice. "Dusty?"

"Yes. Well, actually, I *was* thinking about what happened today. About what an incompetent thing it was for me to do, falling off my horse in the middle of a river."

"Most of us have done that once or twice. Nuthin' to be ashamed of."

"Well, I'm not 'most of us.' I hate not doing things right."

He listened to José's soft guitar for a long minute and then cleared his throat. "Kind of a perfectionist, huh? Don't like to make mistakes?"

"Exactly. That is why I am a good journalist. I like to fix things. I have all my life. I dislike making them worse."

"Always like to be in control, is that it?"

She nodded.

"I hate to tell you this, Dusty, but that's a real poor attitude on a cattle drive. You can't ever predict what's gonna happen with horses and men and steers and the weather. You gotta learn to roll with it."

She looked up from her boot tops just long enough to frown at him.

He cleared his throat. "There is one thing that's going on that is predictable, though. Want to know what it is?"

She nodded again.

"Cassidy. I don't like the way he keeps edging around you, pushing himself at you. Tonight I want you to roll out your pallet under the chuck wagon, next to mine."

"Yes," she said quickly. "I will."

"Not next to Roberto," he added in a low tone. "Next to me. Got it?"

Curly and José began to sing. *As I walked out in the streets of Laredo...*

Out of the corner of his eye, Zach saw a big fat tear start down her cheek. Dammit, she was more shaken about what happened today than she wanted to admit. He wanted to reach over and brush the moisture away with his thumb, but the thought of feeling her soft, smooth skin paralyzed him.

I spied a cowpuncher all dressed in white linen,
Dressed in white linen and cold as the clay.

He watched José's fingers caress the guitar strings and thought of the times he'd touched a woman. Not many. Mostly dance hall girls. Women who were as unlike Dusty as a rusty water bucket was to the moon.

Alex stretched out on her blanket and listened to the rhythmic, slightly wheezy breathing of Roberto outside the wagon wheel. He'd been sound asleep when she laid out her bedroll. She folded her hands across her middle and stared up at the belly pan on the underside of the chuck wagon. Made of dried cowhide, the sling held fuel, wood and something called buffalo chips, which Roberto used to cook with.

Zach was right; she did want to do things perfectly. She always had. It gave her a sense of worth, a sense that her life was something more than the silly, useless existence she'd watched her mother lead. She was nothing like her mother. She needed to excel, she admitted. She wanted her life to matter.

But maybe Zach was right. No one succeeded all the time, not even her. She thought about that until her eyelids drooped shut and her breathing evened out. She woke only once, and that was when Zach crawled in next to her.

He smelled good, like wood smoke.

The next morning it started to rain. Roberto scrambled out of his blankets before it was light, covered himself with a yellow slicker and in half an hour piled biscuits and bacon onto their plates and poured out coffee from the huge speckleware pot he kept on the fire. He washed up the dishes so fast the hands barely had time to finish eating.

Zach watched the chuck wagon pull out in the downpour, followed by Cherry and the remuda. The wrangler didn't mind the rain, Zach guessed. Cherry trotted his mount alongside his band of horses, singing something. Whatever it was, the horses seemed to like it. Cherry had a real connection with his animals.

Before the cattle had covered four miles, the rain turned to hail. Stinging bits of ice drove into Zach's face and he couldn't pull his hat down far enough to protect his cheeks. The wind nibbled its way inside the collar of his sheepskin jacket and coated Dancer's hide with little slushy white balls.

"Sorry, fella." He patted the gelding's neck. "I'll make it up to you tonight." Many times he'd spent an extra long hour rubbing down his horse, sometimes because of bad weather, like today; and sometimes he spent the extra time just because he and Dancer were friends. More than friends. Zach loved the big bay, with his intelligent black eyes and his fondness for ripe apples.

He'd never loved anything in his life more than this horse, not even his first girl back in Colorado, and that was saying something. That flirty female had gobbled him up body and soul and spit him out like a bite of moldy garbage.

But Dancer just loved him back.

Skip galloped past, bundled in a sheepskin jacket with a scarf tied over his hat and under his chin. Zach had to laugh at his point rider; he looked like an old Indian squaw.

The bell steer plowed steadily forward through the mud and the downpour, and the rest of the herd followed, driven on by the shouted commands of the cowhands riding alongside them. Wally, his scout, had ridden in last night and reported that, even with the rain, there was no water in Lost Acres Creek, and that meant an extra-long push to Horse Lake some miles beyond. He wondered where Roberto would set up camp.

Behind him, a subdued Dusty rode her sorrel through a flattened, aromatic patch of wild onions. Zach watched her for a full minute and she never once lifted her head—just stared at the muddy ground. She'd better watch the trail, he thought. Except for Dancer, horses didn't know everything. He'd never ridden a more intuitive mount than the gelding under him.

Dusty began to lag farther and farther behind, but maybe she didn't mind riding drag on a day like this. At least there wouldn't be much dust. There'd be mud, though, and after today's ride she'd sure want a bath. With all this rain, she could just strip and run naked...

He tried to stop the picture that rose in his mind, but it stuck with him until his groin ached.

His belly told him it was suppertime long before he rode up to the chuck wagon. And when he did, Curly strode out to meet him, a scowl on his usually placid face.

"Ya gotta come deal with somethin' that's come up."

"Yeah? What 'something'?"

"You'll see, boss. Damndest thing I ever saw." He jerked his chin over his shoulder. "Over there."

Chapter Nine

Zach rode up to camp and immediately saw an Indian child staring at the herd as it bedded down for the night. He drew rein and approached at a walk.

The bedraggled boy stood his ground, clutching the hand of a younger child, a girl from the look of her longish black hair and feathers. They were both wet and looked cold and hungry. The boy faced Zach and gestured with his hands.

"Cherry!" Zach called across to the wrangler. "Come on over here. You understand any of this kid's lingo?"

Cherry listened to the boy for a few minutes and grunted. "Not a word, boss." He tried a few words in Cherokee and was met with a blank stare. The wrangler shook his head.

Zach dismounted and slowly walked forward. The boy saluted. *Saluted?* This youngster must have had some dealings with soldiers. Zach returned the salute, then knelt down so they'd be at eye level.

"Come on, kid, say something I can understand."

Words poured out of the boy's mouth, but none of them made any sense to him until the little girl rubbed her hand across her belly. They were hungry!

"Roberto, give these two kids some tortillas and maybe some bacon." He stood up and watched the boy carefully fold the warm tortillas, stuff them in the pocket of his ragged trousers and then point behind him, toward the mountains. He wanted to take the food back to his tribe.

"Skip, cut out a cow, a gentle one that's nobody's momma. Tie on a lead rope."

"Sure, boss. Right away."

While they waited, Roberto offered more tortillas and some cold chunks of leftover beef. When Skip rode up with the cow, Zach took the rope, laid it in the boy's hand and pointed toward the mountains. The kid saluted and said some words, then he stepped forward and touched Zach's fingers.

Zach resisted an impulse to reach out and ruffle the boy's black hair. The little girl smiled shyly, and then both children turned away and started across the meadow toward the forest, leading the cow. At the edge of the trees, the boy and his sister turned and waved.

Zach watched until he could no longer see them. When he turned back to the chuck wagon he saw Dusty standing over by the campfire, her eyes shiny with tears.

"Who are they?" she asked.

"Indian kids. Don't know what tribe."

"What are they doing way out here? Where is their home?"

He snorted. "Home? Probably don't have a home anymore since our army ran them off their lands."

"What? Why would they do that?"

He stared at her. "You kidding? You mean you don't know how we—us white men, that is—want everything we see, even what belongs to other people, for ourselves? Where ya been all your life, Dusty?"

Something struck her as odd about the scene. Two small children alone in this wilderness just didn't seem right; her nose for news smelled more of a story. Later, Cherry took her aside and explained.

"Probably an Indian camp off somewheres in one of them woodsy glades we came past. Mebbe the boy and his sister are orphans. Mebbe their father was killed in some raid." The wrangler went on to explain that Indian tribes made war on each other as often as white soldiers attacked. Alex wrote every word down in her notebook.

But she couldn't stop thinking about those two Indian children.

It rained again the next day. By midmorning it was clearing up, but Alex found her horse struggling through what seemed like acres of sticky, hock-deep mud. The thick mess slowed the horse and made her hesitate to dismount for any reason, even to relieve herself behind a bush.

She prayed that Roberto's chuck wagon was parked on a rise with a minimum amount of the chocolate-colored muck to slog through. The thought of crawling underneath the bulky wagon and rolling out her bedroll on top of this sticky, oozy ground made her shudder.

She glanced at the lowing herd. The men riding alongside were moving slowly, and so were the steers. Even Old Blue, the bell steer, plodded slowly through the sea of mud, and the horses... Oh, those poor beasts. She felt sorry for any animal getting splashed and splattered with this viscous black goo. It was thick as molasses. She prayed it would rain again and wash off all that sticky stuff.

Oh, no, maybe she didn't. It would make more mud. It

left her hat brim dripping water down her neck and her canvas jacket feeling steamy and crawly. What a truly miserable life this was! How did the cowhands stand it? One day they baked under a broiling sun and twenty-four hours later hail spit out of the sky and they had to struggle against rivers of raging water.

She marveled at these men. They simply ducked their heads, shrugged their jackets up around their ears and kept riding. And then at night they'd sing and tell more tall tales around the campfire. She couldn't imagine how they kept their spirits up.

She drew in a huge breath and squinted her eyes to see through the mist. She could hardly wait to be warm and dry again, to reach Winnemucca and the railroad train that would take her back to Chicago and civilization.

Her horse sloshed into a brown, rain-swollen creek and slipped and scrambled up the opposite bank. She urged him on up a little lupine-covered rise and lifted her head to scan the horizon. Far off in the hazy distance she spied the chuck wagon and a blazing fire. Roberto already had the iron pot rack erected over the flames and a blackened Dutch oven dangling over it.

Her heart lifted. Bless that wonderful man! She kicked her heels into the sorrel's side and rode straight toward him.

By the time the herd arrived in the relatively dry meadow of rain-flattened, yellow daisylike flowers, nobody felt much like talking, not even Roberto, who usually muttered to himself in Spanish as he bustled around his chuck wagon. Everyone was bone-tired and shivering with the cold.

Alex dismounted and turned the sorrel over to Cherry

to rub down and feed along with the rest of the remuda. The air smelled of sagebrush.

The chilly wind had made her stiff, but she moved around the warm campfire to the cook's side under the gray canvas tarpaulin. "Roberto, would you like some help?" Some nights she peeled potatoes or tried her hand at cutting out circles of biscuit dough, but tonight was different. Roberto took one look at her and clapped both hands to his dusky cheeks in mock horror.

"*Ay de mi, señorita!* No, I don't need no help. You look like…*muy cansada. Pobrecita.*"

Alex deduced that *pobrecita* must mean some kind of chicken. Her feathers must look woefully bedraggled. She thought about what Mama would have said about her appearance and winced.

Roberto waved her away toward the campfire. Her boots squished at every step, and the minute she settled herself on a flat rock near the fire, she pulled them off, along with her socks, and flexed her half-frozen toes before the heat.

She hated being cold! In the wintertime back in Chicago, she left Mrs. Beekin's Boardinghouse for Young Ladies only when she had to walk the two blocks to the newspaper office. When it rained she carried a big black umbrella. When it snowed she bundled up in her long wool coat with its cozy fur hood. She wasn't used to being outdoors for hours and hours in miserable weather, and today had most definitely been miserable!

She felt sorry for whoever Zach would assign to night-herding. The rain had stopped, but the wind was sharp. Curly and rangy, work-hardened Skip tramped up, stomping their boots and beating their gloved hands together. Curly glanced down at her bare feet.

"Betcha never figured it'd be like winter on a summer trail drive, didja, Miss Alex?"

"No, I did not," she admitted. "Sit down and get warm."

"No need. We're used to it." He practically puffed out his chest, and Alex suppressed a grin.

"Why, I remember once—"

"Aw, dry up, Curly," Skip grumbled. "You're just showin' off. Me, I'm colder'n a witch's—"

"Whoa! You talk nice around the lady, or the boss'll have your ba—I mean, your hide nailed to the chuck wagon."

Alex perked up at that. Zach had ordered his cowhands to be polite around her? That made her pause. She thought he wanted her to be as uncomfortable as possible on this cattle drive to teach her a lesson. He'd made it plain as pudding he hadn't wanted her along. Or maybe he didn't like women?

Or maybe he just didn't like *her*?

But he protected you during that dust storm. And he pulled you out of the river and dried your clothes by the fire. And he is protecting you from that lout Cassidy.

The truth was she couldn't puzzle out Mr. Zach Strickland. One minute he was gruff and unforgiving, and then he thoughtfully stood guard with his back turned while she bathed in the creek and gave two hungry Indian children a cow. He ordered her around like a servant, but then he made sure she was protected at night.

The other hands straggled in and stood with their backsides to the fire, complaining about the weather until Roberto banged his spoon around in the iron triangle to signal that supper was ready.

At that moment, Zach rode up and slid off his beautiful bay horse, slapping his rain-spattered hat against his thigh. Water droplets flew off into Skip's face.

"Dammit, boss, watch where you—"

"Dry up, Skip," Zach growled.

"Hey," the rangy blond cowboy yelped. "What burr's got stuck under *your* saddle?"

"No burr, just a tired, wet horse." Zach strode past the circle of hands around the fire pit, whipped out his neckerchief and began rubbing down Dancer's wet flanks. He knew his temper was short. With two days of rain slowing down the herd, any more unexpected delays and he'd miss the cattle buyer he'd arranged to meet in Winnemucca. He couldn't afford to miss the man or he'd end up having to sell the steers at a loss.

And he couldn't do that. He had to clear at least a thousand dollars from this drive to buy his own spread. He'd worked for seven long years to save up enough money for his own ranch, and he'd be damned if rain or anything else was gonna keep him from doing just that. He couldn't afford any more delays.

Roberto's throaty voice cut through his thoughts. *"Vengan, por favor!"*

Curly, Skip and the other hands crowded the chuck wagon, holding out their tin plates for generous dollops of the cook's thick rabbit stew and dumplings. Zach stood last in line with Dusty just ahead of him. He thought he'd instructed the men to let her be first, but she was just stubborn enough to countermand his order and stand in line like everybody else.

A spatter of rain blew in under the canvas roof Roberto had stretched over the chow line, drenching one of the closed cabinet doors. Raindrops slid down the painted surface. Ahead of him, Dusty bent to study the descending droplets.

"I bet I can tell which one of those drops will reach the bottom edge first," she remarked.

"Bet you can't," he said without thinking. He was tired enough not to even notice the wet cupboard doors, much less give a darn, but the words just slipped past his teeth. He rarely passed up a bet of any kind, even if it was about something as inconsequential as a raindrop.

"You're on," she quipped. She sent him a challenging sideways glance and pointed her forefinger at one fat blob of water sliding down the cupboard face. "If I win, you owe me an interview for my newspaper."

"And if you lose?" he asked in a tired voice.

"Then..." she turned back to him and studied his face "...*you* can interview *me*."

"Done." He was too beat to talk her out of it.

"I pick that one," she said. She pointed at a racing droplet that was leaving a wet track on the painted cabinet door. "Now, you choose one."

He poked his thumb at the biggest, most promising-looking droplet, and they both bent to watch. He knew he'd win. His water drop was bigger than hers, so it would be heavier. He knew it would travel faster than her puny little rain driblet.

But it didn't. Somehow his water drop got sidetracked and veered off toward one edge. Hers slid neatly to the bottom edge of the cabinet door.

She grinned up at him. "I won! I will be conducting my interview with you after supper."

"Don't think so," he said.

"Oh," she retorted, a triumphant note in her voice, "I *do* think so, Mr. Strickland."

"Oh, yeah?"

She propped both fists on her hips. "Yeah."

She sounded as if she was trying so hard to be tough he gave a tired laugh. "How 'bout some other night?"

"Nope. Tonight."

"Uh, it's been a long day, Dusty, so—"

"I am getting used to long days, Mr. Strickland. I will expect you to make yourself available at…" she squinted up at the fading twilight "…eight o'clock. Sharp."

"Sorry. Got things to do at eight o'clock."

"What things?" she shot at him.

Hell's bells, didn't she ever give up? "Um…well, I've got to make night-herding assignments, and…uh…talk to Curly about—"

"No, you don't. Sending men out to night-herd takes you less than thirty seconds, and you've been yelling at Curly all day, so you can't possibly have anything more to say to him." She sent him a smile and waited.

Jumpin' jennies. The last thing he wanted to do tonight, or any night in the foreseeable future, was talk about himself. There were things hidden so deep in his soul they'd never see daylight, and the last thing he wanted to do was poke at them.

"I said no, Dusty. No means no!"

She looked up at him with fire in her eyes. "Zach Strickland, I never took you for a coward. You're bossy and hard to please and convinced you're right about everything, but I've never seen you afraid of anything."

"Dusty, hush up, will you? I'm tired and—"

"No, I will *not* hush up! We made a wager, an honest, no-strings-attached wager. And when somebody agrees to a wager, and that someone *loses* that wager, that someone honors the agreement that was made." She paused for breath. "Is that not true?"

"Dusty—"

She propped her hands on her hips. "Well, isn't it?"

He shook his head and turned away. But she wasn't giving up. She grabbed his sleeve and pulled him back to face her. Her narrowed eyes looked like two drops of molten sapphire as she spit a question at him. "Do you or do you not keep your word?"

By this time both Roberto and Jase were listening, and Zach knew he was trapped. On the other hand, maybe after a day like today, with wind and rain and more wind, Dusty would be so tired she wouldn't have the sand after supper to ask him even one question. Maybe he'd be safe from her prying into things that he wanted to keep private.

He tried to put it out of his mind, but after the men had cleaned their tin plates and dropped them into Roberto's wash bucket, he found he was wrong again. She wasn't too tired. She had plenty of energy left to bedevil him. When the last spoonful of stew passed her lips she jumped up, dunked her plate into the bucket of hot soapy water and poked her face close to his.

"In private," she said near his ear. "You won't want to answer my questions in front of your men."

Under his wool shirt Zach began to sweat.

Chapter Ten

Alex tried to suppress her feeling of triumph at having jockeyed their stiff-upper-lip trail boss Zach Strickland into a corner, and now she planned to pounce on him with her interview questions.

A more reluctant subject she had never known. Most men loved to talk about themselves, but not Zach Strickland. Most men bragged about their heroic adventures. But not Zach. Most men, she knew from her shameless eavesdropping on late-night talk around the campfire, liked to talk about women they'd known or wish they'd known, or women they'd loved or left or lost or missed or regretted. But not Zach.

She nibbled the end of her pencil and launched her attack. "Tell me where you were raised, Zach."

They laid next to each other on their bedrolls underneath the chuck wagon, Zach on his back, staring up at the wagon underbelly, Alex on her stomach, propping herself up on both elbows and poking her face close to his.

Roberto snored softly just outside the rear wheel. She could hear José singing something lilting in Spanish as he circled the herd on night duty. It was a mournful song, something about a cowboy and a lost horse…or was it a lost love?

"Zach?" she reminded him.

He heaved a long sigh. "Dusty, it's been a helluva long day. Can't you do this some other time?"

"No, I cannot. I have cornered you at last and you're not going to wriggle out of it." She tapped the pencil against her open notebook. "You can start by telling me about your boyhood."

He sighed. "Didn't have much of a boyhood. I was born in West Virginia. In a cabin on the wrong side of everything. It had a dirt floor and no windows and only two rooms."

He stopped. She waited, and waited some more, until she thought she'd scream with frustration. Finally she nudged his arm with her notebook. "Go on, I'm listening."

He groaned, closed his eyes and continued. "When I was real young, maybe six or seven years old, my daddy sent me to work in a coal mine."

She sucked in her breath. *A coal mine? At six years old?* "Go on."

"It was dark down there. Cold, too. Closed in. And God knew it was hard work pickin' at a coal seam fourteen hours a day."

She winced. "Fourteen hours a day?"

He swallowed. "Soon as I could, I ran away. My…" He stopped and took a breath. "My daddy was drunk most of the time anyway, so I figured he'd never miss me."

"How old were you then?" she asked softly.

"'Bout nine, I guess. Maybe ten. I left home one night

in a snowstorm, just lit out and caught a wagon train goin' west."

"That must have been difficult at such a young age."

"Yeah. Well, I didn't have a choice, really." He stopped again and closed his eyes.

"Why didn't you have a choice?"

He didn't answer.

"And then what happened?" she prodded.

He let out a long, ragged breath. "I ended up tired and hungry on a hardscrabble ranch in Colorado in the middle of winter. Started at the bottom, muckin' out horse stalls and hauling water. Worked up to bein' a ranch hand, and after—"

He broke off. "One summer I headed for Oregon."

He stopped speaking for so long Alex had to poke his arm with her pencil. "And then?"

He bit his lower lip. "Then I worked for an old, used-up rancher, a real mean son of a— He ran too many cows and drank too much liquor. I stuck it out for two years. Ended up bein' his top hand, and then one day Charlie Kingman rode in."

"My Uncle Charlie, you mean?"

Zach nodded. "Charlie hired me on the spot. After a couple of summers he made me his foreman and later the trail boss on his cattle drives. When this one's over..." His voice trailed off.

"When this drive is over?" she prompted.

"When this drive is over, Dusty, I swear I'm gonna have my own spread or die tryin'." Again he fell silent. "Guess I ride hard on everybody because I want that ranch so much."

"You're a tough boss, Zach, but you're fair. The men respect you."

"Maybe."

"Maybe you're hardest on yourself." She had long since stopped taking notes. When he got to the part about riding a wagon west to Colorado when he was so young, she'd folded her hand around her pencil, closed her eyes and just listened to his voice. He spoke softly, but she could hear the pain behind the words. He'd been on his own since he was ten years old. No wonder he was so...so...hard.

And somehow tender, as well.

"Are we done?" he asked, his voice gravelly.

"You mean," she said, keeping her eyes closed, "is my interview over?"

"Yeah. Are we finished?"

Finished? She swallowed. She had a million more questions for Zach Strickland, but some instinct told her to leave it alone for now, not to push too hard or too fast. Zach was a far more complicated man than she'd thought, and she didn't want to scare him off. She'd ask more questions later.

"For now, yes, we're finished," she said quietly.

"Good. I'm tired of talkin'. Never talked about any of this stuff before. Feels real funny."

"'Funny' might be good, Zach." She raised up on one elbow and studied him. One arm lay across his eyes. Had he drifted off to sleep?

"One more question, Zach. Have you...have you ever been married?"

He waited a long time before answering. "Nope. Never been married. About the only thing I ever cared much about besides owning my own ranch is my horse, Dancer. He's the best friend I ever had."

"Do you ever hear from your family? Your father? Or your mother?"

Again he waited a long time. "My mother's dead."

"Oh? How did she die?"

"She was shot," he said. "Don't ask about her again."

She gulped. "What about your father? Is he still alive?"

"Oh, yeah, there's Pa. I don't ever want to hear from him or lay eyes on him as long as I live. And don't ask me why, Dusty. That's between me and him."

Stunned into silence, she quietly folded up her notebook and laid her pencil down. There was much more to know about Zach Strickland, but she sensed she'd touched enough nerves for one interview. There would be other nights.

"Good night, Mr. Strickland," she whispered.

After a long silence he rolled away from her. "'Night, Miss Murray."

Her throat ached for some reason. Maybe she was catching a cold.

But she didn't think so.

He couldn't sleep. This annoyed him because his body hurt all over from a long, wet day in the saddle, and morning wasn't far off. Must be all that palavering he'd done about himself, things he'd never talked about in all his thirty-four years.

She hadn't asked that many questions, but he couldn't seem to stop telling her things he'd kept bottled up inside all this time. He couldn't imagine what she'd find interesting in any of that. And he hoped to hell she wasn't going to write about any of it in her newspaper.

Nah, she wouldn't do that. He didn't figure his life

would be all that interesting to readers back East. She was a good interviewer, though. She had a way of making a man just open himself up.

He rolled over onto one elbow to look at her. She opened her lids once, closed them, and then they fluttered open again and she looked straight into his eyes. She didn't say anything, just smiled kinda funny and let out a long breath. Then she closed her eyes again.

He lay studying her small, pale face in what light there was from the dying campfire some yards away. It wasn't much to see by, but it was enough. *Hell and damn, she is pretty.* Why wasn't she married? Was she engaged? Must be a hundred males sniffing around her, especially in a big-city newspaper office where she was the only woman.

He liked looking at her. Probably several dozen other guys did, too. When he'd been young and scrawny it had always bothered him when a gent cut in on him on the dance floor or muscled him out of the way at an ice-cream social. He didn't like losing. After getting his heart stomped on when he was seventeen, it mattered a lot if some gal gave him a second glance or not.

And it sure as shootin' mattered now. It shouldn't, maybe, but it did. Ellie had waltzed off with a rich rancher from Montana who wore fancy Mexican leather boots and sported ivory-handled six-shooters. She wanted someone successful, she said. Someone wealthy. Not him.

Before he put himself through anything like that again he wanted to have his own ranch. Women at the saloon had sufficed for all these years; he had no business even looking sideways at Dusty.

But he wanted Dusty to like him. Didn't know exactly

why, but he did. He hadn't told her everything. Didn't intend to, either. But then he hadn't intended to tell her about Pa or goin' to Oregon or any of it. She could sure worm things out of him, though. Dusty had a way of makin' him open up a vein and bleed all over her.

He noticed something else about her, as well. He noticed that something about Dusty soothed some of the broken places inside him.

Chapter Eleven

The next morning before breakfast, José's voice jarred Zach out of his thoughts. "Hey, Señor Boss, come over here, *por favor*." Zach dropped the harness he was mending and went over to where the young man stood.

A young Indian boy in a ragged flannel shirt sat atop a black pony at the edge of camp. Zach recognized him. It was the same hungry kid who had appeared with his little sister some days back and left camp leading a cow Zach had given him. What did he want now?

"José, go get Cherry."

The boy sat his horse without moving until Cherry finally tramped over, and then he unleashed a stream of unintelligible words, accompanied by a good deal of pointing.

"If I read the sign language proper, the kid wants you to follow him," the aging wrangler said.

"Huh? What for?"

Cherry watched the boy gesticulate. "I'd guess it's somethin' 'bout a ceremony of some kind back in his camp. He wants you to come."

"Why me?"

Cherry sent him a look. "'Cuz you gave him and his sister that cow, remember? He says it saved his tribe from starvin'."

"Maybe," Zach said. "But I don't think—"

The wrangler stepped in close. "If'n I was you, boss, I'd go with him. Ain't smart to refuse an Indian tribe's hospitality."

He nodded. "All right, Cherry. Saddle my horse."

"Smart man," the wrangler muttered. He started for the remuda corral, and Zach walked over to the campfire, where the hands were now devouring Roberto's bacon and biscuits.

Skip set his tin plate aside and looked up. "What's goin' on, boss?"

"That Indian kid wants me to go with him to his camp," Zach explained. "Some sort of powwow goin' on."

"An Indian camp?"

"Yeah. That's what Cherry says."

Dusty jerked to her feet and began gathering up her notebooks. "How far away is this camp?"

"Hold on a minute, Dusty. You're not coming. Just me."

"Of course I'm coming! My readers will buy up every newspaper in Chicago to read about a real Indian camp."

Cherry rolled his eyes, and Zach turned away from her. "Tough. You're not goin' to this one."

She planted herself in his path. "Why not? Give me one good reason. I won't be any trouble, I promise. Please, please, let me come with you."

Curly appeared at Zach's elbow. "Boss? What's up?"

"I'm going with this Indian boy, but I want you and the boys to keep the herd moving."

"And me," Dusty said from behind him. "I'm going, too."

Curly frowned. "Aw, come on, Miss Alex, I don't think—"

"But I do!" she cried.

Cherry appeared leading two horses, Dancer and Dusty's favorite sorrel.

Zach ignored her, swung up on Dancer and reined away. "Curly, I'll catch up with the herd, probably late tomorrow."

Dusty started to mount, but Curly stopped her. "Yer gonna get hot an' dirty' and plenty thirsty. Might be dangerous, ridin' into an Indian camp, bein' a woman and all."

"Tough." She brushed past him, pulled herself up into the saddle and spurred the gelding forward.

Zach heard the horse, but he didn't slow down. Damn little fool. What made young women from the city so crazy, anyway? Probably rich food and soft beds. And newspaper jobs. *Sheesh.*

She trotted up and fell in beside him. "Where is this camp?"

He shrugged. "If I knew that I wouldn't need to follow that kid ahead of me, would I?"

She didn't answer. Instead, she patted the shirt pocket where her notepad rested and sent him a grin.

Zach gritted his teeth. The boy glanced back over his shoulder, nodded and picked up the pace.

Side by side, they followed the boy's black pony across the wildflower-dotted meadow toward the hills, and after an hour Dusty dropped behind him. He felt halfway sorry that she'd be eating his dust, but not sorry enough to slow down for her.

What the hell would he do with her at an Indian camp? Having Dusty along on a cattle drive was a liability; taking her into an Indian camp was just plain foolhardy. She'd probably scribble away with her pencil, and that was sure to arouse their suspicion.

The trail narrowed and began skirting stands of feathery cottonwood trees and tangles of pale green willows. Meandering streams straggled along in low areas, shallow enough to walk their horses across and clear enough to see small trout darting among the rocks. He could hear Dusty behind him, the steady clop-clop of her sorrel reminding him how much he didn't want her along. No matter how interested she was in the mysteries of Indian culture, having a woman along was a risk.

An Indian camp was always an unknown. On his own he could handle pretty much anything that came up, but Dusty's presence would complicate things. In fact, she could mess up the unpredictable relationship some Indian tribes had with the white man, especially white men driving cattle to Winnemucca or Abilene.

He tugged his hat lower to block the sun. At least she wasn't complaining about the heat or the dust or the pace they were setting. Come to think of it, he hadn't heard Dusty complain about anything on the drive for the last ten days. She was a fast learner, he'd give her that. Or maybe she'd just run out of things to talk about.

She was too outspoken. And she was usually convinced she was right, no matter what anybody said. He prayed that no matter what happened at this Indian camp, she would keep her mouth shut. Either that or watch closely and learn something.

They were coming into a wooded area, and the sun was starting to dip toward the mountains ahead when the boy on the trail kicked his pony into a trot.

"Zach?" Dusty called. Her voice sounded tense.

"Yeah?"

"I need to— Could we stop and…rest the horses?"

"Nope." He let that sink in, then acknowledged that he needed to stop, as well. He stuck two fingers in his mouth and let out a sharp whistle, and the boy pulled up beside a grove of alders.

"Okay, Dusty. You first."

She slid off her mount and sprinted for cover while he walked both horses to the stream. The Indian kid waited.

When she emerged from the trees she sent him a smile. "Thank you, Zach," she murmured. He motioned for her to fill her canteen, walked off behind the nearest tree and unbuttoned his jeans.

Two hours later they rode into a small Indian encampment next to a pretty, slow-moving river. The boy slipped off his pony and disappeared into a large deerskin teepee, and Alex moved her mount up close to Zach's and reined to a halt.

"What do we do now?" she asked.

"Wait," he said.

She gazed around at the Indians who had gathered in knots and were staring at them in silence. Old women with wrinkled faces kept protective hands on half-naked children with huge black eyes. Younger women clad in simple deerskin garments that came below their knees stood in uncertain groups, while men of all ages gathered near them. Their nearly unclothed bodies were painted with broad stripes of red and yellow and black. She was relieved to see they carried no weapons, but they weren't smiling, either.

The air smelled sharp and slightly sour, a mixture of smoke and something pungent. Fires crackled in stone pits situated among the various-sized teepees, but no one was tending the pots hanging over the fire pits. The entire camp seemed to have come to a stop.

She longed to make a sketch of the surroundings and write up some notes. Her hand moved to remove her notepad from her pocket, but Zach stopped her with a quick motion of his arm.

"Don't," he ordered.

"But—"

"Not yet, Dusty. And for God's sake, don't dismount and start asking questions."

"I wouldn't think of it," she muttered. But she did long to explore the camp, peek inside the teepees and sniff whatever was cooking over the fires.

All at once a tall figure emerged from the biggest teepee and strode toward them, the boy at his heels. A feather headdress brushed the man's shoulders and he wore a faded army coat. That gave her pause. How in the world had he acquired such a garment? *Had he killed someone?*

The man stopped in front of Zach, raised one hand, palm up, and spoke some words. She hoped they were friendly ones, but she couldn't tell. He was not smiling, she noted. None of them were smiling, except for some of the younger children.

"Must be the chief," Zach said in a low voice. He raised his hand in the same manner, and the feathered man motioned for him to dismount.

"Stay there," Zach murmured as he slid off his horse. He turned to the chief and pointed at Alex as if introducing her. She would love to know what the chief thought she was. Zach's woman, she guessed. The thought made her face feel hot.

The chief motioned for her to dismount, and the instant her boots touched the ground the entire camp came to life. Women crept up, reaching out to touch her red plaid shirt and peer at her jeans, and the children giggled and pointed. Two of the painted young men came to lead their horses away.

Uneasy, she stepped closer to Zach. "I think we passed muster," he said. "The chief looks pleased, and that kid who came and got us is grinning like there's no tomorrow."

"I'm a little scared," she whispered.

"Well, for God's sake, don't let it show!"

The chief called out something to the other Indians. The women moved to tend the cooking pots, and the men began to don armbands and feather headdresses. The boy motioned for them to sit down by the biggest fire pit.

She followed Zach to the indicated spot, and a large woman with an elaborately beaded deerskin dress pointed at the pot over the fire, then at herself, and then at Alex and Zach.

"I think she's going to feed us supper," he said. He sat down and tipped his head toward Alex. "Sit close."

She sank down beside him and scooted sideways until her shoulder touched his, and he draped his arm over one bent knee. She felt enormously heartened by his presence.

"When can I make some notes?" she asked quietly.

"Not yet," he replied. "Maybe not ever."

The woman stirred the contents of the pot with a long-handled wooden spoon. It smelled rich and meaty, and Alex's stomach rumbled. She hadn't realized how hungry she was. When shallow wooden bowls of a steaming stew of some sort appeared in front of them, her mouth watered.

"Whatever it is," Zach murmured, "eat it."

"Of course," she murmured. "I am ravenous!"

The chief sat down across the fire pit from them, the women served him and the boy, and the men squatted near them and waited.

Alex studied the contents of her bowl. "How do we eat this, with a spoon?"

"Don't know," Zach answered. "Wait."

The chief dipped his fingers into his stew and scooped a portion into his mouth. "Guess that's how," Zach said. He reached into his bowl.

Alex hesitated, studying her supper. It looked thick and lumpy, like beef stew in heavy brown gravy. She fished out a tiny bite and swallowed it. "It tastes very good," she breathed. She downed another, larger bite. "Delicious, in fact."

"Don't talk, just eat. We're guests."

A drum began to beat out an insistent rhythm, and suddenly the men were on their feet, wearing feather headdresses and executing intricate steps forward and then back, moving in a loose circle around the open area of the camp.

She couldn't stand one more minute without a pencil in her hand. Sneaking her notepad onto her lap, she alternated scooping up bites of stew, licking off her fingers and jotting down a few words. She noted the rhythm of the drums using *X*'s and circles, then studied the dancers' steps, described their feathered headgear and sketched the faces of some of the women. She had just started to describe the teepees and some deerskins pegged to the ground on drying racks when Zach laid his hand on her writing arm.

"Stop," he whispered. "Something's happening."

She looked up to see the chief striding toward them with something held in his two hands. He leaned down and draped a necklace made of some kind of animal teeth around Zach's neck. He spoke some words and extended his hand, and Zach reached up to clasp it. The chief smiled.

"Must be thanks for that cow I gave the boy," Zach breathed.

The dancing went on for over an hour and then suddenly stopped. The chief then turned to Zach and gestured toward the smaller teepee next to the big one.

"He's inviting us to stay the night," Zach said.

She sucked in her breath. "Together? In the same tent?"

"Guess so. His hospitality, his rules."

"Oh."

The chief motioned to them again and pointed at the teepee.

"Yep," Zach said. "Together. Like under the chuck wagon in camp."

"But without Roberto," she said in a small voice.

"Yeah, no Roberto." He stood and reached out his hand. "Come on."

He led her to the smaller teepee and ducked inside. Dusty stuffed her notepad and pencil into her shirt pocket and followed.

Zach found he couldn't stand upright except in the center of the teepee, so he settled onto the pile of furs arranged on the far side. Dusty paced around the interior, peering closely at the structure's rawhide seams and gazing up at the smoke hole at the top.

Finally she dropped down beside him, pulled out her

notepad and started to write. After a moment she began pawing through the layers of furs and skins on the pallet where they sat and then scratched some more on her pad.

"Zach," she whispered. "What kind of fur is this?"

Lord God in heaven, never for one moment did this woman forget she's a newspaper reporter!

"Bear, most likely."

She wriggled her bottom on it and he sucked in his breath.

"It's so soft!" she exclaimed. "I didn't know bears were so soft." She scribbled something with her pencil.

"Yeah, they're soft all right." She hadn't yet noticed that there was only *one* pallet.

It was dim inside the teepee, and as night fell, the available light faded into shadows. When Dusty could no longer see to write, he figured she would notice their sleeping situation. And that presented a problem.

He could be gallant and offer her the single pallet, but he honestly didn't fancy sleeping on the bare ground. It was hard, and it would get cold before morning. He pondered what to do, and she went on squinting and scribbling until she could no longer see. Finally she sighed and stowed her pencil and pad back in her shirt pocket.

He waited.

"This is such a grand adventure, isn't it?" she said.

"Yeah."

"I thought going on a cattle drive would be the most exciting thing I've ever done, but now I think maybe it's coming to this Indian camp."

"Yeah?"

"Oh, yes, Zach. I imagine I am the only newspaper reporter in the entire country who has ever seen a real Indian camp. What tribe do you think this is?"

"Maybe Nez Perce."

She gazed around at the walls of the teepee. "Are these structures made of deerskin?"

"Yeah."

"They're quite comfortable inside. They probably shed rain and snow in the winter, too. And stay warm and cozy."

Zach waited, saying nothing. He knew the exact moment their single-pallet sleeping arrangement dawned on her because she suddenly broke off in the middle of describing how the camp smelled. "Kind of chocolaty, with something like vineg—"

He almost laughed out loud.

"Vinegar," she finished. There was a long pause. "Zach?"

Here it comes. "Yeah?"

"There is only one—"

"Yeah," he said yet again.

"Oh. Well, I don't suppose this will be much different from sleeping next to each other under the chuck wagon, will it? Except that…" She bit her lip.

Zach didn't trust himself to say anything, but he was sure smiling inside. More than smiling. He didn't figure Miss Write-It-All-Down would put anything about this sleeping arrangement dilemma in her newspaper. Kinda took the starch out of her, he guessed. Dusty without starch might be good.

"Zach?"

"Hmm?"

"Are you…tired? I mean, are you, um, sleepy?"

"Nope." He was lying through his teeth, but she didn't need to know that.

"Oh." She sounded so disappointed he had to chuckle. Quietly.

"I bet you're tired, though," he offered. "After that long ride."

"Well, it wasn't as bad as riding in all that dust behind a big herd of cows."

"Steers," he corrected.

What now? he wondered. Were the two of them going to struggle to stay awake until one of them slumped over in spite of themselves? In spite of *herself*? He shot a surreptitious look at her, but now it was so dark inside the teepee he couldn't see her face clearly.

She let out a big sigh.

"Tired?"

"Well, yes," she said slowly. "Aren't you?"

He worked hard to keep his voice as noncommittal as he could. "Nope," he said. "Not tired at all."

"Perhaps we should flip a coin to see who gets to sleep on the pallet?"

"You got a coin?"

"Well...no, I don't. Do you?"

He had a shiny new two-bit piece in his pocket, but for some reason he couldn't explain he didn't want to mention it. "Nope," he lied.

"Zach, what are we going to do?"

He stretched his legs out in front of him. "About what?" he said blandly.

"About sleeping tonight," she huffed. "We can't both occupy this little pallet, um, *together*."

"Guess not, if it's gonna tie your drawers up in a twist."

She jerked as if he'd shot her. "What?"

He tried not to look at her face in the gloom, but he

could imagine it, her blue eyes getting all wide and her mouth dropping open.

"You heard me."

"Well, yes," she said, her voice frosty, "but I have never heard such a reference to my…drawers. Really, Zach, it is most improper."

He was glad she couldn't see his face; the smile that tugged at his lips would be a dead giveaway. At this moment, the picture her drawers conjured up in his imagination was making his jeans feel too tight. Not only that, he admitted, but he was enjoying it!

Before he could come up with what to say, she had skittered off onto another subject.

"I wonder what that stew had in it," she mused.

Zach didn't want to tell her. A band of starving Nez Perce would eat anything that walked or crawled, and he suspected the flavorsome supper they'd been served was most likely dog meat. But he wasn't telling Dusty that. Guess they'd eaten that cow he'd given them down to the hooves.

However, he was learning that once Dusty was curious about something, she didn't give up.

"What do you think it was, Zach?"

"Dunno. Tasted good, though." He held his breath, hoping she'd drop the subject.

"Yes, it did. Very rich and flavorful. I wonder what Roberto would think of it?"

He knew damn well what Roberto would think of it. Roberto believed in beef. Period.

She wriggled her bottom around on the furs for a few seconds and then surprised him again. "Perhaps we could take turns sleeping tonight."

"You mean one of us gets the soft bed and the other gets the hard ground?"

"Yes, and then we could trade off. That's fair, isn't it?"

He suppressed a snort. Trade off? Hell, no, he wasn't gonna "trade off" with a perfectly good pallet available.

"Sure," he said. "You can take the first shift."

"All right," she said with some reluctance in her tone. "At least it's a warm night."

"Yeah." It was more than warm; it was getting hotter inside this teepee by the minute. He moved to adjust his jeans over his swollen member, then slid off the pallet. Dusty tipped over onto the furs and stretched out with a tired sigh.

He had just closed his eyes when he heard something, a rhythmic *whump-whump* coming from somewhere outside. It took him a minute to pinpoint the source; the sounds were coming from the teepee next to theirs.

Whump-whump, whump-whump.

Dusty sprang upright. "What is that noise?"

It took only sixty seconds for him to figure it out. Whoever was in the next teepee was hard at making the oldest form of whoopee known to man. Probably the chief and his woman. He gritted his teeth and hoped Dusty wouldn't guess what it was.

She listened hard for a few minutes. "Zach? Is someone...?" Her voice trailed off as understanding sank in. "Oh. Oh, my."

They listened in silence as the thumping went on and on. And on. Zach's groin began to ache.

Dusty didn't move, just sat motionless without speaking.

"Why don't you get some sleep?" he suggested. He noticed his voice was a bit hoarse.

Whump-whump.

"Oh, yes," she said in an uneven voice. "I guess I should."

All at once the pounding ceased, and a woman's voice gave a high, choked cry. Zach closed his eyes. That was followed by a man's guttural shout, and right then Zach thought he would come apart.

Dusty said nothing. Quietly she lay back down on the furs, and he tried to keep his breathing steady. He stretched out full length on the hard ground and clenched both hands into fists. *Don't think about it.*

Thank God she wasn't asking any more questions. Guess she'd figured it out to her satisfaction, and that thought made him hot all over. The idea that they were both thinking about the same thing at the same time had him rock hard and hurting.

It was going to be a long, long night.

Alex would most definitely not be writing about this in the *Chicago Times*! She would also never mention it to Aunt Alice. Imagine explaining to her mother's sister how she laid next to Zach Strickland in over-attentive silence, listening to…*it*.

But she had to admit it was certainly educational. So a woman cried out when… She pressed her fingers against her mouth. And a man shouted?

She wondered what it felt like.

Oh, no, she didn't. She must stop thinking about it this instant!

And she did, for maybe four minutes. And then she lay staring up at the patch of star-studded sky visible through the small teepee opening over her head. Was Zach doing the same thing, thinking about…it? She couldn't ask him. She couldn't even admit she was awake and gazing up at the stars and having all these disturbing thoughts. It was too embarrassing.

She folded her hands across her midriff and closed her eyes. *Dear God, please, please let me clear my mind and go to sleep.*

Hours later she rolled over to find Zach's hard, warm body lying beside her. In fact, he was snugged up right next to her on the fur-covered pallet, and he was sound asleep. His breathing was slow and even, and one arm was stretched above his head. The other arm was curved over her middle.

Well. So much for taking turns!

In spite of herself a spurt of laughter bubbled up. What a newspaper story this would make! Her readers would gobble up such an Indian camp episode and beg for more. She felt her cheeks grow warm, and then hot. The rest of her body did the same, and all the while Zach softly inhaled and exhaled beside her.

No one would ever know about this, not even the *Chicago Times*.

And no one would ever, ever know how it was making her feel.

Zach opened his eyes when sunlight pouring through the smoke hole at the top of the teepee hit his face. He groaned and started to roll over, but a soft, curvy body was in his way. *It's Dusty!*

She was sound asleep, with her butt snuggled up against his groin, and for a fleeting moment he wondered if he'd died and gone to heaven.

Oh, heck no, he wasn't dead! He was tantalizingly, achingly alive. Very gingerly, and with considerable regret, he edged off the fur pallet and away from her. Then he sat up.

What now?

Now he had to wake Dusty, find their horses and head back to the herd. He laid one hand on her shoulder and jiggled it.

"Dusty, wake up."

She mumbled something and scooted away from him.

"Dusty. The chief wants to adopt you and keep you here with him for the next fifty years."

"What?" She sat up so fast her head bumped his shoulder. "What did you say? The chief wants to...?"

He chuckled. "Woke you up, didn't it?"

She scrubbed one hand over her face. "I swear you said—"

"Musta been dreaming," he said. "Come on, get up. We're ridin' back to the herd."

"Oh, thank the Lord, Zach. This has all been very interesting, but I am starting to miss all those silly cows."

"Steers," he corrected.

By the time he found their horses, saddled and ready, she was wide-awake, but Zach was feeling like he needed a good night's sleep. He'd spent half the night trying to keep himself from crawling onto those furs and wrapping his arms around her, and the other half praying she wouldn't wake up when he did.

"Mount up," he ordered. To his surprise she obeyed without a word.

He shook hands with the Indian boy who had brought them to the camp, and then the chief motioned him aside and said some words Zach didn't understand. Whatever it was, it made the boy laugh. The chief then tipped his head toward Dusty, grinned and made a motion with his hand that Zach understood instantly.

The boy's laughter followed them until they rode out of camp and headed east. After no more than five minutes, Dusty twisted in the saddle.

"What did the chief say to you?"

"Haven't a clue," he said quickly. "I don't understand their lingo."

But he sure understood the chief's hand gesture. He'd try not to think about it.

After six dry, dusty hours on the trail, they caught up with the herd bedded down at the edge of a broad sun-scorched meadow of brown tickle grass and tumbleweeds. It was almost suppertime, and both Zach and Dusty were saddle weary and hungry.

Cherry took their horses and clucked over the state of the animals. "Oughtn't let a saddle set on a horse overnight," he muttered.

"The Indians led our mounts off when we got to their camp," Zach explained. "I figured they'd take care of them."

"Indians don't use saddles, boss. What would they know about takin' care of 'em?"

Dusty headed for the shallow stream near camp to wash the grime off her face, and Zach talked to Curly and the other hands and tried not to smell whatever Roberto had bubbling in the Dutch oven hung over the campfire.

Skip clapped him on the back. "Hey, boss, what did them Indians want, anyway?"

"Wanted to thank us for that cow we sent them."

"Did they feed you?"

"Yeah. Good supper. Not as good as Roberto's beans, though. We've had no breakfast and nothing but a few rounds of jerky all day, so we're pretty much famished."

"Famished, huh? Sure came to the right place, boss. Roberto made cherry pie for dessert."

Dusty popped up at his elbow. "Pie?"

Zach swallowed a laugh. "You sure you don't want some more of that good Indian stew instead?"

She swatted him with her hat.

Chapter Twelve

For the next few days the sun poured down like maple syrup, making the air thick and heavy and hot as blazes. It was hard to breathe. Things were pretty much dried out; the wild buckwheat fields were already going to seed and rabbit brush was beginning to thin out.

They covered seventy miles without finding water. Creeks were dried up. Water holes were so low there wasn't enough for the herd and all the horses, too. Zach shook his head. Cattle could only last three days without water.

It was good it wasn't raining, but now it was beginning to look like a real honest-to-God midsummer drought. Guess the storms had moved off to the south. Well, it figured. The closer they got to the Nevada border, the closer they were to the high desert, and that was dry as old buffalo bones.

He gazed around him and let out a long breath. It was six o'clock in the morning and already the sky looked like a big blue bowl tipped upside down over his head. The air smelled of dust and sagebrush.

He turned Dancer away from the herd to check on

Dusty. Idiot girl was riding drag along with José and Jase. That left a sour taste in his mouth, but he couldn't talk her out of it. And by now he knew better than to give her an order. She'd just stick her chin up and insist she was making notes for her newspaper. Then she'd go on doing whatever she pleased.

Dusty always wanted to experience everything, and that included riding at the back of the herd with the stink and the dust and the flies. He shook his head again, and wished he could stop thinking about her.

That evening after Juan filled his supper plate he settled himself at the campfire next to Alex. "Cattle nervous tonight," he remarked.

She sent him a glance. "It's been an extra-long day with no water to drink. I'd be nervous, too."

"Boss send extra men out for night duty."

She wondered who he had sent. Cassidy, she hoped. When that man was anywhere near her she felt her skin crawl; he never seemed to stop staring at her.

She focused her attention on the beans and biscuits on her tin plate and tried to decide who to interview after supper for her newspaper column. Anyone but Cassidy.

Zach was pacing back and forth at the edge of the campfire, his hands jammed in his back pockets while she and the young cowhand ate in companionable silence.

Suddenly Juan leaned toward her. "Boss have also nerves."

"Oh? What about?"

Just as Juan opened his mouth to reply she heard a sharp crack, like a tree branch breaking off. Juan frowned, and then everything happened at once. She heard a low rumbling sound, and suddenly he leaped up, his plate clattering onto the ground.

"Stampede!" someone yelled.

Juan began to run. The next thing she knew Zach was beside her, grabbing her arm and yanking her upright. Her supper plate spilled beans all down the front of her jeans.

"Get in the wagon!" he shouted. He dragged her away from the fire and shoved her toward the chuck wagon. "Roberto! Take her!"

The gray-haired cook scrambled up past his cabinets and cupboards and extended his arms down to her. Zach gripped her around the waist and shoved her up toward him.

"Hurry, *señorita*!" The cook tugged her up and pushed her into the cramped wagon interior.

Zach spun away and raced for his horse, along with all the cowhands around the fire. The men grabbed their mounts, flung themselves into the saddle and pounded off, kicking up clouds of dust.

She saw Cherry struggling to drive the remuda away to the north, and then she heard a noise, a grumbling wave of sound that grew louder with each passing second.

"What's happening?" she screamed to Roberto.

"The cows, they run," he shouted.

Zach kept wondering why he wasn't getting trampled by the maddened animals on his right. He could feel the heat of their massed bodies, hear the sickening thunder of hooves in his ear. Damn, but he didn't need this. He needed to sell every last steer in Winnemucca.

He kept to the left of the herd, avoiding the wall of

charging steers at his elbow. There was no time to waste, but he knew if his horse went down he'd be trampled in seconds. He rode hard alongside the bellowing herd and hoped to heaven that someone up near the front was working to turn the cattle in a circle and bring them to a stop.

His ears hurt with the noise, but he kept moving alongside the pounding steers and prayed Dancer wouldn't stumble and dump both of them under all those hooves.

"Turn 'em!" he yelled to the riders ahead.

"Tryin'!" someone yelled back.

His horse was wheezing, but he kept spurring him to keep going. He couldn't see much except dust and shadows, and he kept pulling Dancer out of the way of the stampeding steers. It sounded like a damn freight train was coming right at him.

Alex could see nothing through the thickening dust, but the ground beneath the wagon began to shake. Roberto grabbed the curved iron brace over their heads. "Hold on!" he yelled.

She grasped the handle of the locked cabinet where Roberto kept his medicine bottles and Zach's emergency cash. The noise grew deafening, and when she peeked out the back she screamed. A swirling mass of bawling, maddened cows was headed straight for the wagon.

"Can they stop them?" she yelled.

Roberto cupped his hands to make himself heard. "They will try to turn them."

"How—"

The wagon started to shudder. "Roberto!" she shrieked. He lunged for her, pulling her head down against his shoulder, but she couldn't stand not seeing what was happening and she wrenched free.

The writhing sea of animals raced straight toward them, and Alex stopped breathing. *I'm going to die out here.*

The herd thundered forward, so close she could see their fear-crazed eyes. Off to one side, three cowhands struggled to steer the animals, cracking their whips and shouting. She could feel the heat of the cows' bodies, and their rank smell made her gag. In another second the wagon would be overrun, trampled under the hooves of a thousand maddened steers.

Oh, God, they would smash it into the earth, and her right along with it. She waited, unable to look away. The cattle surged closer, and Roberto grabbed her shoulders and tried to pull her down.

At the last possible second the sea of cows split in two and swirled around them on either side. The chuck wagon groaned and shuddered and suddenly began to list to one side.

"We're tipping over!" she screamed. She shut her eyes and waited to feel those sharp hooves slice into her body.

A whip cracked, and cracked again, and a man kept shouting. Gradually the noise and the heat receded and all at once it was quiet.

"Madre mia!" Roberto breathed.

"Is it over?" she asked shakily.

"Si, is over. We are most lucky." He reached out and patted her trembling hand. "I find whiskey, okay?"

She looked into his wide brown eyes and tried to smile.

It took the rest of the night to round up the steers and settle them down. Zach satisfied himself that he'd lost no cowhands and that Dusty and Roberto were safe, even though they'd been directly in the path of the runaway herd.

He tripled the night-riders, but he couldn't help wondering what had started the stampede off in the first place. He'd heard a sharp sound of some kind, but what was it? A snapped branch? A gun shot? Maybe he'd never know.

He found a shaken Dusty nursing a glass of whiskey Roberto was just topping up. She answered his questioning look with a brief nod and a wobbly smile that made his insides hurt.

Chapter Thirteen

First thing the next morning, Zach's point rider galloped up. "Boss! Boss!"

"What is it, Curly?"

"We're missing some steers. About a hundred head."

Zach's belly tightened. "Maybe they got trampled. You find any dead carcasses?"

"Nope. You think it was Indians?" Curly asked.

"Don't think so," Zach said. "An Indian would take only what he could eat, and you'd never hear him. And an Indian would be real careful not to start a stampede."

"You're right, I guess."

"Besides," Zach continued, "Indians couldn't get away with a hundred head of cattle before the soldiers from Fort Hall would run across them."

"So…" Curly ran his hand over his stubbly chin.

"Yeah." Zach ground his teeth. "Rustlers."

"Pretty slick, huh? Nobody saw a thing, not even the night-riders, until the herd started runnin'."

Zach bit the inside of his cheek. José and Cassidy were night-herding last night. He'd trust José with his life, but Cassidy? He spurred his horse to the back of the straggling herd.

Dusty was riding alongside José and Cassidy, her bandanna tied over her mouth and nose. He stepped Dancer up close. "You okay?" he yelled.

"Yes," she shouted, nodding. "Fine."

He dropped back and fell in beside the man he hadn't yet decided about. "Cassidy?"

The big man drew rein. "Yeah?"

"You were night-herding last night, weren't you?"

"Yeah. Why?"

"See anything?"

"Nope. Why?"

"After the stampede last night, Curly ran a tally. We came up short a hundred head."

"Maybe Indians ran 'em off. Or you coulda lost 'em during the stampede."

Zach shook his head. "Maybe. But I figure it was rustlers." He watched Cassidy's face, but the cowhand's wind-burned features revealed nothing. Without proof, Zach wasn't about to accuse a man.

"José? You see anything last night before the cattle stampeded? Hear anything?"

The Mexican shook his head.

"Keep your eyes open," Zach said. He shot another look at Cassidy and reined away. Sure hoped his scout up ahead could find water today. Either that or a hundred stray steers. Wally could usually find a water source blindfolded. Steers, he didn't know about. But right now, finding water was more important.

The chuck wagon had rattled away to the east shortly after their dawn breakfast, followed by Cherry and the remuda. Now, twelve hours later, a dirty, exhausted crew came up on a rise and began cheering. The herd smelled water, kicked up their hooves and pressed forward.

"Run 'em parallel," Zach shouted. *"Parallel!"* If the hands just let the whole mass of cattle surge forward, the thirsty steers would trample each other. He wanted them in a long line parallel to the water source, not bunched up on top of each other.

He trotted on up over the rise. Oh, man, just look at that! A sparkling blue lake nestled in a wide green meadow dotted with red and orange Indian paintbrush and carpets of desert primrose. Beyond the lake, the chuck wagon was parked between two stands of cottonwoods, and Cherry had corralled the remuda close by.

If it weren't for Dusty's presence on this drive, the hands would be tearing toward the water, ripping off their shirts and jeans as they went. Zach chuckled. Good thing tomorrow was Sunday. They'd hold up for the day and give everyone a chance to get clean and wash out their dirt-stained duds. Give himself a chance to shave.

That night Roberto celebrated by baking three dried-apple pies for dessert. Zach had just dug his fork into his second piece when he looked up to see two riders on the horizon. He set his plate down and stood up.

The strangers headed straight for the camp without slacking their pace. Talk around the fire dwindled and then died.

"Dusty," Zach said in an undertone. "Make yourself scarce. Get into the chuck wagon."

"But—"

"Now," he ordered.

Roberto strode forward, grasped her arm and steered her toward the wagon. Zach watched her climb inside, and then he turned to face the unidentified riders.

"Curly," he said without turning. "Get a shotgun."

When the two horsemen were thirty yards away, he started toward them.

Both men looked travel-weary and unshaven. Both wore sidearms. They reined up ten feet in front of him, and one leaned down over his saddle horn.

"Howdy. Name's Gibson. Orren Gibson. You missing any cattle?"

"Yeah, about a hundred head."

"Us, too. About seventy steers. I was driving them to Abilene."

"I'm heading for Winnemucca," Zach volunteered. "Name's Zach Strickland."

"How about keeping your eyes peeled for some loose Double Diamond steers?"

"Sure. Most of mine wear the Rocking K brand, but we've got some other brands mixed in."

"We'll watch out for yours, Mr. Strickland."

"Much obliged. Care for some apple pie?"

"No, thanks. Got some miles to cover before dark."

When Zach returned to the campfire, the plate of pie he'd left was scraped clean. "Hey, who ate my pie?"

No one said anything, and then Dusty's fork clattered onto the empty tin plate. "I ate it," she announced.

He frowned down at her where she sat beside the campfire. "How come?"

"Because you sent me off to hide in the chuck wagon. It was extremely cramped in there, and I missed dessert. And an exciting news story."

He stared at her. "I give the orders around here. I expect my hands to follow them."

"I'm not one of your hands," she retorted. "So I ate your apple pie." And then she grinned up at him.

Zach walked over and leaned down to her level. "In

that case, Miss Murray," he said with a chuckle, "you owe me one."

Jase laughed out loud. "What're you gonna ask for, boss? Maybe she'll bake you another pie, huh?"

"I don't want a pie."

"Oh?" she asked, her voice wary. "Then what do you want?"

He bent even lower and placed his mouth near her ear. "I want to ask you a bunch of questions, like you asked me the other night," he breathed. "In private."

Hours after Roberto had washed and dried the tin supper plates and forks and scoured out the Dutch oven, Zach assigned night-herding duties, rolled out his blankets and crawled under the chuck wagon. The cook was snoring away just outside the rear wheel, and Dusty was asleep. Or pretending to be.

He touched her shoulder. "Dusty?"

"Mmmff."

"Dusty, wake up."

"I'm awake," she said in a sleep-fogged voice.

He propped himself up on one elbow and spoke to the lump under the blue blanket. "You ate my pie, remember? So tonight it's my turn to ask questions."

She struggled into a half-upright position. "Now? It's the middle of the night!"

"Now."

"But—but I'm half asleep. I don't think well when I'm half asleep."

"Good. I don't want you to think well. I want you to talk."

She flopped back onto her bedroll and closed her eyes. "Very well, Mr. Strickland. What do you want to know?"

Everything. "Tell me about yourself, Dusty. Where were you born, for instance?"

"Chicago," she murmured.

He should have guessed that. He'd bet she had been rich as Croesus as a kid. "What about your parents?"

No answer. But he could hear her breathing, and it wasn't as even as it had been before. He knew she was awake, so he waited.

"My...my father never wanted me. He wanted a son, and he never let me forget it. When I was born, Mama told me he took one look at me and slapped her across the face. Then he said, 'She's a damn girl and I don't want her.'"

"Ouch," Zach said.

"Papa didn't care if I lived or died. All my life I worked hard to get him to notice me, to approve of me... but he never did."

"What about your momma?"

She huffed out a long breath. "I don't like to think about Mama very much. She hadn't wanted a child at all," she said, her voice muffled. "Mama was...well, vague, I guess you could call it. She was very beautiful, but she couldn't really *do* anything. She had servants, so she never *had* to do anything."

"You grew up rich, huh?"

"In some ways. In other ways I was as impoverished as the beggars in the park. I wanted to be nothing like my mother, nothing at all."

"And? What did you do instead?"

"I did things Mama couldn't have done. I went to college. I was just sixteen, and I finished in two years. And then when I was almost nineteen, I got a job. That absolutely scandalized Mama, but I did it anyway. Working at the newspaper made me feel worthwhile. Foolishly, I thought that having a career, excelling at a major newspaper like the *Chicago Times*, would earn me Papa's acceptance."

"But it didn't," he hazarded.

"No, it didn't. It was quite the opposite. I wasn't a boy, you see, and—" Her voice broke.

In a way Zach regretted asking. But in another way he felt a warm knot deep inside, an understanding of this young woman he wouldn't have thought possible a month ago. He'd seen what Dusty was like on the outside, and he'd had some hints about what made her tick. Now he was beginning to know who she was on the inside.

He reached over and laid the back of his hand against her cheek. "Go back to sleep, Dusty. And thanks."

The next morning, after a breakfast of bacon and beans, the men slipped off to the small lake. Alex listened to the splashing sounds and raucous shouts of their obvious enjoyment and let out a deep sigh. She felt sticky and dirty and a little saddle sore, and she needed a cool bath as much as the men. But she would wait until after supper when it grew dark and she could bathe without attracting attention.

She thought about it all through Roberto's excellent roast rabbit and spicy chili beans. She also thought about the fact that Cassidy's eyes still followed her every move. Something about the man made her more than uneasy. He frightened her.

After supper, Zach walked over to the wash bucket to dunk his tin plate and coffee mug, and Alex rose and followed him. "Zach," she said quietly, "I'd like to go for a swim in the lake."

"Now?"

"Yes. But…" She cut her eyes to where Cassidy sat by the fire, watching her. "I need you to—"

"Stand guard," he finished for her. He glanced over at Cassidy. "Is he botherin' you?"

"N-no, not really. He just, well, he keeps looking at me."

"Gather up your soap and stuff. I'll walk you down to the lake."

While he waited for her, he spoke again to Roberto. "Tuck a pistol under your pillow tonight. And don't tell Miss Alex."

"Something it is wrong?" the cook wanted to know.

"Not wrong, just iffy."

"*Que?* What means 'iffy,' *por favor*?"

"It means keep your eyes open. You savvy?"

"*Si*, Señor Boss, I savvy." He, too, shot a look at Cassidy.

Dusty didn't say much on the short path through the cottonwoods to the lake. There was enough moonlight to see, and she moved a few yards ahead of him, walking at a quick march and singing under her breath. She must be thinking about her bath.

He was thinking about it, too. He was half worrying about Cassidy and half worrying about why he felt like humming at the thought of Dusty taking a bath.

When they reached the lake, he leaned his back against a sugar pine trunk, facing away from the lake, and took up his lookout post. Dusty disappeared, and in a few minutes he heard a soft splash and a happy-sounding laugh. Without thinking he turned around.

She was standing knee-deep in the water, just standing there with the moonlight shimmering on her naked body. He stopped breathing. He watched her unbraid her

thick hair, lift it in both hands and spread the dark wavy
mass about her shoulders. Then she clasped her hands
over her head and stretched up, arching her bare back.

She was so beautiful she made him ache. Sweat prick-
led his neck. Oh, God, he wanted her. *He wanted her.*

Slowly she turned away from him, raised her arms
again and dived into the water. He watched as the ripples
spread and washed toward him in widening circles until
his eyes burned, waiting for her to stand up and move
toward him. She must not catch him watching, but he felt
frozen in place, unable to turn away and break the spell.

No, not unable, Strickland. Unwilling.

His heart had flown outside his body somewhere. Part
of him wanted to call it back; another part of him, a part
that was feeling kinda shaky all of a sudden, wanted to
toss it over the moon.

He waited, unable to turn away, and she finally waded
to the shallow water at the edge of the lake, her wet
hair fanning her shoulders in a dark waterfall. Then she
began braiding up her hair again.

He was damn sorry when she put on all her clothes.

All the following day Alex felt Zach's eyes on her.
By ten o'clock it was beastly hot, the sun like a steaming copper pot over their heads and the air so heavy
and still it was suffocating. How did the men stand this,
hour after hour?

The horses were rotated every few hours, but there
was no respite for the riders.

The shouting, yipping men drove the herd through
wide, flat meadows that smelled of sage and narrow,
steep-sided canyons where the earth beneath their feet
was red gravel and the only thing to break the monot-

ony were lumpy black rocks and an occasional stand of spindly pine trees.

She could not imagine a more desolate landscape. Nothing moved in the shimmering heat but cows and horses and clouds of stinging knats and men. And one woman, as hot and sweaty and miserable as she had ever been in her life. Even the hawks perched motionless on the tall pine branches.

Just as she thought she could not force her aching body to ride one more mile, she spotted Roberto's chuck wagon far ahead, parked near a sprangly oak tree. Listlessly, she rode toward it.

Roberto looked up when she reined to a halt and dismounted. "Señorita Alex," the cook said with a grin. "You want taste of my stew?"

She was hungry, but she was too hot and parched to even think about putting something warm in her mouth. "Thank you, Roberto, but I want to wash first."

Cherry appeared and gathered the sorrel's reins in his leathery hand. "You come with me, Miss Alex. I got a nice private horse trough you kin use to cool off. Just filled it, so the water's clean."

"Thanks, Cherry. I don't even mind sharing it with your remuda."

"No soap, though," he cautioned. "That'd give all my horses the scours for sure."

She laughed, snaked a dishtowel from the rack on the side of the chuck wagon and followed him to the rope corral. She knew Cherry's thoughtful gesture wasn't because she'd made a friend of him the night she'd interviewed the old wrangler. Patient, thoughtful Cherry was just being Cherry.

Chapter Fourteen

Three more long, scorching days dragged by. In the evening, lathered horses walked into camp, their heads drooping, and the tempers of all the hands grew short. Zach seemed unusually curt, especially to her. The heat was draining them all, and Alex worked extra hard not to let anything nettle her, especially Zach's disinterest. She knew she would never survive many more weeks of this; every day was an ordeal worse than the preceding one. She began to worry that she could not last.

But what choice did she have? There was nothing to do but keep moving forward with the herd and hope for the best.

Now she had something else that nagged at her. Since the night Zach had questioned her about her parents and her work at the newspaper, he had changed. She would swear he was avoiding her, but she didn't know why. She drew in a gulp of the gritty air and tried to stuff down her disappointment.

She had confessed to Zach something she had kept buried for years, how her father had wanted a boy and how Mama hadn't wanted a child of either sex. And after that, the tall, rangy trail boss had taken to sleeping by the campfire, next to Cassidy of all people, and Roberto had continued to sleep next to her under the chuck wagon at night.

Zach seemed distant, as if he disliked something about her, but what? The fact that she came from a well-to-do background? The fact that she was a newspaper reporter? Or, more likely, that she was a female tagging along on an all-male cattle drive.

The next night after supper, when the hands had left the campfire and rolled out their bedrolls, she cornered him. "Zach, what is wrong?"

He looked up, and then focused everywhere but on her. "Nuthin'," he said shortly.

She flinched at his tone. "I don't believe that for one minute."

"Got things on my mind." He looked over her head, staring at the herd bedded down in a dry meadow a few dozen yards away.

"What things?" she persisted.

"Just…things." He sent her a quick look, then studied the scuffed toes of his boots. "The men are gettin' tired. And you already know I lost a hundred head of cattle to some damn rustlers."

She knew instinctively it was more than that. Something else was bothering him. But what? Even Roberto shrugged his shoulders when she asked him. "Boss never act like this before. He maybe sick."

The next night Alex watched Zach's plate of beans and biscuits disappear as usual, along with three cups of black coffee, and she knew he wasn't sick. Then, without a word, he stalked off to inspect the herd. Much later he returned to question Cherry about the remuda, and then he tramped around and around at the edge of the campfire until Juan intercepted him.

She couldn't hear what was said, but Juan returned to the fire with a shrug, just as Roberto had. Alex decided to put it out of her mind and concentrate on her note-taking. Tonight, she decided, she would interview Roberto.

The chuck wagon cook told her he had come from Mexico when he was just a boy, worked as a vaquero until he married and then settled down in Arizona with his wife and baby son, José.

"José?" she asked. "*Our* José?"

"No, not this José. My José. He die of fever, and my wife, she die, too. And then I come to live with my sister, Consuelo. *Our* José," he explained, "he is Consuelo's son. My nephew. Juan, he is also my nephew."

"How did you become the chuck wagon cook?"

Roberto laughed. "Consuelo, she teach me. Then Mr. Charlie, one year he take me on the roundup. You know what is roundup?"

Alex twiddled her pencil between her thumb and forefinger. "I think so. You ride around and stick those awful hot irons on all the cows, is that right?" She shuddered.

Roberto chuckled. "You know not much of cattle ranching, *señorita*."

"I know absolutely *nothing* about cattle ranching. I belong in a big city, not on a ranch."

"But, *señorita*, even in big city, one can know what happen in life. *Que sera*, no?"

Alex smiled into the older man's dark eyes. "No, Roberto. Sometimes one *doesn't* know what happens in life." She flipped over a new page in her notebook. "Roberto, tell me something."

"Anything, *señorita*. Is good to learn."

"How do you decide what to cook for supper every night?"

"Ah, is easy, Señorita Alex. See that?" He tipped his gray head toward a large canvas-covered mound in one corner of the chuck wagon. "Is beef. I keep cool with water splashing so not dry out or spoil, and each night I slice off some." He chopped his hand downward.

While he talked, Alex scratched notes.

"Then I cook chili with beans or beef stew or just plain beef steaks."

She nodded. "I do like your chili, Roberto. I never tasted anything so spicy back in Chicago."

He laughed and reached out a work-gnarled hand to pat her shoulder. She wanted to ask him again about Zach, why he was suddenly so unfriendly, but the cook got to his feet, gathered up his roll of bright-colored blankets and headed for the chuck wagon. "*Buenas noches, señorita.*"

Alex closed her notebook and stared into the campfire. How many days had she been following these noisy, smelly cows around this godforsaken countryside? Three weeks? Four? Funny how easy it was to lose track of time out here so far away from civilization. No clocks. No deadlines. No late hours spent proofreading her newspaper columns.

And no concerts. No theatrical performances. No libraries. And not one horse race!

But she couldn't say she was bored, not with colorful characters like Cherry and Roberto and Curly, whose hair was as long and straight as a sheet of newsprint. And, she had to admit, the most interesting activity of all was watching the trail boss, Zach Strickland.

Or it had been until he got so moody and standoffish.

She massaged the back of her neck. She would thank all the powers of the universe when they reached Winnemucca and she would have a hotel room with a bathtub. And the train. Oh, my, yes…the train that would carry her back to civilization. She would put all this aggravation behind her, gather up her overflowing notebooks, travel back to Chicago and write her newspaper columns. She intended to impress the socks off her editor at the *Times*.

Then she would put her sore bottom and her stiff shoulders and her hurt feelings behind her. She wouldn't miss any of this one bit. And that included Zach Strickland!

Endless long hot days without water had Zach gritting his teeth and praying, something he never did. For one thing, the good Lord couldn't care less about one herd of cattle, and for another, the good Lord couldn't care less about *him*. All his life he'd had to fight, for respect, for acceptance, even for survival. He hadn't believed in "turn the other cheek" since he was ten years old and had left home for good.

And now he was fighting for the money to start his own ranch. He reached to pat his mount's sleek neck. "You hear that, Dancer? We're workin' damn hard for this, aren't we? We might not be rich, but we sure as blazes can be independent."

A steer veered away from the herd and lumbered off toward the hills. Zach touched Dancer's flanks, grabbed his lariat and raced across the plain after the animal. It was full-grown, four hundred pounds of grass-fed beef on four hooves, and it wasn't easy to run down.

He galloped beside it for a dozen yards, then loosed

his rope. The lariat sailed out and settled neatly over the horns, and Zach yanked it tight. Dancer backed away and the steer bawled. Zach lifted the rope off the horns and re-coiled it as the animal headed back toward the herd.

"Good work, boy. That's another forty dollars for our ranch." He began to ride parallel to the herd, whistling as he thought about the spread he planned to buy when he returned to Oregon with his share of the profits.

He'd build a big barn to start with, then a bunkhouse with a potbellied stove for heat and later a ranch house.

He kicked Dancer into a gallop and headed off in a wide circle to work off his excitement. Just as he turned back toward the plodding herd, his mount stumbled hard and Zach was thrown out of the saddle. He landed flat on his back and for a minute he couldn't draw breath.

He turned his head to one side to see Dancer not three yards away, waiting for him to get up. It took him another minute before his lungs started to work again; then he picked himself up, dusted off his hat and took a step toward his horse.

Dancer did not move. And then he noticed that the black gelding was standing perfectly still, but his fore-leg was bent funny.

Zach felt like throwing up.

Curly stopped his story mid-sentence, staring at something past her shoulder, and Alex looked up. Slowly the cowhand stood up. "Damn," he said under his breath.

She twisted to see behind her and heard José mutter, *"Madre mia."*

Zach was coming across the meadow, walking very slowly and leading his black horse. Even from here she could see the animal was limping badly.

One by one, the men around the campfire rose in silence.

"Aw, no, not Dancer," Skip whispered. "Zach's practically married to that horse." He started forward.

"Don't," Cherry snapped. "Let him alone."

"Gosh, Cherry, you can see that black's leg is busted."

"I see it," the wrangler said, his voice quiet. "Let Zach deal with it."

Alex stared at the dusty figure coming toward them. He'd pulled his hat down so his face was half hidden, but what was visible was his mouth, grim and unsmiling. He led the horse to the chuck wagon and dropped the reins.

"Roberto."

"Si?"

Zach's face was stony. "Get my revolver."

No one spoke, and Alex's heart constricted.

Cherry walked over to him. "You want me to do it?"

Zach shook his head once. Roberto held out the gun and Zach grasped the butt, then turned away and picked up the reins.

"Oh, no," someone murmured. "My God, no."

Zach led the beautiful black horse away across the meadow, moving slowly, as if his legs were made of lead. Alex's eyes burned.

She watched him stop, loosen the cinch and lift off his saddle. All the time he seemed to be talking to the animal, running his hand over its neck, its flank. Finally he leaned his forehead against the muzzle for a long minute, and then he brought the gun up.

Alex covered her mouth with her hand.

The sharp retort of the revolver made her shoulders jerk, and Roberto stepped near. "Do not look, *señorita*." But she couldn't stand not to.

After a long moment, Cherry started forward to meet Zach. Without a word, Zach laid the gun in the wrangler's hand, dropped the saddle at his feet and turned away.

Her throat aching, Alex watched him walk slowly toward the stand of cottonwoods half a mile away.

Cherry spoke over his shoulder. "Curly, Jase, get a shovel."

Zach didn't return for supper. Eventually the subdued hands dunked their plates in the wash bucket and sat around the campfire smoking in silence. No one felt like talking. And Roberto's special raisin pie went untouched.

Curly made the night-herding assignments, then sat with his head bent, braiding a new rawhide lariat.

Alex stood it for as long as she could, then she rose, moved out of the firelight and walked across the meadow toward the cottonwood trees.

Chapter Fifteen

She found him sitting motionless, his back against a tree trunk with his long legs bent, his battered gray hat on the ground beside him. His hands hung loose across the tops of his knees. He didn't look up.

She knew he had heard her approach, but he didn't move. She stepped forward and stood in front of him without speaking, and then she moved between his splayed legs and dropped to her knees.

He reached for her. She pulled him forward, pressed his head against her breast and held him in silence.

An hour passed, maybe two; she didn't know and she didn't care. In all that time Zach said nothing. She didn't know what else to do other than just hold him, be there with him. Some instinct warned her not to talk.

Finally he lifted his head, looked into her eyes and nodded tiredly. Slowly he smoothed one hand over her hair, then did it again. Then he reached to one side to pick up his hat and stood up.

She rose with him, stepped close beside him and took his hand. Without speaking, they turned toward camp. Her throat was so tight it ached.

* * *

In the morning, Alex balanced her tin plate of fried potatoes and bacon in one hand and accepted a brimming mug of coffee with the other.

"Boss not eat breakfast," Roberto confided.

"Where is he?"

"Not know. Not sleep in camp last night."

She looked up into Roberto's worried face. "Where did Curly and Jase bury the horse?"

"Close by. Under big oak tree."

"Then that is where he is," Alex said. "I am sure of it. But…"

Roberto's salt-and-pepper eyebrows rose. "But? But what, *señorita*?"

"Roberto, I think we should leave him alone. Right now he needs to be by himself."

He gave her a long look. "You are correct, I think, *señorita*. Señor Strickland is much man."

Much man? What did that mean?

She thought about Roberto's description all morning and well into the afternoon as the herd plodded slowly through the hot, dry sagebrush-dotted desert.

When the sun burned directly overhead, a lone rider on a spirited paint swung in ahead of the herd. She knew it was Zach; she recognized the way he sat on his horse.

He made his way back to Juan, who was riding the flank position, and reined up beside him. They spoke together briefly, and then Zach touched his hat brim and rode up to Alex.

He thumbed back his Stetson and gave her a slow nod. "Dusty." His voice sounded raw.

She fished in her shirt pocket and thrust two breakfast biscuits toward him. "Here."

"What's this?"

"You didn't have breakfast. You must be hungry because you skipped supper last night, too."

He pinned her with clouded green eyes. "Yeah, I did. Thanks. You don't miss much, do you?"

"I am a newspaper reporter, Zach. I have trained myself to notice things."

The ghost of a smile touched his tight mouth. "I'm obliged to you, Dusty." For just a moment the shadow lifted from his eyes. "For more than just the biscuits."

He touched his hat and reined his horse away to join Curly and Skip, who were riding point. But he ate both biscuits and washed them down with the whiskey Roberto had poured into his canteen.

Zach tried to keep his mind busy thinking about the weather and finding water. And about his missing cattle. It would be simple enough to stampede a herd and in the confusion run off a hundred head of maddened steers. Hungry Indians would take maybe one or two beefs, not a hundred. Besides, they didn't need to stampede a thousand head of cattle; they could sneak up on an animal, quiet as a shadow, and lead it away without a sound.

Cattle didn't just escape or get lost in a stampede. When they started to run they pretty much kept together in one roiling mass. And nobody had seen or heard anything unusual that night, except for the sharp sound that had started them off. Zach figured it had been a gunshot. But who had fired it?

Orren Gibson's cattle were missing, too, but Gibson's herd hadn't stampeded, and that told Zach it had to be rustlers. Made his head ache to think about it.

He slowed his mount to ride beside his point man. "Curly?"

"Yeah, boss?"

"You got any theories about our missing steers?"

"Could look for them in the canyons up ahead."

"They could have been driven off anywhere. Why check the canyons ahead?"

"Because a canyon's a good place to hide a hundred head of cattle?" Curly offered.

"Worth a look, maybe."

"Yeah?" Curly said. "And then what?"

"Go after 'em?" Zach muttered.

"You crazy?"

"Not last time I looked, no. I don't fancy ridin' unarmed into a canyon, but I don't fancy losin' a hundred steers, either."

Curly huffed out a laugh. "Didn't figure you did, boss. But might be you wouldn't be alone. We got plenty of guns stowed in the chuck wagon."

Zach gave a short nod. "Right. Pass 'em out to the boys after supper tonight. And let's keep a sharp lookout."

That night Alex sat in front of the campfire with Jase and Skip, trying to keep her mind on the interview she was conducting. Idly, she twiddled a stubby pencil while Jase explained how he'd grown up in Boston and made his way out West when his folks died. He'd been married three times and divorced twice; his last wife had died in childbirth, along with the baby. She noticed that Jase rarely smiled.

Skip Billings, on the other hand, had an annoyingly sunny outlook. Nothing had bothered him since he'd mustered out of the Union Army after the War and realized he was still alive and whole. He'd taught himself to read and write, carried a collection of dime novels

in his saddlebag and spent his days singing the praises
of the Lord and General William Tecumseh Sherman.

She listened with half an ear, forcing herself to ask
pertinent questions and take notes, even though her mind
was occupied elsewhere. Still, she had a job to do. She
sat up and squared her shoulders. "And then what happened, Skip?"

Usually she enjoyed conducting interviews, but tonight she found talking to the men unusually draining.
What she wouldn't give to crawl into her blankets and
close her dust-irritated eyes. But she'd stick it out until
she had all the information she needed about both men
carefully written down in her notebook. She stifled a
yawn and straightened her spine.

Cassidy, she noted with relief, was not in camp.
Maybe Zach had assigned him to night-herding; whatever the reason, it was a relief when he was gone.

Jase leaned close. "You look plumb tuckered, Miss
Alex. You 'bout done with your questions?"

"Yes, we're finished." She wanted to learn why each
of the men she interviewed had chosen the hard life of
a cowhand. She was beginning to realize that the more
they talked, the more they revealed about their real reasons, and she resolved to listen even harder as the men
answered her questions. No one liked to admit their most
private feelings. Especially the trail boss, Zach Strickland.

When she stood up both Jase and Skip rose. "'Night,
Miss Alex."

She arched her stiff back, stuffed her notebook in the
back pocket of her jeans and circled the camp to work
out the ache in her spine. Sleeping cowhands lay in a
haphazard ring around the fire pit, and she took care not
to scuff her boots and wake them.

The far side of the chuck wagon, where Roberto lay snoring, was shrouded in darkness. She was moving quietly through the shadows when suddenly someone stepped into her path.

"Where ya goin', pretty lady?"

Cassidy! Her blood went cold.

"Been waitin' for ya."

She couldn't bring herself to look at him, so she kept her head down, her eyes focused on the toes of her boots.

"C'mon, say somethin'." He laid one thick hand on her arm.

She yanked it away. "Leave me alone."

"Aw, don't be that way, honey." He grabbed her shoulder, and before she could cry out, he planted a wet, sloppy kiss on her cheek.

She pummeled the arm holding her, but he tightened his grip. She lifted her boot, intending to stomp on his toes, but suddenly she felt his smelly body jerk away from her.

"Take your hands off her," Zach ordered, his voice tight.

"Aw, boss, I was just—"

"I said let her go."

"Hell if I will. You kin go to—"

The next thing she heard was the crack of a fist hitting something solid. Bone, she hoped.

"Here's your pay," Zach snarled to the unsteady cowhand. He flipped a twenty-dollar gold piece at him. "Now get out."

"Wait a damn minute, boss…"

"You heard me," Zach said. "You're fired."

Cassidy sullenly moved away.

Zach turned and laid a hand on her shoulder. "You all right, Dusty?"

"Y-yes."

"You sure? You look kinda pinched."

"Well, perhaps I am not really all right."

He gave her a long look. "Don't worry about Cassidy anymore. He won't be back."

At least, he hoped he wouldn't. He'd hate to have to kill the man.

The next night during supper, Cherry appeared unexpectedly at the campfire. Usually he stole off to the remuda at night, preferring the company of his beloved horses to that of a bunch of sweaty cowhands.

"Boss," the old man panted. "Ya gotta come with me."

Zach looked up from his plate of beans and corn bread. "What's up, Cherry? Got a sick mare?"

"Naw. Horses are all fine. But somethin' ain't so fine, so you'd better come have a look-see."

Zach knew better than to second-guess his wrangler, so he set his plate aside, got to his feet and walked with him out to the rope corral where the horses were bedded down for the night.

Cherry stopped and pointed ahead.

Zach blinked at the two figures facing him. He recognized one, the young Indian boy who'd guided him to his camp. The other was a full-grown man with a turkey-feather headdress and a necklace of what looked like buffalo teeth. Not the chief, who Zach would recognize. Another Indian. Both were mounted on sleek Indian ponies.

"Look hostile to you?" Cherry murmured.

"Maybe. Maybe not. Sure wish you spoke their lingo."

"Me, too. Don't fancy losin' any of my horses just 'cuz I cain't understand a word they're sayin'."

"How's your sign language?"

"Better'n most, I guess."

The tall man dismounted and walked toward them. The boy followed, then caught up, and the man laid his hand on the boy's scrawny shoulder. Maybe father and son.

"Neither one of them look too well fed," Zach intoned. "But if they'd wanted food, they would have come into camp."

"Mebbe," Cherry muttered.

Zach moved forward and raised one hand. The man pointed to himself, then to the boy, and then swept his arm toward the hills to the north.

Zach nodded. "I think the camp's in those hills. Might be they moved it after that powwow they invited me to."

"Mebbe," Cherry said.

The boy pointed to his pony, then to the man's horse and pantomimed riding.

Zach nodded again. "They were riding somewhere," he said to Cherry.

The man pointed then to the herd of cattle bedded down nearby, then back to his horse.

"Whazzat mean?" Cherry wondered. "They want another cow?"

Zach shook his head. "No. If they did, they'd just take it and make no fuss. I think they've seen something. Maybe some of our cattle." He gestured to the east and then west.

The man shook his head.

Zach then pointed south. Another shake. "North?" He pointed.

This time both the man and the boy nodded. The boy broke into a stream of unintelligible words and held up three fingers.

"Three men, I'd guess," Zach breathed. "They've seen something, all right." He watched the boy's motions a moment longer. "On horseback."

Again the man pointed back to the herd of steers.

"With some cattle. Cherry, they've just told us our cattle were rustled by three men, and we can find them someplace north of us."

"North! But we're headin' east, aren't we?"

"I think it might pay us to take a detour for a few miles."

He strode toward the man and offered his hand. Then he signaled for the boy to follow him. When he reached the two riders on night duty, he called out an order. "Curly, cut out a heifer and get a rope around its neck."

"Sure, boss." Curly eyed the young Indian boy. "Still hungry, huh?"

Zach watched the boy lead the cow back to what must be his father, and they both mounted their ponies. Before they rode off, the man trotted his horse up to Zach, leaned down and extended his hand again. Then the two reined away.

Zach watched them ride off, the calf trotting along between them. "I'll be damned," he breathed. "You just never know about people, do you?"

"Sure don't," a beaming Cherry exclaimed. "Look what that Indian feller gave me!" He held up the buffalo-tooth necklace.

"Let's go back and finish our supper," Zach suggested.

Back in camp, Cherry took a good deal of joshing about his new necklace, but he just grinned. "Didn't know I could speak such good Injun lingo, didja, boys?"

"Nope," José returned with a laugh. "Now you learn Spanish, no?"

"Naw," Skip offered. "Now Cherry gets to practice readin' Indian signs so's he can track our missing steers."

"Already done that," Cherry crowed. "Our missing cattle's north of here, right, boss?"

At Zach's amused nod, Cherry rose dramatically and pointed toward the hills in the distance. "That's where we're headin'!"

"That true, boss?" Skip queried.

"Yeah," Zach said.

"How come?"

Zach caught Cherry's eye. "Indian savvy."

"Huh? Whazzat mean?"

Zach turned toward a jubilant Cherry. "You tell 'em, Cherokee. I'm going to bed."

Chapter Sixteen

At the end of another long, hot, miserable day, Alex rode up on a little rise and suddenly there was a sparkling clear stream ahead of her. Cottonwoods and gray-green willows grew in a frothy border along the banks, and sparrows chattered among stands of chest-high cattails and wild plum bushes.

She rode toward it for another quarter hour, dragged herself out of the saddle and stumbled over to the chuck wagon where she gobbled a double helping of tortillas and beans. She had just finished when Zach dusted off his hands and came toward her.

"You okay, Dusty?"

"Yes, I'm fine, just tired. And filthy. And at the end of each day my— I'm sore."

He just looked at her, and she could see he was trying not to smile.

"I know exactly what you're thinking, Zach."

"Yeah?" He reached around her to slide open one of the drawers in the chuck wagon. "What am I thinkin'?"

"That you were right. That I'm a…how did you put it? A city girl. A green head."

"Green*horn*," he corrected.

"Greenhorn," she acknowledged. She watched him lift a flask of whiskey out of the drawer, uncork it and offer it to her.

"Here, have a swig of this. Might help your sore— Might help some."

She tipped the bottle to her lips, swallowed and began to cough. "I find it amazing that cowboys drink this awful-tasting stuff," she said when she could talk.

Zach chuckled. "You're not a—"

"I know," she said. "I'm not a cowboy. Believe me, I know that. But never in a million years did I think a cattle drive would be so…well, so…difficult. Full of heat and dust and…difficulties."

He laughed and downed a gulp from the flask, re-corked it and then uncorked it again and took another long swallow. "Yeah, you're a real greenhorn, Dusty. Cattle drives can be rough." He again handed her the whiskey.

"But," he continued, "I've watched you for almost two hundred miles. You'll do to ride the river with."

"Wh-what does that mean, 'ride the river with'?"

He looked at her for so long with those mossy green eyes she felt goose bumps pop out on her arms.

"It means you haven't whined or ridden a horse to death or gotten drunk or shot anybody. It means you'll do to ride the trail with."

"Oh," she said softly. *"Oh."* His words made her dizzy with happiness. She couldn't stop smiling at him. *Yes, I would like that, riding a trail with—*

Oh, no, she wouldn't! What was she thinking? She didn't want to ride anywhere ever again. She couldn't wait to get back to Chicago and clean sheets and four-course dinners and tea every afternoon.

"Now," he said, "let's—" He broke off when he heard a horse gallop past. "Night-herders," he murmured. "Showing off again."

She stifled a hiccup of laughter. "Let's what?"

"Go to bed."

This time she laughed outright.

"Oh, hell, Dusty, you know what I mean."

"Yes, I do. It's just that it sounds so—"

"Rude," he finished. "Sorry. Guess I'm a little tired." He dropped the whiskey flask back into the drawer and pushed it closed. "'Night, Dusty."

"Good night, Zach."

She wrapped herself up in her blankets under the chuck wagon and lay listening to Roberto mumbling in his sleep on the other side of the wagon wheel. She had just closed her eyes when Zach crawled in next to her and began to smooth out his bedroll.

She reached out a hand to stop him. "Cassidy's gone," she reminded him.

"I know," he said.

"So I no longer need protection."

"I know."

"Well, then, why—"

"Shut up, Dusty," he said in a gravelly voice. "Just go to sleep."

Zach lay awake, staring at the under-ribs of the chuck wagon and wondering what the hell he was doing. Dusty could scramble up his brain worse than a mess of Roberto's eggs. He couldn't wait to get to Winnemucca and dump her on the eastbound train. Her luggage from the ranch could follow on after her. She made him sweat in ways he didn't want to think about.

He closed his eyes and tried to clear his mind. Lord knew he hadn't had a good night's sleep since that Sunday afternoon back at the Rocking K when he'd first laid eyes on her. How many more days before he could dump her on a train and be rid of her?

He swallowed a groan. A better question was how many *nights*? It wasn't that he didn't like her, he admitted. The problem was that he *did* like her.

He liked her. Way too much.

In the morning he hastily gobbled a big breakfast of Roberto's sourdough flapjacks and bacon and rode out with Curly to scout the route ahead. He didn't feel like talking, so his companion's bleary-eyed grunts and pointing fingers suited him just fine.

Ten miles out, Zach reined up his gray and sat sniffing the air.

"What's up, boss?" Curly asked. "You smellin' perfume?"

"Nope. Smoke." He turned the horse in a circle, scanning the sky overhead.

"I don't smell nuthin'. Don't see nuthin', either."

"Over there." Zach pointed north toward an area of rocky hills where a curl of smoke rose.

"Indian camp, maybe?"

He shook his head. "Indians take care not to let smoke mark their camps. They dig their fire pits a foot deep so they can't be seen." He kicked his mount into a trot. "Come on, let's ride over there and find out."

The sparse grass and huckleberry bushes gave way to sagebrush and greasewood that gradually thinned out to gray-and-black expanses of rock. Sparsely wooded canyons ran deep into the hills. Zach headed straight for the thin spiral of blue smoke.

"Comin' from one of them canyons," Curly said.

"Yeah. I think I see which one." Zach pushed his horse up a steep, gravelly hill, then reined up. Ahead of him was a narrow trail that overlooked a box canyon.

All of a sudden he was peering down at a mooing herd of steers. Rocking K and Double Diamond brands were plain as day.

Well, damn.

Three men were hunkered down over a fire, and that fire was not heating coffee; it was heating up branding irons.

Curly spit off to one side. "Looks like they're aimin' to rebrand those steers."

"Looks like," Zach agreed.

"What're we gonna do, boss?"

"Stop 'em." He turned his mount and started back down the hillside. "Losing those steers could cost me my ranch. After all these years of scrimpin' and savin' to buy some land, I'll be damned if I'm gonna let that happen."

Alex woke suddenly when Roberto shook her shoulder. "You will miss breakfast, *señorita*. Everyone else has eat and gone."

She sighed, stretched her stiff muscles and crawled out of her warm bedroll. Not only were cattle drives hard on one's derriere, one never got enough sleep! Or enough time to wash her face and comb her hair.

Still, she reasoned as she picked up her tin plate, Roberto's meals always tasted good, and now that she'd befriended the cowhands, she was waited on hand and foot.

That made things more bearable, even if she did feel a tad guilty about enjoying their attention. Even if it was still dark, there were some compensations, she supposed.

She'd just forked up a big bite of pancake when Zach and Curly galloped up. "Skip! José! Get your rifles. Juan, ride east till you catch up to the Double Diamond herd. Tell Gibson we've found his missing steers."

Zach dismounted, disappeared into the interior of the chuck wagon and emerged a moment later carrying a rifle and a shotgun. Around his hips he buckled a gun belt with a big, mean-looking revolver, and all at once Alex felt uneasy. He tossed the shotgun to Skip, jammed the rifle in the leather scabbard attached to his saddle and remounted.

Thunderstruck, she watched Curly and José retrieve their rifles, and suddenly it dawned on her what was happening. Zach was going after the men who'd stolen his cattle. Now she felt more than just uneasy.

She stood up, her tin plate of uneaten pancakes clutched in her hand. Four men armed with guns were riding off to do battle over a few lost cows? Surely this was the ultimate in idiocy.

Cherry hastily saddled a horse for Juan, and with a whoop the young cowhand clattered off. Zach and the other two grim-faced men loaded their weapons, heaved themselves atop their horses and rode away.

Alex sank back down beside the fire and shook her head. "Idiots," she murmured. "Men are idiots."

Jase frowned at her from across the fire pit. "Don't say that, Miss Alex."

"Well, they are! What is so important about a few cows? Why risk your life to get them back?"

Jase brought his coffee mug over to her side of the

campfire and stood looking after the men who had just ridden off. "Ya ought never tell a cattleman that his steers ain't important, Miss Alex. At forty dollars a head, that's four thousand dollars Charlie's gonna lose unless Zach can get 'em back."

"Oh."

"Is more, too," Roberto said at her elbow. "Boss need money for buy his own ranch. This he want very much."

Chastened, Alex took a small bite of pancake. Another thing she didn't like about cattle drives was how easy it was to say the wrong thing. Suddenly everything tasted like dust.

Roberto set a mug of coffee on the ground beside her. "But is true," the cook admitted. "I, too, do not like the guns."

She dawdled over her breakfast until Roberto began to pace back and forth from the wash bucket to the fire, and then she hurriedly gulped the last of her coffee and rose to drop her tin plate into the soapy water.

She helped the cook wash up the dishes and dry them, and then he packed up the chuck wagon and it rumbled off after the scout, Wally, and Cherry and the remuda that traveled with the herd under his watchful eye.

The aging wrangler managed to give loving attention to each animal in his care, and he always picked out an even-tempered mount for her. Reluctantly she mounted the roan Cherry had saddled for her today and joined the cowhands trotting alongside the herd.

Because they were now short-handed, she ended up riding alone in the left flank position, but by now the cattle were so docile, tossing their heads and swishing their tails to drive away the flies, that they lumbered after the bell steer with little prodding, and she had little to do but think.

Hours passed. As she rode, she scanned ahead, watching for Zach and the other men, but morning turned into afternoon and there was no sign of them. When the sun was like a boiling orange ball over her head and the air was so hot she thought she would melt, she ate the rolled-up pancake she'd slipped into her shirt pocket and told herself not to think, just keep going.

Zach reined up on the rim of the box canyon and sat gazing down at the branding operation. He and his three hands, with dust-covered hats and rifles laid across their laps, were quiet for some minutes. "Ain't gonna be easy, boss," Curly remarked at last.

"Maybe not. But I want those steers."

"Ya might wanna live till we get to Winnemucca, too."

Skip spit off to one side. "Shut up, Curly."

"Is no mystery what they do, *señor*," José offered, his voice flat. "Change brand so not recognize."

"Yeah," Curly said. "Then they sell 'em like they owned 'em and go home with the money."

"Over my dead body," Zach growled.

"Don't want your body dead, boss," Curly grumbled. "Gotta go about this real careful-like."

Zach said nothing for a long minute while he studied the steers, the angle of the sun and the three men working on the canyon floor. "Curly, you think you could pick off one of those men from up here?"

"Sure. Easy."

"If you miss, you know you'll probably hit me, instead."

"Like I said, it's easy. Hold on a second, boss. You ain't thinkin' of goin' down there alone?"

"Yeah, I am." He watched the men below him for a few minutes longer. "Just me. When the sun's in their eyes, you three spread out along this rim and cover me."

"*Si, señor.* But is most foolish."

"Don't think so, José. It's four thousand bucks worth of smart." He lifted the rifle onto his lap and reined his horse away.

"Don't worry, José," Curly said. "Boss knows what he's doin'. I hope," he added under his breath. "Let's spread out, like he said."

Zach slowly picked his way down the steep, rock-strewn incline, taking care to make no noise. At the canyon entrance he reined up, checked the ammunition in his Colt and dismounted. Above him, his men's rifle barrels glinted in the sun. With any luck the rustlers were so busy with branding they wouldn't look up.

Maybe.

Out of nowhere a picture of Dusty floated into his mind. He didn't want to get himself killed for obvious reasons. He wanted to go back to Oregon with a pock-etful of cash, buy his ranch and start breeding cattle. He'd waited all his life for this, and he'd be darned if he'd give it up.

And...

And there was another reason he didn't want to get killed. If he was dead, he'd never see Dusty again.

Careful not to step on twigs or dry leaves, he worked his way down to the canyon floor and around in back of the three horses tethered to a low-lying cottonwood branch. Carefully he slid his pocketknife out and sliced the lead ropes. Then he shoved a big cocklebur under each saddle blanket. In silence he crept back to his hidden position, picked up a rock and tossed it over the heads of the rustlers.

The men spun toward the noise, and Zach stepped forward.

Alex waited up long past supper, along with a somber-faced group of men who made a show of nursing mugs of coffee and idly whittling sticks instead of crawling into their bedrolls. She wasn't fooled. They were as worried as she was about Zach and the three other men who had galloped off so many hours ago.

Roberto paced and hovered and filled coffee mugs, but finally he took himself off to bed. "Must cook breakfast before the sun come," he announced. "Everyone should sleep."

As long as she lived she would never understand how the old man managed his grueling schedule. She could scarcely remember the luxury of sleeping until eight o'clock back in Chicago. Nine o'clock on Sundays. But for the past few weeks, every single morning at the first gray finger of dawn she was roused by the cook's shout of "Come and eat." Long before the sun even turned the sky pink, Roberto was hard at work. She would have to ask him how he managed it.

A cattle rancher's life looked like endless drudgery. Definitely not for her.

Cherry ambled into camp, poured himself a mug of coffee and settled his wiry frame next to her. "Any news?"

"No," she breathed. "It's been hours and I'm about to jump out of my skin."

He leaned in close. "You worried?"

She nodded. "Everybody is. I wish I had something to take my mind off what's happening out there."

Cherry nodded. "Might be able to help you there, Miss Alex. I'll just bet you don't know much 'bout how I keep the remuda together, do ya?"

"Well, no, I don't. I never thought much about it."

"Tonight's a good night to think 'bout it, don'tcha think? Gotta have somethin' to take yer mind off…you know. And mebbe it'd be interestin' fer yer newspaper readers."

"Oh, Cherry, what a good idea!" She pulled a new notepad and a pencil from her shirt pocket.

The wrangler slurped two swallows of coffee and drew a dramatic breath. "Well, Miss Alex, I gotta tell ya, it ain't easy bein' in charge of a bunch of horses for a Rocking K trail drive. That's 'bout thirty mounts fer a crew this size, and keepin' 'em fed and watered and happy ain't somethin' just anybody kin do."

Jase groaned. "Aw, g'wan, Cherry. Anybody can do it. All you gotta be is plumb crazy."

Cherry snorted. "Dry up, Jase. What you know 'bout horses would fit in yer ma's thimble."

"My ma ain't got a thimble!"

The men went on wrangling, and Alex's thoughts began to wander. Where was Zach now? Was he sneaking up on some lowlife rustlers hidden in some camp somewhere? Was he in danger? *Could he get killed?*

She went cold all over. Zach could get hurt. Shot, even. *Oh, God, he could die.*

All at once she wanted to fill up her coffee mug with some of Roberto's whiskey. The stuff tasted awful, but it might ease the sharp pain lancing across her chest.

"Roberto?"

She didn't even have to ask. The cook, who obviously hadn't been able to sleep, lifted her half-empty mug away, and when he set it down beside her it was full. When she took a sip she realized what the old man had done. She downed a big gulp, and her eyes watered.

"Gracias," she choked out.

"De nada," he murmured.

It helped some. She wrenched her thoughts away from Zach and gradually became aware of Cherry's voice, still talking about his remuda.

"Gotta get up before any of the other fellas even crack an eyelid and get them horses saddled up for ya, and then drive the rest to wherever Wally's picked out for the next camp. That's maybe fifteen miles. Then I got to—"

"Sometimes," Jase interrupted, "it feels more like twenty or thirty miles. And we're working hard all that way. All you're doin' is trottin' along easy-like."

"That's all you know," Cherry said. The wrangler picked up his narrative again, but once again Alex couldn't keep her mind on it.

Zach, don't do anything brave or foolish. Nothing was worth dying for, especially not a bunch of cows. There were much more important things to do in life. Beautiful things. *Oh, please, God...*

"Are you listenin', Miss Alex?" Cherry asked.

"What? Oh, yes. The remuda. Tell me more, Cherry."

The wrangler sent Jase a hard look and cleared his throat. "Then, when I get them horses to Wally's picked-out spot, I got to rope off a corral for them an' brush all of 'em down and take care of 'em after you boys run 'em half to death."

Alex had never seen Cherry so worked up about anything before. The wrangler was trying his best to keep her mind off Zach and the other three men out there somewhere risking their lives for a bunch of stolen cows. Steers, she amended.

She gulped another big swallow of her whiskey-laced coffee and closed her eyes. *Darn it all, Zach Strickland, if you don't ride into camp pretty soon I will never forgive you!*

Zach aimed his rifle at the man in the center of the three hunched over the branding fire.

"Hands in the air, gentlemen. Drop your sidearms."

"What the—" The tall man went for his revolver, but a bullet from the canyon edge thudded into the ground a scant yard in front of the man's worn boots. He hesitated, and another shot from above whined into the dirt even nearer to his feet.

The other two men threw down their guns and backed toward the fire, where four branding irons lay heating in the coals. Zach stepped forward and snagged their revolvers out of the holsters, then hurled them into the sagebrush.

"You're gettin' off easy," he said. "In these parts, cattle rustlers don't live long." He signaled to Curly up on the ridge.

"Now," he continued, "you gentlemen have a choice." He waved one arm at the brush. "You can catch your horses and ride on out of here, or you can walk. Either way you're gonna run into my companions, and they're well armed." He paused. "Which *you* aren't. Now, strip down to your long johns."

The men stared at him. "Howzzat?" one of the men blurted out.

"You heard me. Strip."

Zach watched the men peel off their duds and scramble into the scrub to retrieve their mounts. The tall one climbed onto his horse and was promptly bucked off.

"Cockleburr," Zach said, his tone conversational. "One for each of you." The others fished under their saddles for the thorns, sent Zach an angry scowl and then mounted up.

"Walk 'em," Zach ordered.

"Y-yessir."

He kicked dirt over the branding fire and eyed the milling steers. Sure enough, a new brand had been burned into the hides of about half the animals, turning the Rocking K into a crude Circle V. He figured a little less than half the herd wore Orren Gibson's Double Diamond brand, now rebranded into a heavy Bar W. They'd be easy to separate out.

By the time Curly, Skip and José reached him, the three rustlers had skedaddled.

"Gosh, boss, how come you let 'em go?"

"Had no choice, Curly."

"Sure ya did. Coulda strung 'em up for cattle rustling."

"Maybe. But that'd take time. Besides, the steers are all I want. Let's move 'em out."

He caught his horse and swung up into the saddle. Hot damn, looked like he'd maybe saved his ranch. Even better, he was gonna live another day, so he'd get to see Dusty again.

He could hardly wait to get back to camp and crawl under the chuck wagon next to her.

Chapter Seventeen

Long past midnight Alex woke to the sound of thundering hooves and bellowing cattle. Oh, no, not another stampede! She scrambled out of her bedroll and started to climb up into the chuck wagon, then noticed that Roberto was staring off into the dark and grinning.

Her heart jumped as if bitten by a scorpion. "What is it?"

"Boss," he said.

The men woke up and cheered when they saw the ragged herd of steers pound over the hill and head toward them. Roberto tossed an armload of wood onto the dying fire. "Ees beautiful, is it not, *señorita*?"

Cows? Beautiful? Only to a cowboy. But she couldn't help smiling at the four dusty, unshaven men who drove the lowing animals in to rejoin the main herd. They were so tired they were drooping in the saddle, something she'd never seen any of them do before. They tumbled off their horses, tossed their rifles in the back of the chuck wagon and immediately grabbed their bedrolls and rolled themselves up in the blankets.

All except Zach. He stopped to speak to Roberto and

then Jase, stashed his rifle and revolver in the chuck wagon and sent her a tired smile. Only then did he crawl under the wagon and stretch out on his bedroll. He didn't even bother to remove his boots!

She crept in next to him, but he had already fallen asleep. Inexplicably happy, she propped herself on one elbow and watched him. She couldn't help it. He'd laid one arm over his eyes, and although she studied his face for a good hour, he didn't so much as twitch. His breath pulled in and out, regular as a clock, and his chest rose and fell in the same steady rhythm.

What are you doing, staring at a sleeping man?

Back in Chicago this would be purely scandalous! But out here in this rough, untamed land, no one was watching. And even if they were, she didn't care. She liked looking at Zach Strickland.

She released a long breath and was about to stretch out full-length on her own bedroll when his voice stopped her.

"You can build up a powerful hunger in a man lookin' at him that way, Dusty."

Oh, my stars and little chickens, Zach was watching me! She couldn't think of one sensible response. Or even an unsensible one. Before she could open her mouth, he reached his hand up, curved his warm fingers around the back of her neck and pulled her head down onto his chest. In the next minute the gentle rise and fall of his breathing told her he was sound asleep.

A delicious warmth stole through her. Afraid to move for fear of waking him, she stretched out beside him and very carefully laid her arm across his midriff.

Utterly shameless, her mother would have said. But

then she was quite sure Mama had never felt about a man the way Alex was beginning to feel about Zach Strickland.

In the morning, Roberto took one look underneath the chuck wagon, chuckled under his breath and "forgot" to bang his spoon in the iron triangle to announce breakfast.

Zach woke to the smell of coffee and sizzling bacon, and the sound of Dusty's soft breathing beside him. Gently he lifted her arm away from his midsection and slid his body out from under the wagon. How he had slept through Roberto's clattering and clanging while he prepared breakfast he'd never know. Guess maybe he was bone-tired.

And he also guessed he wasn't inclined to move with Dusty snuggled up against him like that. Feeling her so close to him sent an odd prickle up his spine. He shook his head and headed for the spot where his cowhands sat sipping coffee.

"Gonna lay over a day," he announced. "Juan, I know you've only recently come back, but ride again to Gibson. Tell him we're coming with his cattle."

"*Si*, boss," Juan said with a nod. "Señor Gibson maybe two hours ride ahead. When I find him I tell him to wait."

Zach nodded. "Jase, you and Skip cut out the Double Diamond beefs. Then you can drive 'em up the trail till you meet up with Gibson's herd."

Curly sent him a sleepy grin. "What're *you* gonna do, boss?"

"I'm gonna take a bath in that creek over there, wash out my duds and shave off my whiskers while I can still see my chin."

After breakfast, Cherry saddled up mounts for Juan

and the other two hands. Just as they rode out of camp, Dusty appeared.

"Never seen you skip breakfast before, Miss Alex," Curly observed with a bland expression. "Musta not slept good last night."

"No, I—I slept perfectly…well. It's just that I didn't go to bed until—"

"Yeah," the rangy cowhand acknowledged. "Neither did we. Boss says we're gonna lay over a day."

Alex settled herself by the fire pit and gobbled the bacon and biscuits Roberto had saved for her.

Zach had disappeared.

By midday she'd stopped wondering where he'd gone, took her notebook from the bottom of her saddlebag and tramped out of camp to spend the afternoon catching up on her writing. Without a doubt her newspaper articles would capture the attention of twenty thousand *Chicago Times* readers. Maybe more when she reached Chicago and her copy desk.

She tramped upstream along the creek bank until she spotted a spreading cottonwood tree with a thick trunk. The perfect spot.

No sooner had she settled her spine against the gray bark when she heard something, a soft flapping sound. A bird, perhaps. There it was again!

She twisted her head to study the surrounding brush and got a real shock. Two long, jeans-covered legs were stretched out on the opposite side of her tree trunk.

"Zach!"

"Yeah," he acknowledged in a lazy voice.

"What are you doing here?"

"Readin'. I heard you come up from camp. Thought maybe you'd move on past me. What are *you* doing here?"

"I am organizing my notes."

"Sounds mighty dull."

"Oh, no. The information I am collecting on this trip is anything but dull. I intend to create simply fascinating pictures of life on a cattle drive for my newspaper articles."

"Uh-huh."

"What are *you* reading? *Principles of Cattle Herding*, perhaps?"

He laughed. "To be honest, I'm readin' an old book a teacher gave me once." He held up a well-thumbed edition.

"Tennyson? I don't believe it. You are actually reading Tennyson?" For a minute she could think of nothing to say. "You mean you actually *like* reading?"

"Sure. Don't you? Like reading, I mean."

"I do, yes."

"I never went to school, see," he said in a low voice. "A lady on the wagon train coming West was a schoolteacher, and she taught me. Her husband was a professor of some kind. By the time we reached Colorado, I could read and write and cipher and—" He broke off. "How come you're looking at me like that?"

She couldn't answer right away. When she recovered her wits she blurted out the first thing that came to her mind. "Zachary Strickland, you are such a surprising man!"

"Zachariah," he corrected. "Not Zachary."

"Zachariah," she amended softly. "Zachariah. Is that your real name?"

"Yeah. It's from the Bible. Zachariah was king of Israel."

"Oh." She hadn't read the Bible since she was six

years old, and she didn't remember any Zachariah. This man was not only surprising, he was…

She studied his face. Today hc was clean-shaven except for the dark mustache over his upper lip. His longish black hair curled damply over his forehead. Why, he'd had a bath in the creek! All at once she felt sticky from four days of heat and grime and dust and swcat from the trail.

She gazed across the stream to a wide pool with a little waterfall tumbling into it. Perfect. Tonight, after the hands had wrapped themselves up in their bedrolls, she would come back to this spot and take a long, cooling bath.

She picked up her notebook and opened it to a page she'd folded down. "A good journalist," she said aloud, "asks probing questions and writes down each response, word for word."

Zach chuckled and turned his attention back to his Tennyson. "'A young man will be wiser by and by,'" he quoted. "'An old man's wit may wander 'ere he die.'"

He glanced up at her and their gazes met.

"And which are you, Zach? A young man or an old one?"

"Somewhere in the middle, I guess. Not sure if I'm ever gonna be any wiser."

Alex stared at him. Zachariah Strickland was a genuine puzzle, half cowboy and half…what? Who *was* this man? She forced herself to look away.

A better question might be, what is this man to me?

Next day, fifty yards from Orren Gibson's Double Diamond outfit, Zach and Curly dismounted, and to avoid raising dust they walked the rest of the way into the camp. Gibson had invited them to supper as a way of thanking them for recovering his steers. Skip and José lagged half a mile behind with Dusty.

Gibson's handshake was firm, and his thanks for returning his missing seventy head of stolen cattle were heartfelt. The graying ranch owner introduced them all to his cowhands, then when Dusty and Zach's other two hands arrived, he introduced everybody all over again.

Gibson did a double take at the sight of Dusty. "My Gawd," the rancher exclaimed, "you're a woman! What're you doing out on the trail with this bunch of drovers?"

Zach felt a stab of something close to alarm. Jealousy, maybe.

"Working," she replied. "I am a newspaper reporter. My editor wants a story about a Western cattle drive."

Gibson's eyebrows shot up. "A reporter! You mean your daddy isn't a cattleman?"

"Oh, no. My daddy is—" She broke off. "I don't actually know what my father is," she said quietly. "Or where."

Gibson ran his hand over his chin. "I meant no offense, Miss Murray. It's just that it's mighty unusual to find a woman on a cattle drive."

"Señorita Alex, she is not ordinary woman," José announced.

"I can see that," Gibson replied. The man was looking at her in a way Zach didn't like, but since he was an invited guest, he stuffed down his annoyance and tried to ignore what it was doing to his gut. But when he caught one of the Double Diamond hands, an awkward youngster called Sandy who was no more than sixteen years old, staring at Dusty with his mouth hanging open, Zach stepped in close.

"Shut your mouth, kid," he intoned. "And mind your manners around the lady."

One of Gibson's other hands, an older man called O'Leary, executed an awkward bow over Dusty's extended hand, and Skip made the mistake of snickering. Zach jabbed an elbow into his rib cage.

A meaty back strap of beef from a slaughtered steer turned on a spit over a bed of glowing coals, and around the perimeter lay pots of chili beans and ears of sweet corn roasting in their husks.

"Made a detour near a farm coupla nights back," Gibson said at Zach's questioning look. "Came away with sweet corn and a bushel of apples. Cook's makin' pies for dessert."

Curly groaned in appreciation and José rolled his eyes and rubbed his belly.

"Gentlemen," Gibson announced. "Make yourselves comfortable and let's eat."

The cook slapped thick beefsteaks and ears of corn onto their plates. Every one of Gibson's men jockeyed to sit next to Dusty, but Curly and Jase elbowed them aside with good-natured grins and flanked her. Silence fell as the men dug in.

Zach found himself on the opposite side of the fire pit from where she settled. Gibson sat next to him, and it took Zach exactly half a minute to figure out why. It was more than a neighborly gesture. From over here, the Double Diamond owner could look his fill at Dusty and there wasn't a darn thing Zach could do about it.

Supper was excellent, ending with slices of apple pie at least four inches thick, but the cook's coffee couldn't hold a candle to Roberto's. Zach sipped his mug slowly and talked cattle with Gibson.

Then the kid, Sandy, suggested they have some music and some dancing, and Zach watched every male in camp leap up to be first in line to claim Dusty. A banjo appeared, then a fiddle, and José unstrapped his guitar from behind his saddle. The older man, O'Leary, produced another guitar.

Gibson studied the crowd around Dusty and rapped his spoon against his tin plate. "Let's have a Virginia reel. That way everybody gets a turn with Miss Murray."

The musicians strolled into the moonlit night and the music rose. Bandannas tied to one arm signified which cowboy was playing the part of the woman, and the men formed two lines facing each other. Gibson extended his hand to Dusty and ceremoniously conducted her to the head position.

The two lines swept forward and bowed awkwardly, then Dusty and Gibson met in the middle and joined hands while everyone else, even the grinning cook, clapped and hoorahed. Zach tried not to watch her.

"Any louder and they'll start a stampede," he grumbled under his breath. And right at that moment he realized something he'd been pushing to the back of his mind for weeks; he was jealous. Green-eyed, irrationally, possessively jealous.

He tossed the dregs of his coffee into the fire and strode away from camp to study the stars overhead.

"Hey, boss," Jase yelled. "Why aren'tcha dancin'?"

Good question. Why wasn't he?

Because… He swallowed hard. Because he wanted to touch Dusty so bad it hurt. The thought of holding her in his arms, looking into her upturned face, sent a cavalry detail of butterflies into his belly and made his knees feel funny.

You coward. You've been close to her before and sur-vived. He'd never forget that day when she got dunked in the river and he'd undressed her by the fire. He'd tried hard not to look, but…it was a memory he'd keep stuck deep in his heart for the rest of his life.

Then he thought about the night he had to put Dancer down, when Dusty had found him grieving under a pine tree and had reached out and just held him, saying nothing.

But dancing with her would be different. Dancing with her would be just her and him, moving close together on purpose. With his body touching hers.

He couldn't do it. But, oh, God, he hungered to be with her. Touch her. His groin ached with it.

He refilled his mug from the speckleware coffeepot, resettled himself by the campfire and closed his eyes.

You're scared.

Damn right I'm scared. No man in his right mind would fall in love with a city girl from Chicago who's spent half her life hankering after a career in the newspaper business and the other half achieving it.

The music changed from the Virginia Reel to a waltz. Zach opened his eyes to see a gaggle of cowhands, his own included, whooping it up and clumsily stepping around and around together. Dusty was dancing with Gibson, then with Curly, then Sandy, then…

He couldn't keep track of how often someone cut in on her and whisked her away from her partner. She slipped out of one man's arms and into another's so many times he got tired of keeping track.

"Boss!" Curly yelled.

Zach ignored him.

And then Dusty broke away from her current partner,

a lanky cowhand with a droopy blond mustache, and moved toward him. She walked steadily, unhurriedly, straight to where he sat, and stopped in front of him.

He set his coffee mug on the ground and stood up.

Chapter Eighteen

"You're not dancing," Dusty observed.

"No."

"Why not?"

"I...uh...can't dance."

She propped both hands at her waist and cocked her head. "Can't?" she accused. "Or won't?"

Zach avoided her accusing blue eyes. "Can't," he lied.

She laughed. "You're lying, Zach. That schoolteacher taught you to read and write. I bet someone taught you to dance, too."

He studied the toes of his boots.

"Zach," she said softly. "Dance with me."

"Dammit, Dusty..."

She took a step closer and smiled up at him. "Dammit, what?"

"Oh, just dammit. Come on." He reached for her hand and walked her past the cowhands gathered at the edge of the clearing, kicking up their heels in a spirited polka. In the shadows beyond the campfire he turned her into his arms.

The top of her head only came up to his jaw. He drew

in a long breath and groaned inwardly. She smelled of apples and something spicy. Cinnamon, maybe.

He rested his chin against her hair, slipped his hand behind her back and pulled her close. Slowly they began to move.

"Zach?" she said quietly.

"Hmm?"

"They're playing a polka."

"Yeah, I know."

She laughed softly. "But we are waltzing."

"I know."

She didn't say another word, just ignored the music and followed his lead. They circled in the shadows around the edge of the clearing where firelight licked at the darkness. The warm air was scented with grass and apple pie.

They danced in silence until the fiddler began a two-step and then another polka. They kept waltzing. At last Dusty looked up at him and he bobbled a step. "Sorry," he murmured.

"You do dance, Zach. Very nicely, in fact."

"Maybe. Good instructor, I guess."

"The schoolteacher?"

He hesitated. "Nope."

"Who, then?"

He said nothing for a full minute. Finally he opened his mouth and gave her the only answer he could come up with. "Don't recall her name. I was only fourteen."

"Was she someone special?"

He clamped his jaw shut and didn't answer. He hadn't thought of the woman, a dance hall dolly whose name he couldn't recall, for twenty years, and she sure wasn't what was on his mind at this moment.

Dusty was on his mind. With every breath he took, there she was, stuck in his brain like a toothache he couldn't shake off. It was a sweet, insistent pain that had him clenching his jaw and starting to sweat.

But he didn't want to let her go. What he *did* want... His heart somersaulted into his stomach. He wanted *her*. He wanted her more than he'd ever wanted a woman in his life.

Forget it, Strickland. Wrong lady. Wrong time. Wrong place. Wrong everything. Never gonna happen.

Alex could feel the tension in his body as they danced and hear his ragged breathing. Something was bothering him. He should be feeling proud of himself and the other three men who had rescued Orren Gibson's stolen cattle and driven them back with no loss of either cowhands or cows. Curly had told her everything, emphasizing that they had succeeded because when they discovered the rustlers, Zach had kept his head.

Roberto was right, she thought. Zach Strickland was "much man."

And he certainly *could* dance! True, he had kept waltzing through two polkas and a lively two-step, but when the musicians did play a tune in waltz time, he never missed a beat.

But, oh, my heavens, this one is the slowest waltz I have ever danced. And as they drew farther into the darkness at the edge of the firelight, he moved slower and slower. Finally he drew her to a complete stop.

He didn't move and neither did she. Instead, they stood together, barely breathing, as the fiddle's plaintive melody washed over them. She recognized the tune. "Lorena."

Zach stood motionless, one hand holding hers and the other lightly pressing her backbone. Alex stared at the top button of his blue shirt, watching the pulse throb in the hollow of his tanned throat, and waited for him to say something.

But he didn't.

The music seemed very far away, the melody rising and falling over the scrape of crickets and the song of an evening sparrow. She did not want to move, did not want to break the spell. An expectant feeling built under her rib cage until she felt she might burst.

He said nothing for a long, long minute. And then, very deliberately, he brought her hand up to rest against his chest and folded his fingers around hers. Under her knuckles his heartbeat thudded in a driving pulse that matched the thrumming of her blood.

Something was happening between them, something magical. Something beautiful. Never in her life had she felt so filled with light, as if at any moment she would float up off the face of the earth. She wanted to savor the feeling the way she would an exquisite, elusive scent.

Her breathing stopped. *What is this wondrous feeling?*

She wanted to be close to him, and that was perfectly scandalous! Her mother would never...

She caught herself. Mama had never waltzed with a man in the firelight. Mama had never known a man like Zach Strickland. Alex knew with sudden clarity that her mother had missed something that was of value in life.

She closed her eyes, afraid to breathe for fear he would release the hand he kept pressed to his chest. She stood without moving and inhaled deeply. He smelled faintly of wood smoke.

God forgive her, she wanted to crawl inside his skin. She made an unconscious motion closer to him, and in the same moment he pulled her against him and bent his head. She raised her face to his and felt his mouth cover hers, his lips warm and insistent. In the space of a heartbeat she was lost.

If he lived to be a hundred, Zach would remember this moment for the rest of his life. He'd kissed his share of women. None of them had felt anything like Dusty, all fire and soft velvet.

Her mouth opened under his, and when he went deeper, her arms came up around his neck. A heady realization zinged through him. *She wanted this. She wanted him!*

His brain exploded. He couldn't think, could only ask with his lips for what he needed and take what she offered. God help him, he didn't want this to end. He lifted his head briefly, felt her warm breath wash against his cheek and without thinking he caught her mouth under his once more.

He kissed her until his senses reeled and his body trembled with need. When he lifted his lips from hers, he knew he was a different man.

He held her close for a long minute, felt her heart flutter against his chest and her breathing grow ragged. Then, without speaking, they turned and moved together toward the campfire.

He wanted to take her hand, but he didn't. Instead, he walked her past the cowhands who were still stomping about in their awkward two-steps, past the musicians and past Orren Gibson, until they reached the fire pit.

He settled himself on a wide log and pulled her down beside him, close enough to brush her shoulder with his.

Only by gritting his teeth could he keep from touching her. When his breathing began to return to normal, he spoke the first word that came to his mind.

"Dusty."

"Don't say anything," she murmured.

Suits me, he thought. After what had just passed between them, he had no idea what to say to her.

Curly and José ambled up. "Boss, you think maybe we should be headin' back?"

Zach nodded. The two men wandered off to find Skip and retrieve the horses, and when they returned he shook hands with Orren Gibson and helped Dusty climb into the saddle. Then they headed back to the Rocking K camp, Curly, José and Skip riding on ahead.

Zach and Dusty followed slowly, walking their horses side by side in the moonlight and not speaking while he tried to sort out what was happening. It was hard to understand why he suddenly felt so different. Something had shifted inside him.

Chapter Nineteen

Alex lay awake for hours, waiting for Zach to roll out his bedroll next to her under the chuck wagon. Her body still tingled from his kiss.

What on earth should she say to him? She hadn't had one coherent thought since he had lifted his mouth from hers hours ago. Maybe he hadn't, either. She could think of no other reason why they had not spoken a single word since then.

Where was he? She longed for some acknowledgment of the extraordinary thing that had happened between them. She closed her eyes and tried to think, but only one thought made any sense. Tonight was the end of something and the beginning of something else, something she couldn't begin to name.

Three feet away, outside the wagon wheel, Roberto was singing softly under his breath in Spanish. It made her ache inside. It made her want to stay awake and wait for Zach.

An hour passed, then another, and still he didn't come. Maybe he hadn't enjoyed their kiss as much as...as much as she had. She bit her lip at the thought.

Nothing in her entire life had ever been like those few toe-curling moments she had shared with Zach Strickland. It was magical. Beautiful. But, she admitted, she was relatively inexperienced about kissing. Maybe it hadn't been all that special for him.

Near dawn she fell asleep, only to wake again when Roberto crawled out of his bedroll and began rattling around in the chuck wagon. She gave up trying to get any more rest, rolled up her blankets and helped Roberto cut out biscuits and fry bacon. She ate breakfast with the hands and climbed onto the saddled roan Cherry brought for her, even though her sleep-deprived body ached at the prospect of having to stay upright in the saddle until suppertime.

She didn't see Zach until almost noon, when she glimpsed him riding point alongside Curly. Later she saw him spur his horse after a wandering steer, but the long, scorching hours dragged by and he came nowhere near her.

Why?

Her spirits sagged.

That night after supper she lingered around the campfire with the hands, waiting for Zach to ride in and join them. But he didn't. Even Roberto was puzzled.

"Ees not like Señor Boss to miss supper," he complained. "And tonight I make my beef stew and dumplings, his favorite."

She kept her eyes on the Dutch oven hanging over the fire pit, expecting that any minute Zach would stride into camp and load up his plate.

"Where's the boss?" Curly wanted to know.

"Yeah," Skip chimed in. "It's sure not like him to miss a meal."

Cherry looked up from his coffee mug. "Hope that gray gelding I fixed him up with hasn't stumbled into another darned gopher hole. Don't fancy watchin' him have to put down another horse. 'Bout broke my heart when he had to shoot Dancer."

Alex's heart skipped at the memory. Then Juan spoke up. "I see him before."

"Before what?" Skip demanded.

"Before supper. He reads a book."

Alex jerked. A book! *Well, then, he must be all right. He's just not interested in eating supper with us.*

And maybe he's not interested in you.

Did a man really set a woman's body on fire like that and then just wander off and read a book? She dashed the rest of her coffee into the fire and got to her feet.

Damn him! Tears stung at the back of her eyes. *Reading a book?* What kind of man did that? Kiss a girl until she was dizzy and trembling, and then go off and read a book?

She stomped off for a long walk, circling the campfire four times before Roberto fell into step beside her. "Something is wrong, Señorita Alex?"

"N-no. Well, yes."

"Not want to eat dessert?"

"Dessert?"

"Cobbler I make from peaches."

"Oh."

Roberto took her arm and brought her to a stop. "You have bad words with Señor Boss?"

"No. No words." She would give anything for even *one* word from Zach.

"Ah." The old man nodded wisely. "Ah," he said again.

"You come eat some peaches, Señorita Alex. Is good for having no words."

She looked into the cook's velvety brown eyes. Roberto saw much more than he ever let on. She wondered what he read in her face, and after a moment, when he smiled broadly, she had her answer. Roberto saw everything. *Everything*.

"All right, Roberto, I will come and eat your peach cobbler."

The cook nodded. "*Bueno*, Señorita Alex. *Mucho* smart."

In minutes she was spooning bites of tender peaches and crunchy sweet topping into her mouth and listening to José tune up his guitar. All at once she had a thought that made her breath catch. She laid down her spoon.

Oh, please, please don't play "Lorena."

Her eyes burned. She picked at her cobbler until she couldn't stomach another bite, listened to the sad ballad José was softly singing with his guitar and wondered what to do about her aching heart.

For the next three days the cattle rumbled on, drawing nearer and nearer to their destination, and Alex watched the man she now suspected of stealing her heart. Never in her life had she wanted to belong to anyone the way she wanted to belong to Zach Strickland.

She knew it was foolish, letting herself be so undone by one single kiss. Well, yes, maybe it was, but she didn't regret it. As the herd got closer to Winnemucca, she resolved to store up all the memories she could for when she went back to Chicago.

She rode long hours under the searing sun, watching Zach from a distance. Little by little she noticed how his eyes followed her until he saw her watching him, and then he would quickly look away.

And that was how she realized what Zach was working so hard to hide from himself. He cared about her. Zach Strickland wanted her the way a man wanted a woman. She knew instinctively that was what was frightening him. He was in love with her.

She couldn't help smiling inside. Zach was withdrawing from her because he didn't *want* to be in love with her! Some woman had hurt him in the past, and now he was protecting his heart.

She laughed aloud and kicked her horse into a trot alongside the sea of lowing cattle. True, there was no future for this just-discovered connection between Zach and herself, but just knowing that this wondrous feeling was shared between them made her happier than she could ever remember.

And at the same time, it made her sad. When the drive ended, she would be leaving, going back to Chicago and her newspaper.

She caught sight of his tall, lean frame moving gracefully on his horse and a shocking stab of pure animal hunger shimmered into her belly. Up until this moment she had hated this cattle drive—hated the long, hot hours in the saddle and the dust clogging her throat and the bugs crawling into her hair. Some days she even hated her newspaper editor for sending her along on this venture.

This whole ordeal had been a kind of baptism of fire, and more. It had brought her to an awareness of what life was really all about, of the bonds between people, of the feeling that could bloom between a man and a woman.

Of course, a permanent relationship with Zach Strickland was not possible. She knew that. When the drive was over, she would return to Chicago and he would start that ranch in Oregon he wanted so much. He had scrimped and saved and struggled to buy that ranch. And she had fought long, hard years for her career as a newspaper reporter.

They weren't so different, really. They both wanted to follow their dreams. The problem was that her dream was in Chicago and his was in Oregon. When the drive ended she would never see Zach Strickland again.

That realization didn't dampen her feelings for him, or her happiness at knowing that he cared for her. It did give her pause, however. She did not want her heart broken. But…well, maybe it would be worth it to have known this man.

In camp, Zach was still ignoring her, but now Alex understood why. Unless, of course, she was mistaken about his feelings. That thought brought her up short. A good reporter never jumped to conclusions, especially about a man's most private feelings, but…she still felt lighter than air. All afternoon she thought about Zach and that kiss they had shared, and the bubble of joy inside her refused to go away.

That evening, during a supper of Roberto's chili beans and corn bread, Jase promised to show her how to throw a lasso. The minute she dumped her supper plate in the wash bucket, he produced a braided lariat and beckoned to her.

"Come on, Miss Alex. You said you wanted to learn ropin'."

She stood up, stepped over José's long legs and followed the slim blond cowhand to a spot half a dozen steps from the campfire. She would pay extra-careful attention to Jase's instructions; her newspaper readers would gobble up an article on lasso throwing.

From outside the circle of cowhands, Zach surreptitiously watched Dusty and chuckled at her attempts to control the whirling lariat. It flopped into the dirt or went lopsided or spun off sideways. Why did she want to learn to throw a rope in the first place? Then he figured maybe she'd want to use the knowledge in a newspaper column she'd write someday.

A shadow slid over his heart.

He took a sip from the mug of cold coffee in his hand and kept watching. She sure didn't give up easy. She worked with Jase for two hours, until she could rope a rock and then a hunk of firewood. And then, unexpectedly, she danced over and dropped a lasso over his shoulders. With a triumphant squeal, she pulled it tight.

The hands cheered, and Dusty's face shone with pride. He shrugged off the rope, and she immediately re-coiled it and looked for another target. She lassoed Juan, then Skip, even Roberto, who was caught lounging near the wash bucket. With her every success, the hands cheered and whistled.

It sure was obvious his men liked her. She'd won their respect by just hanging in there during the hot, dusty days on the trail, and then she'd won their hearts. Nothing surprising in that, he figured. She'd done the same with *his* heart.

A choking rush of an emotion he couldn't identify closed his throat into an ache. *What am I going to do when I have to put her on the train back to Chicago?*

After another half hour she coiled up the lariat and handed it back to Jase. "Gentlemen, I am going down to the stream now for a bath," she announced. "Juan, would you stand guard for me?"

Without a word he stood up, and Dusty moved to the chuck wagon, hauled out her travel bag and walked off toward the creek. Juan started after her, but Zach gave a short whistle to stop him and took his place. No way were any of his hands, even one as polite and well-behaved as Juan, going to watch Dusty take a bath.

No one was going to watch her but himself.

The night was warm and peaceful with a fat, almost-full moon hanging low in the sky and a million frogs croaking from somewhere near the river. Dusty moved along the faint path through grass so thick it felt like a Turkey carpet, and Zach followed silently, keeping to the shadows twenty paces behind her.

Quietly he stationed himself near a spreading oak tree, settled his back against the trunk and watched her peel off her jeans and shirt. When she got down to her smallclothes, he wished he *wasn't* watching.

Aw, hell, he did and he didn't. A twinge of guilt nibbled at his conscience for spying on her, but he sure didn't want to stop. In fact, he admitted, he *couldn't* stop.

Chapter Twenty

Alex waded out into the stream until the water reached her knees, then dived forward into a deep pool. Oh, what heaven to wash away days of salty perspiration and dust! She sighed with relief as the cool water sluiced over her itchy mosquito bites, then she soaped her skin, un-braided her hair and scrubbed her scalp until it tingled. After she rinsed away the bubbles, she rolled over on her back and floated.

Millions of stars winked above her. The tree branches over her head looked like ghostly sailing ships in the silvery moonlight, and she fancied the jagged black boulders tumbled at one end of the pool were huge sea captains standing guard over her.

A cattle drive might not be so bad if she could take a bath every night. As it was, she had forgotten what it was like to smell scented powder or perfume. Even her hair smelled of sweat and dust. With one hand she gath-ered it up on top of her head and wished for a ribbon or even a piece of twine to secure it.

She had worn the single braid down her back for so many weeks her curls had straightened somewhat, but the thought of ever taming the mass of waves into a semblance of a proper coiffeur made her laugh.

These past weeks spent herding a thousand hulking cows along a trail for days on end had been an unexpected ordeal. The experience had changed her. She had come to know the cowhands, and she prided herself on winning their respect. She suspected that some of them even genuinely liked her.

But, she sighed, then there was Zach Strickland. He liked her, even though he didn't want to. But the fact that he felt that way about her made her happier than she could ever remember, almost as happy as seeing her first newspaper column in print. She laughed aloud, and then she froze when she saw the shadow leaning against a thick tree trunk suddenly straighten up.

Oh, poor Juan. Good-natured and patient, the young man had faithfully guarded her privacy for the better part of an hour without complaint. Feeling safe from prying eyes, she splashed gleefully around and around in a wide circle.

But the shadow against the tree was now moving toward her. Her breath stopped. "Juan? Is something wrong?"

"There's nothin' wrong," a low voice replied. "And it's not Juan."

She trod water and peered through the darkness toward the voice. "Zach! What are you doing here?"

"Watchin' you take a bath."

"I thought that Juan—"

"Juan was busy."

"But—"

"And I wasn't."

"Then you should be really standing guard," she reminded him, "not watching me." She tried to make her tone accusing, but secretly she was glad it was Zach. She didn't even mind the fact that he was watching her.

What on earth was the matter with her? No man had ever laid eyes on her naked form, but here he stood with both hands propped on his hips, calmly studying her as if she were a pony or a heifer. Of course, she was chest deep in the water, so he couldn't see much.

Then a deliciously shocking thought settled in her brain. What if she *were* standing up? What if he *could* see all of her? What would he do?

What would *she* do?

On impulse she splashed into an upright position and turned to face him. For a long minute he didn't move, just stood at the edge of the river and stared.

And then he started toward her.

She looked like some kind of water nymph, a magical creature right out of a Tennyson poem, and Zach had to remind himself to keep breathing. Water sheened her pale skin, making it look so shimmery she looked like something from another world. She was the most beautiful thing he had ever laid eyes on.

For an instant he wondered if he was dreaming. No, he sure as hell wasn't dreaming. This was Dusty Murray, Charlie Kingman's niece from Chicago. He swallowed hard.

His Dusty. Oh, God, she was beautiful. He took another step forward, half expecting her to dive into the deep part of the river or vanish into thin air to escape his gaze. But she didn't move. Instead, she stood motionless as droplets of water slowly rolled down her shoulders and her breasts. The only sound was an insanely happy evening sparrow twittering in the branches above his head. Yeah, maybe he *was* dreaming.

He realized she was watching him, and his chest tightened until he couldn't draw a breath. What was she thinking? Did she know that he...?

Yeah, she knew. She had to know. And she wasn't afraid.

Very deliberately he stepped deeper into the stream. Heedless of his boots and his trousers, he strode toward her until the water came up to his thighs.

She waited without speaking. When he was close enough, he dipped his knees, lifted her into his arms and splashed toward the bank. "Where are your clothes?" he whispered.

"I don't know." She raised her head from his shoulder and looked into his eyes. "I don't care, either."

He blinked. "You know, if I live to be an old man, I'm never gonna understand you, Dusty."

"Good." She breathed the word in his ear, and it was all he could do to keep on walking.

"You know what you're saying?" he murmured.

"Yes."

"I mean, are you sure you know what you're *doing*?"

She hesitated. "Y-yes, I think so."

"Damn right." He found an area of thick, soft grass, dropped to one knee and laid her down. Then he toed off his boots and stretched out beside her.

"Your jeans are wet," she whispered.

"Yeah. Keeps my blood from overheating. You want to tell me why you're not kicking and screaming?"

"You know why, Zach. Because I'm in love with you." She pulled his head down until her lips met his.

"And," she said after a long, delicious minute, "you're in love with me."

He jerked in surprise, not because it wasn't true, but because she said it so calmly, so matter-of-factly. "Yeah," he murmured. "Damndest thing." He kissed her until his body threatened to explode, and then he kissed her some more. He knew it was risky. Dangerous, even. He didn't care.

She looked up at him, her eyes soft as a summer morning and her mouth kiss-swollen. "Zach," she breathed, "show me what comes after kissing."

He swallowed hard. "You don't know, do you." It wasn't a question. She shook her head. "You sure you want me to show you?"

She gave him a smile that melted his insides. Hell's bells, here she was, warm and willing in his arms and eager for more, and he was hesitating. *What is stopping him?*

"I know we have no future," she whispered. "And I don't care. I just want to know what it would be like with you. You know, to…to…"

"Make love with a man," he supplied.

"Not just any man," she murmured in his ear. "I want it to be with you."

He groaned deep in his throat. "I can't, Dusty. I can't make love to you and put you on the train back to Chicago and never see you again. Can't do it."

"It will be hard anyway, Zach." She began to unbutton his shirt. "So kiss me, and then show me what comes next."

"Wait." He cupped her face between his hands. "There's something I want to say to you."

"Yes?" She tugged his shirt free of his jeans and spread it open across his bare chest. "What is it?"

He caught her hand to stop her, but not soon enough. She bent her head and ran her tongue over his nipple, and he sucked in his breath.

"I'm getting light-headed," he said with a chuckle.

"Hush, Zach. I want to touch you."

He gritted his teeth. "Dusty, I gotta say this. You're the most exasperating, wonderful, maddening, admirable bundle of woman I've ever known. And, dammit, I'm in love with you so deep I can't see straight."

"Well, then," she breathed. "I'm in love with you, too, and I…I want you to make love to me."

He brought both hands up to cup her breasts, and when she made a small sound he bent and very slowly ran his tongue over one nipple.

"Oh." She sighed the word and he smiled against her soft skin. *"Oh,"* she said again.

"You like that?"

"Yes." She licked her way across his chest. "Do you?"

"Oh, God," he groaned. "Don't ask. And don't stop."

She laughed softly, pushed his shirt off his shoulders and ran her lips down to the waistband of his jeans.

He caught her hand. "On second thoughts, you'd better stop."

"May I not touch the rest of you?"

Zach shut his eyes and fought for control. "In a minute." He set her apart from him, got to his feet and peeled off his jeans and his drawers. It was pretty obvious he was aroused; he wondered what she would think about that. He dropped down beside her.

"Show me," she murmured.

"Yeah. I will, in a minute." He got his breathing under

control, then trailed his lips from her breasts to her navel and then moved lower. She caught on quicker than he was ready for.

The little sounds of pleasure she made almost undid him. He licked and sucked her flesh the way he'd thought about doing for weeks, and after a while he didn't care about anything other than the woman moving under his tongue.

He kissed the soft skin of her belly, and he heard her breath hiss in. He dragged in a shaky gulp of air and pressed slow kisses on the back of one knee, then ran his tongue over her inner thigh.

"Oh, my." She sighed.

"Good?"

"Yes. It makes me feel...funny inside."

He drew back. "Funny, huh? Funny bad or funny good?"

"Funny good," she said.

He couldn't help smiling, and kissed a path across her belly. Then he moved lower.

"Funny very good," she murmured. "I have never before wanted a man to touch me, but..."

He lifted his head. "But what?"

She breathed out a long sigh and tangled her fingers in his hair. "But now," she said, her voice quiet, "I want it very much."

"Yeah, me, too," he breathed. "I want it a lot."

He ran his tongue over the most intimate part of her, lingering just long enough to tantalize, and she stretched her arms over her head and smiled up at the stars. "Your breath stirs me there."

"Where?"

"Anywhere," she whispered. "Everywhere."

He spread her slick inner lips with his tongue, and

when she drew in a quick hiss he dipped one finger inside her.

"Yes," she breathed. She moved against him. "Yes. *Yes.*"

"Dusty, are you sure about this? I can stop now."

"Don't stop, Zach. Nothing has ever felt this wonderful. It makes me want more. It makes me want... everything."

He rose over her and nudged her legs apart. "You sure about 'everything'?" he whispered.

In answer, she reached her arms around him and pulled him closer.

He probed gently at her entrance, and when she moved her hips to meet him, he slowly entered her partway, withdrew and then thrust deep. She didn't cry out, just gave a quick gasp, and then she was moving with him and he was kissing her, her tongue sweet in his mouth and hungry at the same time.

He couldn't stop, couldn't get enough of her. Until the day he died he would never forget the feel of her body under his, the hot silky sheath that enveloped him, inviting him deeper. He'd never known anything like this. Part of him was singing with delight; part of him was scared to death.

She was murmuring something, his name, he realized. Suddenly she sucked in her breath, and then her body went still and she cried out. He buried himself deep and held on as spasms racked him and his breathing turned into a sob.

He wondered what the hell was happening. He'd never felt anything remotely like what he was feeling now. He wondered if she felt it, too.

When he could talk he turned his head and put his lips near her ear.

"Dusty?"

"Yes, Zach?"

"What just happened?"

She gave a soft laugh. "You don't know?"

"Hell, no. Never felt anything like this in my life."

He could tell she was smiling because the skin of her cheek moved under his mouth.

"Is it always like this?" she asked. Her voice sounded drowsy and soft.

He shook his head once and kissed her slowly. "No. It's never like this."

He kissed her again, and all at once he felt like crying. "It's never like this."

Two unforgettable hours passed, and at last they pulled on their clothes and walked quietly back into camp past the cowhands sound asleep in their bedrolls. Roberto snored a few yards away from the chuck wagon.

In silence they crawled underneath the bulky wood structure and wrapped themselves in a single blanket. Zach hooked an arm around her middle and pulled her close. "'Night, Dusty," he murmured. He pressed a long, soft kiss behind her ear, then curled his body around hers and slept.

Chapter Twenty-One

In the morning, Alex managed to eat her biscuits and bacon without staring at Zach, at least not too obviously. He went about making his trail assignments as usual, but later, instead of riding alongside his point man as he usually did, he spurred his gray gelding to the back of the herd and fell in beside her.

He didn't say anything, but she was acutely aware of his tall, rangy frame moving close to hers, and that was conversation enough. Surely her entire body was glowing! The cowhands must've seen the change in her; maybe they even guessed the reason why. But hour after hour passed on the trail and not a word or a look from any of them revealed that they knew anything unusual had happened.

But it had. She felt different today. She knew what it was like to be loved by a man.

As the day wore on, Zach rode beside her, and they spoke sporadically of the dust, the harsh sun, the hot wind that came up in the afternoon. Inconsequential things. Occasionally he galloped off, lariat swinging, after a rebellious steer straying from the herd. But he always returned.

All that afternoon, even though nothing particularly significant was said, she felt the unmistakable bond between them, and that had her smiling in spite of the heat and the hard saddle chafing her bottom.

Could Zach see the glow she felt inside? If he did, he gave no indication of anything unusual, other than the expression in his moss green eyes when he looked at her. At last she understood what the word *poleaxed* meant. He looked…well, dazed.

She herself must look positively besotted. She worked hard to keep her mind on something other than his body moving only a few feet from hers, and by suppertime, she was feeling a bit faint and dizzy with fatigue. Or maybe it was desire?

For dessert that night Roberto outdid himself by baking tarts made from dried cherries. And then Zach surprised everyone, most of all Alex, by volunteering for night-herding duty.

Curly goggled at him. "You serious, boss? You ain't never rode night duty before. How come—"

"Gettin' close to Winnemucca," Zach responded, his voice even. "Want to do my fair share."

Curly's bushy blond eyebrows went up. "But you're the boss!"

"Yep," Zach said with a grin.

"Aw, well, I guess you kin do what ya want."

"Gotta remember how to do it," Zach replied with a laugh. "Next year I'll be drivin' my own herd to market." He shot a look at Alex, then refocused on the cherry tart on his plate.

The truth was Zach didn't think he could lie next to Dusty all night without touching her, and the thought of sleeping anywhere else didn't sit well with him. He wanted to be close to her, even if he couldn't...

Oh, Jupiter. At least night-herding would give him something to do besides sweat all night wanting her. For the hundredth time he wondered how he was ever going to stand watching her climb on board that train back to Chicago.

The three hours he spent riding in slow circles around and around the slumbering herd passed more slowly than he could ever remember. By two in the morning, when Juan came to relieve him, he was so wound up he couldn't sleep anyway, so he crawled in next to Dusty under the wagon and just lay quiet, watching her breathe in and out.

The next morning he was completely wrecked. Served him right, he guessed. *You damn fool. You had to go and tumble hat over spurs for someone you're never gonna see again.* Guess he was seventeen kinds of a fool.

But he wasn't sorry. He would never be sorry.

As they got closer to Winnemucca, Alex noticed that the landscape began to change. The flat plain that had been punctuated with rivers and streams and trees and rolling green hills in the distance gave way to endless flat acres of wildflowers. It was still desert, but yellow and orange dandelions bloomed beside the trail, along with purple sage and something with tiny golden daisylike blossoms that covered rounded gray bushes and made them look almost fluffy.

Gradually the land began to look more populated. Neat little farmsteads and ranches were scattered here and there in the wide valleys and flat, dry landscape. An occasional herd of sheep or goats blundered into their path, followed by a single serape-draped sheep-herder and his dog.

By the time they rode into Winnemucca, Alex was so tired and sweaty she didn't care if she ever saw another cow again for the rest of her life.

The town was made up of mostly wind-scoured wooden buildings with false fronts, including at least a dozen saloons and the Silver Spur Hotel. Huge livestock holding pens sprawled near the rail yard. It was the driest, windiest place she had ever visited, and after ten minutes of riding along the main street behind a thousand head of cattle, all she wanted was a long hot bath to wash off the dust. She also needed to pay a visit to the dressmaker, if there was one.

Roberto had arrived hours before with Cherry and the remuda, which now filled three large stables at the edge of town. The cowhands spurred forward, driving the herd toward the holding yards where the lowing steers and heifers would be jammed in head to tail, waiting to be loaded into the chute.

When the last cow had joined the rest of the penned herd, Alex walked her roan to the stable, where Cherry stood waiting. She slipped out of the saddle, handed her horse over to the wrangler and turned to find Zach at her side.

"Some of the boys are stayin' out at camp with Roberto and the chuck wagon. I want you in the hotel."

"Is there some reason? I could stay with the cowhands, too, Zach. After all these weeks I feel at home with them."

He took her elbow and walked her out of earshot. "I'm stayin' at the hotel, Dusty. I want you there, too."

Her heart kicked. "Oh. Yes, then I will stay at the

hotel." She resisted adding "where you are," but from the look on his tanned face, he knew this.

"Come on, then. I'll walk you over."

When the gray-haired clerk at the hotel desk spied them, he flipped open a fresh page on the register. Alex stepped away and stood apart, watching out the front window as the wind kicked up the ruffles of a child's pinafore. That reminded her that she needed some ruffles of her own. She hoped the dressmaker would be accommodating.

"How many rooms you want, mister?" the hotel clerk inquired.

"Two," Zach said. "One for me and my men, here…" he gestured at Curly and Skip standing next to Alex "…and one private room."

"Fer yourself, huh? Must be the trail boss of yer outfit."

"Not for me, no. For the lady."

The clerk's salt-and-pepper eyebrows rose. "Oh, yeah? What lady would that be, mister? Some fancy lady, I reckon. We don't allow no fancy—"

"Dusty?" Zach gestured for her to join him at the hotel desk. "This is Miss Alexandra Murray, a reporter for the *Chicago Times*," he told the clerk. "The private room is for her."

The clerk frowned at her. "'Miss,' huh? You sure don't look like any lady I've ever seen."

Alex sent him a tired smile. "What kind of ladies have you seen?" she asked sweetly.

"Real ones," he blurted out. "You know, ones wearin' skirts and petticoats an' hats an' proper gloves, not grubby jeans and dusty shirts."

Her eyebrows went up. "That makes one a lady, does it? Petticoats and hats?"

"Well, yes, ma'am, it surely does."

"Have you ever heard the old saying 'beauty is only skin deep'?"

"Sure I have," he snapped. "So what?"

She smiled at him. "And what about this one. 'Clothes don't make the man.'"

"Uh…" His plump, smooth-shaven cheeks grew pink.

Dusty's smile widened. "Clothes don't make the lady, either. Just because I am wearing jeans and a shirt and leather boots doesn't mean I am not a lady, now, does it?"

The clerk shot Zach a harried look and swallowed. "No, ma'am, I agree, it don't."

"Doesn't," she corrected. She planted both elbows on the counter in the most unladylike gesture Zach had ever seen her make and fluttered her eyelashes, something else he'd never seen her do.

"Well, then, sir," she said, her voice like rich cream, "along with my private room I would like a bath brought up. We *ladies* like to keep clean."

Curly and Skip guffawed. Zach managed to keep a straight face, but he let Dusty go on with her teasing until the clerk was apoplectic, and then he stepped in.

"Okay, Mr.…?"

"McMullen," the harried clerk blurted out.

"Mr. McMullen," Zach acknowledged. "That's two rooms we need, one of them a single. And a bath. I assume you have hot water?"

"Oh, yessir, sir. And maid service. One hot bath comin' right up."

Dusty accepted the key and followed the clerk's young helper up the stairs, with Curly and Skip at her heels. Shaking his head in amusement, Zach went outside to the men's bathhouse next door, where he scrubbed himself till his skin stung and got a shave. When he was so clean he squeaked, he reentered the hotel and met Jase and Skip in the lobby. He couldn't help joshing them about their newly trimmed mustaches.

Then he went in search of Ned Palmerston, the cattle buyer he had arranged to meet.

An hour later he stepped from the Rocky Rooster Saloon into the street with four hundred dollars in gold to pay the men and a bank draft for forty thousand dollars. A thousand dollars of that money was his cut as trail boss. That, plus what he'd saved up over the years, ought to be enough to buy good land and some stock to start his own ranch. The thought made his heart almost fly out of his chest.

The bank teller agreed to wire the money to Charlie Kingman at the Smoke River Bank, and Zach felt so relieved that the drive was over he swung on down the street whistling "Streets of Laredo." He couldn't wait to change into some clean duds and take Dusty out for a thick, juicy steak dinner.

Curly and José waylaid him in the hotel bar, where he paid them the money they'd earned, plus a little extra. Naturally they insisted on buying him a shot of Red Eye.

An hour later he pulled on new jeans and a clean blue shirt and went downstairs to the hotel dining room to meet all the other hands, except for Cherry, and wait for Dusty. Five o'clock, she'd said. "After I visit the dressmaker and curl my hair."

On the drive he'd seen her only twice when her hair hadn't hung down her back in a single thick braid. The last time was the night he'd made love to her, and her hair had been wet, not curly.

Oh, damn, remembering that night is getting me hard.

He walked around for a few minutes to get himself under control, then entered the hotel dining room and settled down to wait for her. Knowing his hands would want to join them, he chose the big round table in the center of the room, right under the tinkly glass chandelier.

Five o'clock came and went with no Dusty. After another half hour, a spiffed-up Curly and Juan wandered in and joined him. He paid Juan his wages, and as the rest of the hands straggled in, along with Roberto, he counted out some more gold coins. While they waited for Dusty, José and Jase, each bought him another whiskey.

"Sure takes a woman a long time takin' a bath, don't it?" Curly complained. "I'm gettin' mighty hungry, boss."

"Do not complain, Señor Curly," Roberto cautioned. "The *señorita* she is wear man's clothes for over a month. Now she wants to look like a—" He broke off, his brown eyes widening, and rose out of his chair.

Curly frowned at the cook, and then his mouth dropped open. "Hel—" he muttered. He shot to his feet, followed by Juan and the other hands around the table. Zach had his back to the dining room entrance, so he didn't see the reason. He stayed seated and went on sipping his whiskey.

Dusty glided across the room, shaking off a bevy of obsequious waiters, and sent Roberto a wide smile. Then she floated toward the table of gaping cowhands, all of whom were now on their feet and swiping off their broad-brimmed hats.

Zach stared up at his men. What the—

"Señor Boss," Roberto hissed. "Look behind you."

Zach twisted his head in the direction the cook pointed. Nah, that wasn't Dusty. But he had to admit the woman moving toward them was the prettiest female he'd seen in a long, long time.

"Must be dreamin'," Curly breathed.

Roberto barked out a laugh. "Ah, no, Señor Curly, is no dream."

Zach shot a look at Curly. "You'd think you'd never seen a good-lookin'—"

"Gentlemen," a feminine voice drawled. "Do sit down."

The eight men sank back into their seats, and very slowly Zach got to his feet, hoping his tongue wasn't hanging too far out of his mouth. The vision in ruffly yellow silk moved to his elbow.

My God, it is Dusty. She looked so beautiful it made his mouth go dry.

She even *sounded* beautiful with the soft swish-swish of petticoats under her billowing yellow skirt.

"May I join you?" she asked with a laugh in her voice. She headed for the empty chair across from Zach. Roberto, on his right, leaned toward him. "Say somet'ing, Señor Boss," he intoned. "Is not polite not to speak."

He wasn't real sure he *could* speak. The other men all managed polite greetings, then tumbled over each other to draw Dusty's chair out for her. When the waiter appeared, Zach was still standing, speechless at the sight of her.

"Sir? Is something wrong?"

Without taking his eyes off the vision now seated across the table from him, he shook his head at the waiter and dropped into his chair.

"Sir?" the waiter persisted.

"What? Oh, no, nothin's wrong."

Not true. *Everything* was wrong. His head felt muddled and his body was beginning to ache in places he couldn't afford to think about at the moment. God, she was so beautiful, and he was so much in love with her, his brain was trussed up like a branded heifer.

And she was leaving in the morning!

She held his gaze across the table. "I do apologize for being late," she said. "I had to visit the dressmaker and then get a hotel maid to press the creases from my gown and..." she looked straight into his eyes "...curl my hair."

Zach swallowed hard. "You look beautiful, Dus— Miss Murray. It was worth the wait."

Curly gallantly snapped open her linen napkin and unfolded it for her. Juan, on her other side, signaled the waiter to fill her water glass and Skip stretched an arm across the table to slide his own menu in front of her. Zach sat dumbfounded, unable to think of a single thing to say.

She gave a delighted laugh. "Have you all ordered dinner already?"

"Nope," Curly assured her. "We was waitin' for you."

"Well, then..." She studied the offerings. "I bet you're all having steak tonight, am I right?" She grinned.

"No, Señorita Alex," Juan said. "We have had enough beef this past month. We have fried chicken."

"Well, I want a big juicy steak!" she announced. "I want to commemorate this cattle drive with something special. Something I'll remember for the rest of my life."

She looked across the table straight at Zach, and he noticed that her eyes were shiny.

Chapter Twenty-Two

Alex twirled her spoon in the dish of chocolate ice cream and scooped up a ladylike portion. "Gentlemen, before I go back to the city, there are two things I've always wanted to do."

"What's that, Miss Alex?" Curly asked eagerly. "If you wanna dance with a top hand, I'd sure be willin'."

She smiled, caught Zach's puzzled look and shook her head. "I want to visit a real saloon."

There was a moment of stunned silence. Curly recovered first, clearing his throat and leaning forward. "Aw, that's easy, Miss Alex," he said. "What's the other thing?"

She swallowed a mouthful of smooth, cold ice cream. "I've always wanted to sit at a poker table. And play a game of poker."

"Poker!" Curly's brow furrowed.

"Poker," she said calmly. Zach stared at her from across the table.

Skip hesitated, taking his time to formulate his question. "You, uh, got any money you're hankerin' to lose, Miss Alex?"

She gave the wiry cowhand a wide-eyed look. "Of

course I have money. On this cattle drive I have earned, let's see…almost six weeks' salary from the *Chicago Times*."

"Yeah?" Skip intoned. "How're you gonna pay up if you lose?"

Alex leaned toward him across her ice-cream dish. "You have my word, Skip. *If* I lose at poker, and you will please note that I said *if*, you have my word that I will send you any money I may owe. That is," she said with a twinkle in her eye, "if any one of you can manage to vanquish me at the poker table."

"You mean 'win a hand,' Miss Alex," Curly corrected.

"Oh, yes," she said quickly. "Anyone who wins a hand from me will be paid, I promise."

She risked a quick look at Zach. He was frowning, and that gave her pause. He probably disapproved of ladies who played cards. Or was it visiting the saloon where the poker tables were located that bothered him? She didn't care. She was feeling reckless tonight.

Liar! You are feeling numb with grief tonight.

She couldn't look at Zach for fear she would burst into tears.

Curly self-consciously straightened his leather vest. "You gonna write about us in your newspaper?"

"Yes, of course I am. That is what I was sent out here to do, write about life in the West and some of the interesting char—cowboys on a cattle drive. That's why I interviewed each one of you."

She caught Zach's wary expression across the table. He hadn't wanted her to interview him, and when she had finally cornered him, he'd told her things about himself that broke her heart. She knew she could not ever speak of these things. Much as she longed to write about the tall, good-looking trail boss, she would protect his privacy. She would leave Zach out of her columns.

She wrenched her mind away from him and forced her attention back to the matter at hand, playing a game of poker after supper.

"Now," she said, anticipation in her voice. "Who is going to accompany me to the saloon?"

The entire table of men jolted to their feet. All except Zach, who sat with a half-worried, half-bemused expression on his face. Oh, how she enjoyed surprising this serious, upstanding man she'd fallen in love with.

She stood up slowly and watched his face change as his gaze moved from her mouth to her breasts and then to her eyes. She saw his desire for her, and it sent heat washing through every inch of her body. If he only knew what she was thinking, he would have her up the stairs and into her room and in his arms before she was a minute older.

She could feel her cheeks burning.

"Wait a minute," Curly exclaimed. "We wanna have our pictures took with Miss Alex! There's a photography place right next door to the saloon. C'mon." Ostentatiously he offered her his arm.

"Very well, gentlemen, a photograph it is. Curly and I will lead the way."

Full of himself and a fine dinner, the muscular cowboy led the way to Henslee's Photography Studio. Zach reluctantly followed them.

The proprietor was just locking up his shop, and when he caught sight of them from inside his front window, he waved them off. "Closed," he mouthed.

Curly tapped on the glass. "No, ya ain't," he insisted. "Open up."

The photographer cracked the door open a scant inch. "I told you, mister, the studio is closed."

Skip shoved the door forward another inch. "Well, open it back up! Got some famous people out here wantin' their picture took."

At that, the door swung wide open and a short, pale man with thick glasses stepped forward. "Famous? Who're you talkin' about, sonny?"

"Her," Skip and Curly said together. Skip extended his hand and pulled Alex forward.

The photographer's eyebrows went up. "Oh. Didn't see you there, Miss. Uh…are you fam—I mean, are you someone I should recognize?"

"She sure is," a chorus of male voices assured him. "And we're all famous, too. Or we're gonna be, soon as Miss Murray gets back to Chicago."

"Chicago, hmm? What, exactly, is it about Chicago that is significant, miss?"

"Chicago," she said demurely, "is where the *Chicago Times* is located." She paused. "The newspaper I write for."

"Oh," Mr. Henslee said.

"And publish photographs for," she added.

"Oh?"

She smiled at him. "Giving the photographs I publish in the newspaper full photography studio credits."

"Oh! Well, then, why don't you all step right in here and let me set up my camera."

Zach took her arm and conducted her inside, and the entire crew of the Rocking K crowded in behind them.

"This way, miss," Mr. Henslee invited. "And…" he cast a doubtful eye over the cowhands "…gentlemen." He pointed to a backdrop of blue drapery. "Stand right over there, please. And you, Miss Murray, is it?" He pulled an ornate wooden chair forward. "Please be seated."

She settled herself in the chair and rearranged her skirt. Zach stepped up beside her and rested one hand on the high carved back. The other hands fell in behind them, jostling for positions near Alex.

"I dowanna stand in back," Skip complained. "Can't see over Curly's big fat head."

"Aw, shut up, Skip. Shoulda growed more when you was young. Guess you didn't eat enough beef."

"Hold still, now," Mr. Henslee insisted. He disappeared underneath his black camera hood. Alex could see how difficult it was for the men not to fidget. Surreptitiously, Zach moved his hand to rest on her shoulder.

"Hold it. Hold it…" A puff of gray smoke wafted into the air, and the photographer waved the men away.

"And we'd like one more," Zach announced. "Just Miss Murray and me."

"Aw, c'mon, boss. We're gonna take her to the saloon."

Mr. Henslee's eyes popped. "The saloon!" he spluttered. "Really?"

"Really," Zach said sharply. "Get on with the picture taking."

The photographer directed him to sit in the fancy upholstered chair with Alex now standing behind him. When he disappeared under the camera hood, she stepped in close and grazed his shoulder with her hand.

"Hold still, now." Henslee called out as she gently pressed Zach's shoulder.

"Got it!" the photographer announced when the smoke cleared. "Y'all can pick 'em up tomorrow morning."

"We'll pick them up tonight," Zach said quietly.

"Miss Murray is catching the eastbound train tomorrow morning."

"Sorry, mister, that won't be possible. It takes time to develop photographs, you know."

"How much time?"

"Well, let me see. I'd say at least three or four hours."

"That gives you till midnight, Mr. Henslee. Unless…"

Alex picked up her cue. "Unless you want it noted in the *Chicago Times.*"

The eyebrows went up again. "Want what noted?"

"That there was to be a photograph accompanying my article, but…" she smiled sweetly "…the photography studio was…late. And that Henslee's Photography Studio is slow to…" She let the sentence trail off suggestively.

Henslee sighed. "All right, all right. Your photographs will be ready by midnight."

Juan stepped forward and offered his arm. "Come, Señorita Alex. You want to see saloon? I escort you."

"And me," Curly added.

"And me, also," Roberto said. He tipped his head close to hers. "Is risky what you do, *señorita*. Men don' like ladies in saloon."

"Aw, she's got us to protect her!" Curly blustered. He led the way out of Mr. Henslee's studio and into the Rocky Rooster saloon.

Zach watched Dusty disappear through the bar's swinging doors on Juan's arm with a sinking feeling in his gut. She'd sure surprised him on this drive. She'd surprised all of them, he admitted. And, he thought with a wry grin, she'd won a wagonload of respect from his men.

That was unheard-of for this bunch of hard-bitten ranch hands who'd rather make fun of their cohorts than say anything even halfway nice. He'd heard them say plenty of nice things about Dusty when they didn't know he was listening.

Lord God, he would miss her. He couldn't imagine riding four hundred miles back to Smoke River without her smile and her questions and her prettiness and her sass and her soft blue eyes meeting his over the campfire.

Hell and damn, Strickland, you need a drink!

When he entered the saloon the scene that met him made him laugh out loud and then tightened his throat into a knot. Dusty sat at a big round corner table like a queen holding court. Curly was just sliding a glass of what Zach assumed was whiskey, watered down, he hoped, in front of her, and Juan was leaning in, probably explaining what it was.

Zach took the empty chair across from her, crossed his long legs in front of him and settled down to watch. Mostly, he admitted to himself, he was settling down to just watch Dusty and nurse his aching heart.

It was hard to sit so close to her and not touch her. Hard to acknowledge that Dusty had won not only the hearts of his rough Rocking K trail crew, right down to his chuck wagon cook and Cherry, his aging horse wrangler, but his own heart, as well.

It was doubly hard to face the fact that it was ending.

Dusty studied the glass of whiskey before her for a long minute and glanced around the table at the avid faces of his men. Then she bit her lip, drew in a long, determined breath and raised the whiskey to her lips.

She'd had a sip of liquor before, Zach remembered. A nip from the watered-down bottle Roberto kept hidden in the chuck wagon. But that would be nothing compared to a full gulp of the real stuff.

As the liquor hit her throat, Zach saw her eyes widen, and then she swallowed. Or tried to. She didn't cough or sputter like he thought she would. Instead she blinked hard and tears rose in her eyes and hung on her lashes like big trembly diamonds. She swallowed hard and closed her lids for a long moment. Her lips tightened and then her eyes opened again.

Zach felt his own eyes sting. *Go ahead and cough, honey. Get rid of that stuff burning your throat.*

But she didn't. She sat without moving a muscle while every single cowhand, even the usually imperturbable Roberto, leaned forward, waiting. Finally she opened her mouth.

"That tastes perfectly awful," she rasped. She picked up her glass and took another swig. After a long moment she asked an unexpected question. "How can any of you drink this stuff? It tastes like…like…"

"Horse piss?" Curly volunteered with a chuckle.

"Printer's ink," she shot back.

"Ain't never tasted printer's ink," Skip said.

"Ain't never tasted horse piss, neither," Curly retorted.

The men laughed, and Curly vacated his chair and sauntered back to the bar.

Zach heard him tell the bartender to pour him a shot of "horse piss." His point rider sure had a sense of humor. Even Dusty laughed.

"Gentlemen," she said, her voice hoarse. "May I have another whiskey?"

Skip blinked at her. "You ain't serious, are ya, Miss Alex?"

"Of course I am serious. An elephant," she enunciated carefully, "never gives up."

In that instant Zach knew his life was over. The minute Dusty climbed on that train tomorrow, nothing else would matter, not riding back to Smoke River, not Charlie Kingman, the man he'd come to admire, not savoring Consuelo's cooking, not even owning his own ranch.

Yeah, he'd worked like an idiot for years, scraping his hard-earned pennies into a mason jar under his bunk and drawing and redrawing plans for his own horse corrals and barns and a ranch house. When he got back to Smoke River he'd by God have enough money to do it.

But somehow, all of a sudden it didn't matter. Inside he felt empty as a flour barrel. And lonely? Lord God, he missed her already.

Dammit, what he wanted more than he'd ever wanted anything in his life was Dusty.

Curly returned with a second glass of whiskey and set it down in front of her. She looked up, and suddenly Zach saw her eyes go wide and the color drain from her face.

Juan shot to his feet, followed by Skip and then Jase, all staring at something behind him. Zach swiveled around to see what it was, and his gut twisted.

Cassidy.

Chapter Twenty-Three

"Howdy, boys," Cassidy drawled. "Figured you'd get here sooner or later."

Zach let out a muttered curse, and his men immediately closed ranks around Dusty, screening her from view.

Zach stood up. "What do you want, Cassidy?"

The big-bellied man ignored the question. "Looks like I timed it just right."

"Just right for what?" Zach snapped. As far as he was concerned, the man was all hat and no cattle.

Cassidy slicked back his overlong brown hair. "Just right for gettin' what's owed me."

"Nothing's owed you. I paid you off the night you left camp, twenty dollars in gold."

"Mebbe. See, the way I look at it, you had no cause to run me off like that."

"Guess I see it differently," Zach replied evenly.

"Guess you do at that. Now Miss Murray, sure as shootin' she wanted me to stick around. But you poked yer trail bossy nose into her affairs and—"

"Get out," Zach ordered.

Cassidy pushed back his jacket and ostentatiously

stroked the Colt stuffed under his belt. "Now, I really don't think you wanna order me outta here, Strickland."

"Yeah? Why's that?" Zach kept his eyes on the man's face, not on the hardware. Even Cassidy wouldn't shoot an unarmed man. Or would he?

"Well, 'cuz this here saloon's a public place. I got as much right here as you or anybody else. Now, I figure you owe me some more money, Strickland, so let's have it."

"What'd you do with the twenty dollars in wages I gave you?"

Cassidy barked out a laugh. "Had to spend half of it buyin' a horse off yer wrangler to ride out of camp. Drives a hard bargain, that Cherry does."

"When you give Cherry back the horse, you'll get your ten dollars back."

Cassidy's close-set black eyes narrowed. "That ain't the way I figure it, mister."

"I don't care how you figure it. I'm telling you to move on."

"I will iff'n you pay me another twenty bucks."

Zach gritted his teeth. "I don't owe you another twenty. I pay my top hands that much, and you're no top hand."

"Yeah?"

"Yeah. Move along, Cassidy. I fired you once. Don't figure on doing it twice."

Cassidy ran his forefinger over his bristly chin. "Now hold on just a damn minute. I been waitin' here for more'n a week to see that pretty lady travelin' with you. Thought she was maybe sweet on me."

Zach opened his mouth, but before he could speak, Dusty's voice rose from behind the wall of surrounding cowhands.

"You're wrong, Mr. Cassidy. This lady was never sweet on you."

Cassidy blinked. "That you, Miss Murray? Never expected to find you in a saloon." He made a quick lunge forward and butted Juan away from his protective position in front of her.

"Well, now." Cassidy grinned when he caught sight of Dusty. "That's more friendly-like. What're you doin' here in a saloon, pretty lady?"

"Research," came her cool response.

"Oh, right. Plumb forgot you was a newspaper writer. You learnin' anything interestin' tonight?"

"Yes, I certainly am. This may be a public place, Mr. Cassidy, but I do not believe you are welcome here."

"Mebbe. Mebbe not. I'll mosey on when Strickland here pays me what he owes me."

"Pay him, *señor*," Roberto muttered. "Get rid of him."

"Hell if I will," Zach replied.

Cassidy shook his head. "Well, I'll make you a deal, Strickland. I'll leave if you let me have one hour with Miss Murray. One hour *alone*."

"No," Zach said, his voice hard. He wouldn't let this man within twenty feet of Dusty.

"Let the pretty lady answer for herself, why don'tcha? Might be she'd fancy—"

"No," Dusty sang out. "She wouldn't."

"Lissen, there's a good number of you fellers and only one of me. But…" he patted his Colt "…this one is armed."

"Señor," Roberto hissed at Zach's elbow. "Someone will get hurt. Why you not pay him?"

"Because. That's—"

"Extortion," Dusty supplied. She raised her voice.

"Besides, I am not the kind of lady who spends time with a man for money. Leave me alone, Mr. Cassidy."

"Like hell, I—"

On impulse Zach spun toward the man and dropped him with a single punch to the jaw. Then he bent over, yanked the man's pistol out of his belt and hurled it over the batwing doors into the street. Roberto grabbed the unconscious man's shirt and Curly gripped his belt; together they heaved Cassidy after his gun.

Quick as a cat, Juan scrambled toward the door. "Not smart to leave angry *hombre* with weapon." The cowhand disappeared, then returned within minutes and handed the Colt to Zach.

Dusty stood up. "Gentlemen. Has this interruption stopped our poker game?"

Zach watched her move gracefully past the whole ugly incident to put the men at ease, and he shook his head in admiration. There'd been lots of times in the past month when the woman he'd thought was Charlie Kingman's citified, pampered niece had surprised him. Tonight was sure no exception.

Settled once more around the table for the poker game, Dusty garnered advice from Skip, seated on her left, and from Juan on her right. Juan pretended he knew nothing about poker, but back at the Rocking K Zach had noticed something. After most of the bunkhouse card games, Juan made a trip into town to visit the Smoke River Bank.

He shook Juan out of his thoughts and leaned back to watch the game. He didn't worry about Dusty losing money; he just wanted her to have a good time. If she did lose, he didn't want her to owe money to anyone but him.

So he motioned Juan to deal him in. Later, he decided,

he'd visit the sheriff, tell him to keep an eye on Cassidy. Right now, he wanted to play poker.

Nah, he didn't give a peacock's hind feather about playing poker. The truth was he just wanted to be near Dusty, stick to her as close as he could get until she got on that train tomorrow.

He laid down the cards Juan dealt him and closed his eyes. God, tomorrow morning the train was going to take her away from him.

"Boss?" Jase jogged his arm. "You okay?"

He opened his lids to see Dusty watching him, her face grave and those blue-blue eyes of hers beginning to shimmer with unshed tears. She knew. She knew what he was feeling and what he was thinking. And she knew how he was hurting inside.

"Yeah, I'm okay," he said. His voice came out rougher than he intended. "I'm thinkin' the sheriff oughta know about Cassidy."

Dusty caught on to five-card stud pretty fast. So fast that when everyone dropped out of that hand, it ended up being just him and Dusty. "Why, Zach," she said with a laugh. "I do believe I am learning this game to your disadvantage."

He just looked at her. Her voice betrayed nothing, but her eyes were full of something that made breathing difficult. In her eyes he saw longing. And pain. He couldn't hazard a guess about what his own eyes showed.

She came within an ace of beating him out of a big pot. Then, while the hands cheered and hurrahed, she won the next hand. And then the next two hands.

After that, things went all to hell. Dusty cleaned him out. Yeah, he had to work hard to keep his mind on the game, but the truth was she won fair and square. She kept her face set in a perfect poker-player's bland expression. But her eyes...

He couldn't stand to look into her eyes.

She scooped in her winnings, practically bouncing up and down in her chair, her eyes as wide as a kid's at Christmas. Guess she liked winning.

Maybe because his pride was a bit stung after he'd lost the last three hands to her, Zach challenged her to one final hand. "Just the two of us," he said. "Double or nothing." If he won, Dusty would forfeit all her winnings, which amounted to around three hundred dollars. If Dusty won, he'd have to write her an IOU.

She accepted his challenge, sending him a slow smile across the table, but he had to laugh at the gleam in her eye. Dusty was competitive. No matter what she was doing, she liked to come out on top.

He prayed to God he would win the hand because he needed that money. It was part of the hard-won thousand dollars he'd earned to start his ranch. With that, plus the money he'd salted away in the bank, he could purchase four good horses and four or five heifers and a young bull to start his herd. Maybe he wouldn't eat too much for the first couple of years, but he had to have stock.

No one around the poker table said a word as the cards were shuffled and dealt for the final hand. And no one spoke when Dusty traded in three of her cards. Zach claimed only one.

She studied her hand. "All right," she announced, her voice grave, "I will speak."

Juan leaned over and whispered something to her.

"Oh, of course." She grinned. "I mean I will *call*," she amended.

Zach spread his three queens in front of him. Dusty

looked down at them, and then her blue eyes flicked up to hold his for a long moment. There was some kind of message in her gaze, but he couldn't read it.

Then she leaned forward and spread two tens and three jacks on the table.

Hell in a handbasket, she had a full house! And that sure beat his three queens.

The hands cheered. Stunned, Zach just sat there. "Curly, get me a piece of paper and a pencil." He scratched out an IOU, walked around the table and pressed it into her hand.

Then, to his surprise, she did something he would remember for the rest of his life. She glanced at his IOU, looked up and held his gaze for a long minute. Finally, she smiled at him and tore the paper up into tiny pieces. She dropped them on the poker table, then rose and smoothed out her skirt. The men stood up, as well.

Zach couldn't seem to get his brain in gear. She'd just won hundreds of dollars from him in an all-or-nothing poker hand, and then she'd tossed it back into his lap. He shook his head. Guess he'd never understand her, not in a million years.

But, he thought with an inward groan, it wouldn't be the first time he'd scratched his head over Miss Alexandra Murray. And it sure didn't change the way he felt about her. Nothing would ever change that.

"Gentlemen," she purred. "I believe I will retire now. You are loading cattle tomorrow, and I am returning to Chicago."

The men shuffled out of the saloon, and after a moment, she started for the door. Zach stepped up and grasped her arm. "Dusty, wait a minute. You won that hand fair and square, and I always pay my debts."

She stood on tiptoe and whispered near his ear, "I can't take your hard-earned money from you, Zach. Really, I should be paying you! After all, you didn't want me along on this cattle drive in the first place."

He heard the words, but the only thing he really understood was the tremor in her voice. Leaving was going to be as hard for her as it was for him.

She walked on into the hotel foyer and swept up the stairs. He followed her. When he caught up with her, he reached for her hand. "Having you along on this drive, riding the trail with you…it was worth it, Dusty. You know that."

"Yes," she said softly, "I do. And I also know how much you want to start your own ranch. That takes money."

"Yeah, but—"

She stopped short and pulled him around to face her. "Zach, for heaven's sake, let's not argue about it. Not on my…our last night."

That stopped him cold. *Their last night.* He'd spent all evening shoving that realization to the back of his mind. He'd never worked so hard to forget something in his life.

"Dusty…" She looked up, and he saw that her eyes were all shiny with tears. All at once, whatever he was going to say to her died on his lips. Instead, he folded her into his arms and held her close.

"I can't think about tomorrow," he said against her hair. "I had a hard time thinkin' about it for the last three hundred miles, and right at this moment I'm not doin' much better."

"What are you going to do now?" she asked after a long silence.

"Go down to the bar and get a double whiskey."

"Bring me one, too."

He choked out a laugh. "I'll bring you a lemonade, Dusty. Not another whiskey. I don't want to send you off on the train tomorrow with a hangover."

"Very well." She sighed. "Leaving will be…" She swallowed. "Leaving will be hard enough, won't it?"

He couldn't speak. *Hard* didn't even come close. He looked at her for a long moment. "I'm going out for a walk. I'll be back in an hour."

She studied his face and tried to smile, then said only one word. "Promise?"

Zach stood at the bar between Curly and Roberto, staring into the tumbler of whiskey he was twirling around and around in his fingers. Suddenly he didn't want it. He'd already downed three whiskeys tonight; he figured that was enough. He didn't need a headache tomorrow, either.

Besides, when he went upstairs Dusty would be waiting for him.

Curly clapped him on the back. "Sure been a helluva drive, huh, boss?"

Other voices chimed in from the cowhands strung out along the length of the polished mahogany bar. "Sure has," Skip agreed.

"Lotta fun, too, with Miss Alex along," Jase added.

"What you think, Señor Boss, the *señorita* will come with us next year, maybe?" Roberto's large brown eyes looked hopeful.

"I don't think so, Roberto. Miss Murray's life is in Chicago, not out here in the West."

"But she like all of us, don't she, *señor*?"

Zach clenched his fingers around his whiskey glass. "Yeah, she likes all of us." He took a gulp of liquor.

"But her newspaper job is back East. And it's real important to her."

"Why she need a job, *señor*?"

"Yeah, why?" Curly echoed. "Women out here don't have jobs."

"Some do," Skip reminded him. "Just not the kind Miss Alex would know about."

The buzz of voices droned on around him, but Zach shut them out and tried to think. Images of Dusty danced around in his brain. Dusty gobbling beans and corn bread along with the other hands. Dusty nibbling on her pencil stub and scratching away in her notebook. Dusty standing hip deep in the river, her hair tumbling down around her shoulders, her skin sheened with water.

Oh, God.

He shoved his drink over to Curly, clapped Roberto on the back and slid off the bar stool.

"'Night, boys. Don't forget, we're loadin' cattle tomorrow morning early."

He swung toward the saloon door and headed up the stairs two at a time. At the door to Dusty's room he hesitated, sucked in a long breath of air and walked in.

Chapter Twenty-Four

Alex was almost asleep when she heard the door of her hotel room open.

"Dusty?"

She sat up in bed. The faint glow from the kerosene lamp on the nightstand illuminated the figure standing with one hand on the doorknob. "Zach?"

"Can I come in?"

"Of course you can come in. I thought you'd never get here!"

He set his hat on the dresser and moved toward her. "I forgot to bring you any lemonade. Or sarsaparilla, either."

"I didn't really expect any. I did expect you, though."

"That's good. I didn't fancy breakin' down your door."

"Would you have, really?" she asked in a hushed tone. "Broken down the door?"

He sat down close to her on the edge of the narrow bed. "Damn right."

She laughed softly. "That is extremely gallant of you, Zach. Like rescuing a princess locked in a tower."

"Desperate, maybe," he murmured. "Not gallant." He

pulled her leather-bound notebook out from under his thigh and looked at her enquiringly.

"I was writing down my notes from tonight," she said. "You know, about playing poker."

"And drinking whiskey," he added with a chuckle.

"I don't think I will ever, ever do that again. Whiskey tastes worse than… It tastes like furniture polish."

"You drink a lot of furniture polish, do you?"

She looked up at him. "Not anymore. I did once when I was growing up, though. Mama cried and carried on for a week."

He slid his forefinger under her chin and tipped her face up to his. "Dusty?"

"Yes, Zach?"

"Stop talking."

He kissed her, moving his warm mouth over hers so slowly and deliberately it made Alex want to weep. When she could breathe again she unbuttoned the top button of his shirt and pressed her lips into the hollow of his throat.

He bent away from her to blow out the guttering lamp on the nightstand, and her notebook slid off the bed onto the floor. He ignored it. Instead, he finished unbuttoning his shirt. In the dark she heard his boots thunk onto the carpet, followed by his leather belt.

My heavens! A man was undressing in her hotel room, and she wasn't the least bit perturbed! *Something has happened to you, Alex. Something wonderful.*

Before she could untie the ribbon on her nightgown, he reached for her. "Least you're not wearin' a corset," he breathed against her mouth. "You know something?" he asked after a long minute, his voice gravelly.

"Tell me." She kissed his closed eyelids.

He expelled a long breath. "I sure as hell don't want you to get on that train tomorrow."

"Oh, Zach," she said, her voice breaking. "You know that I—"

"Marry me, Dusty."

Silence. She moved in his arms but didn't speak.

"Zach. Oh—" Her voice broke, and Zach steeled himself. He knew what she was going to say. He didn't want to hear it.

"I wish…I wish I could marry you, but…"

He gave a low groan. "No, you don't wish you could." He put his hands on her shoulders and drew back slightly. "Let's not tell each other lies, honey. The life you want is back in Chicago writing for your newspaper."

"And your life is raising cattle on a ranch in Oregon."

He let his breath out in a long sigh. "I've wanted a ranch, my own ranch, ever since I was eleven years old, Dusty. I've always wanted it."

"You know what I've always wanted?"

"A heifer named after you?" he joked.

"You'll think it's plain silly, especially since it has nothing to do with writing newspaper articles. But I've always wanted a ruffly apron with two big pockets in front. A pink one."

"Kinda frilly for a newspaper writer, don't you think?"

"Yes, I guess it is. I don't know why I want it, really. I live in a boardinghouse and I don't ever do any cooking. I don't even visit the kitchen."

"Sometimes we just want something. The reasons don't have to make much sense. I guess everyone gets a little crazy now and then."

She pulled him down next to her, and with a groan he stretched his long frame out beside her. She smoothed her fingers over his bare chest. "This bed is...well, it's rather small, isn't it?"

"It's big enough." He began touching her, moving his hands slowly over her thighs, pushing up her nightgown. She closed her eyes at the pleasure of it.

"Take this off," he murmured.

She did, and he kissed her in places that made her moan.

"Zach," she whispered. He lifted his head. "Remember the night you told me about your father?"

"Yeah. Kind of a funny time to bring it up, though."

"Will you tell me why you don't want to see him?"

He released a ragged sigh. "You sure you want to hear this?"

She wrapped her arms around him. "Yes. I want to know."

He tucked her head under his chin and cleared his throat. "Pa kept a rifle over the door of our cabin. One day when I was about nine, I came home and he was yelling and pointing the gun at my mother. I went for the rifle and..."

He pressed his hand against her head, then tangled his fingers in her hair. "When Pa pulled it away from me it went off. The bullet went through my mother's heart."

"Oh, Zach. How awful for you. And that's why you never went back, because of your father—"

"I don't trust him not to kill me, too. He knows I'm the only one who witnessed what he did."

She was silent a long time, moving her hand back and forth over his chest.

"Dusty? Are you sorry I told you?"

"No. Zach, I want to tell you something. I see why you don't ever want your father to know where you are.

I am not going to mention you in any of my newspaper columns. Ever."

His mouth grazed her breast. "Thanks." Then his tongue flicked across her nipple and she forgot everything but the hot, silky way he made her feel inside.

Afterward, when they lay in each other's arms, she drew in a shuddery breath. "Zach?"

"Yeah?"

"What happens tomorrow?"

"You mean before your train pulls out? Well, early in the morning we'll run the cattle up the chute and load them into rail cars. Should take till around noon."

"Could I watch?"

He chuckled. "Thought you'd seen enough steers."

"That's true, I've seen a good number of them."

"Thought you just loved drivin' a thousand head of cattle across the desert and through rivers," he teased, his voice lazy.

"I did not love that part, no. But…"

He lifted his head. "But?"

"But I did love knowing you. Loving you."

He said nothing for so long that Alex thought he hadn't heard her. Finally he nestled her head into his shoulder and again laced his fingers in her hair.

"Dusty, honey?"

"Yes?"

"I think you can love a place like you love a person. You understand what I mean?"

"I do understand, yes."

"Lord knows I've never said this to a woman before, but I'm gonna say it now. I will love you until the day I die, Dusty. You know that, don't you?"

She couldn't speak over the ache in her throat. She

watched his bare chest rise and fall with his breathing and felt as if she were drowning.

"I've always wanted to mean something to some-body," he whispered. "Tomorrow…" He hesitated. "Tomorrow I'm not sure I'll be able to walk away from you."

"Yes, you can, Zach. You have to."

With a choked-off groan he reached for her again.

Chapter Twenty-Five

Before Dusty woke up, Zach pulled on his jeans and a shirt and fished his boots out from under the bed. He locked the door behind him and walked from the hotel down two blocks to the sheriff's office.

The craggy-faced lawman removed his feet from the littered desk and gestured to an empty chair. "Can I do somethin' for you, Mr. Strickland?"

Zach blinked. "How'd you know who I am?"

"Because one Herman Cassidy paid me a visit last night and lodged a complaint. Described you pretty good."

"Complaint about what?"

"Oh, the usual. You know, assault. Said you punched him pretty good. I figure it was mostly humiliation talkin', but with a guy like Cassidy, you never know. Kinda likes to blow things out of proportion."

Zach nodded. "Actually, I came on another matter."

The sheriff grinned. "Figured that, Mr. Strickland. Name's Davidson, by the way."

Zach studied the man behind the desk. "Yeah, it was assault, all right. He threatened one of my...trail crew with a shiny new-lookin' Colt."

"Maybe stolen," Davidson muttered.

"Maybe. Cassidy rode with my trail crew out of Oregon till I fired him."

The sheriff's dark eyes flicked up in surprise. "What'd you fire him for?"

"He accosted someone riding with my outfit."

"The woman, right?"

Zach blinked. "How'd you know that?"

Davidson chuckled. "Word is the prettiest girl within five hundred miles is part of your outfit. Newspaper lady, right?"

"Right. Cassidy made a pass at her on the trail, and he showed up at the Rocky Rooster last night and made a nuisance of himself again. I slugged him and my hands threw him out the saloon door."

"Well, you made a mistake not shooting him," the sheriff said slowly. "Now he's hellin' around town talkin' big about gettin' even. And more."

Zach came to attention. "What 'more'?"

"A lot of palaver about Miss Murray, about how he's goin' back East on the train with her."

Zach went cold all over. "Over my dead body."

"Maybe so, Strickland. He's talkin' real loud about killin' you first."

Zach said nothing for a long minute while the sheriff calmly rolled a cigarette and touched a match to it.

"Listen, Davidson, I came in to see you this morning about something else that might concern Cassidy."

"Yeah?" The sheriff exhaled a puff of blue-gray smoke.

"Some miles back I had a hundred head of Rocking K cattle rustled one night. Another drover on the trail, Orren Gibson, lost about seventy head of his Double Diamond stock. Some days later, my boys and I caught up with three men who were busy doing some re-branding."

"And?"

"We got all our stock back."

"What'd you do with the rustlers?"

"Stripped 'em down to their long johns and ran 'em off."

"You didn't string 'em up? Rustling's a hanging offense in these parts."

"Nope. Didn't want to take the time. I figured I'd report them when we got here to Winnemucca. I think Cassidy might have been part of it."

"Got any proof?"

"Nope. Just a hunch. Thought you'd want to know anyway."

"Interesting." Davidson lifted his legs off the desk and clunked his boots onto the plank floor. "Listen, Strickland, you might want to stick close to Miss Murray."

"She's leaving on the eleven o'clock train this morning." He swallowed. "Going back to Chicago."

"Don't let her."

"What?"

"I wouldn't put it past Cassidy to do what he says, get himself on that train."

Zach jolted to his feet. "Sheriff, could you lock him up?"

"Well, yeah, I could do that. Might take some time to find the man, though. That bein' the case, I think you should have Miss Murray delay her departure by twenty-four hours. Take the train tomorrow morning instead."

A rush of irrational joy coursed through him. *Twenty-four hours. Twenty-four more hours with Dusty!*

He reached to shake Davidson's extended hand. "Thanks, Sheriff."

Sheriff Davidson grinned at him. "I'll find Cassidy and question him. You take care of Miss Murray, you hear?"

"No, Zach. I can't."

"Twenty-four hours, Dusty. It's either that or send a bodyguard with you all the way to Chicago."

"No," she said again. But now her voice sounded more thoughtful. "A bodyguard would have to be one of your hands, am I right?"

"Yeah. Skip, maybe."

"But you need Skip. He's your second in command. You need all your men, Zach."

"If it would keep you safe, I'd do without one."

"Oh, Zach, I can't let you do that. I will wait an extra day and catch the train tomorrow."

Zach let out the breath he'd been holding. "Thanks, Dusty."

"But on one condition," she said softly.

"Name it."

"After breakfast, we spend the rest of the day here."

"You mean here, in your hotel room?"

She nodded, her cheeks turning pink. "In…um…in bed."

Late in the afternoon, a loud, insistent pounding on the hotel room door roused them both from sleep. Zach cracked open one eyelid. "What the—"

"Miss Murray?" a muffled voice shouted. "There's a message for…there's a message from the sheriff."

Zach chuckled. "Guess the sheriff knows where I am.

Hope it doesn't compromise your reputation for him to find me here."

She ran a lazy hand over his bare chest. "What makes you think I would care?"

He squeezed her shoulder, then pressed a kiss on her soft skin, rolled out of bed and pulled on his jeans. To stop the insistent banging he padded barefoot across the room to the door and unbolted the lock.

The young hotel assistant, his face scarlet, thrust a folded sheet of paper into his outstretched hand and fled back down the stairs.

Zach unfolded the paper and had to laugh. The message from Sheriff Davidson was short and to the point, consisting of just two words: *Got him.*

"Dusty?"

He turned toward the bed, where Dusty was now sitting up, the sheet clutched to her chin, her eyes wide. "What is it?" she whispered.

"Dusty, let's go for a walk."

"What?"

"You heard me. Cassidy's in jail, and I want to walk down by the river with you. There's some things I want to say."

She put on a pair of jeans and a shirt, brushed her hair and wound it into a bun at the base of her neck and pulled on her boots.

Outside, they passed the livery stables, where Cherry had housed the remuda, and when the stores and houses petered out at the edge of town they skirted the slow-moving river until they came to a little-used path. Half a mile farther it led to a footbridge. The pretty stream that flowed underneath fed into the river somewhere beyond, where it curved out of sight.

Zach guided her to the center of the tree-shrouded bridge. "Look down there," he said. "Can't see around the bend, can you?"

"No," she said.

"I figure that's kinda like you and me. We know what's here today. But we don't know what's around the bend."

"I do know what's around the bend, Zach. Tomorrow I will climb on a train and I'll never see—" Her voice broke off.

"I don't believe that, Dusty. I can't."

"I wish things could stay the same," she breathed. "Why can't this beautiful, precious thing go on forever?"

"You know why, honey. It will always be beautiful and precious. It just can't go on. Nothing stays the same, Dusty. Nothing."

She brushed tears out of her eyes. "I feel like I'm walking off a cliff. The future feels like a big blank wall."

"Well, Dusty, it isn't a blank wall. You'll write articles for your newspaper and I'll buy some land and start my ranch. Neither of those things is a blank wall."

"Oh, Zach," she sobbed. "I'm not strong enough for this."

He put his arms around her. "Dusty, right about now there's just one thing we can do. We're workin' so hard to forget this painful thing, you gettin' on that train, that we're forgetting the good thing. And that's you and me."

"But…" She struggled to get the words out. "But things are never going to be the same. *Never.*"

"Yeah, you're right, honey. Things are never gonna be the same again. But you know what?" He wiped his thumbs across the tear trails on her cheeks.

"W-what?"

"You and I won't ever be the same, either. We've changed each other."

He placed his forefinger under her chin, tipped her face up to his and kissed her, long and deep. He could feel her body trembling, and it just about undid him. He had to hold it together until she climbed on that train, and then…

Oh, hell. Then he would climb on a horse and shut his eyes and let the animal carry him wherever it wanted.

Chapter Twenty-Six

At ten the next morning, Alex rolled over to find Zach gone. She bolted out of bed, dressed hastily in the green bombazine travel suit and black leather shoes she'd purchased her first day in town, and grabbed her tapestry travel bag. Then she sprinted all the way to the train station.

The cattle had already been loaded, so she was surprised to see the cowhands milling around the railroad platform. Juan stepped forward and grasped her travel bag.

"What are you all doing here?" she asked. "Why aren't you heading back to Smoke River?"

Zach's deep voice rolled over her. "The hands wanted to wait and say goodbye to you, Dusty."

"Oh." *Oh.* Tears stung under her lids.

He took her aside and bent to speak near her ear. "Cassidy's still in jail," he said quietly. "Sheriff got a wire this morning that linked him to the cattle rustlers. Your hunch was correct. I didn't want you to be uneasy about it."

Uneasy! Uneasy was getting on the train and leaving him!

She could scarcely breathe. She blinked hard and turned away.

The cattle cars, full of bellowing steers, rolled out of the station to make way for the passenger train behind it. Another engine chuffed to a stop and stood puffing clouds of steam into the cloudless blue sky while a uniformed conductor clanked down an iron step. Juan swung her travel bag up onto the train.

Zach's hand touched her back. "Look over there," he intoned.

The entire crew was lined up, waiting on the platform, Curly, Skip, José…all of them, even Cherry. Her heart swelled.

She went down the line and kissed every single one of their bristly cheeks. Cherry's eyes got all red and wet-looking, and he reached out and patted her head, then turned away and blew his nose. She came to Roberto last. His somber brown eyes looked deep into her own, and she brushed her lips over first one cheek and then the other. "Roberto…" Her tears spilled over.

He took both her hands in his. "Señorita Alex." The old man swallowed hard. "No more cows, eh?"

"No more cows. Roberto, I will never forget you." She kissed him one last time.

"Vaya con Dios," the cook murmured.

Zach walked her away from the gathered cowhands, turned her to face him and laid both hands on her shoulders. "It's real hard to say it, Dusty." His eyes looked shiny.

"I— Oh, Zach." She mopped at her tears with the handkerchief he pressed into her palm, but they kept coming anyway.

"Zach, I want you to know something, and I want you to remember it always."

He looked startled for a moment. "Yeah? What's that?"

"You're much more than a trail boss, Zach. Much more."

He looked down into her eyes without smiling. "And you're much more than a newspaper reporter. You ever think of that?"

He pulled her into his arms and she felt his mouth on hers for the last time. Every bone in her body wanted to turn away from the train, climb on a horse and ride back to Smoke River with him.

"Come on," he said at last. "You're gonna miss your train." He picked her up and set her feet on the iron step, then gave her a little push. She looked down at him through a blur of tears, and he swept off his hat.

For the rest of her life, she thought raggedly, she would always remember that battered gray Stetson.

The engine tooted twice. The railcars gave a clang and a jolt and started to slide on down the track. Zach stood motionless, his hat in his hand, and she held on to the steel pole and leaned out, watching until she could no longer see him.

Then she made her way inside the passenger car, found an empty seat and had a good cry.

Chapter Twenty-Seven

Several months passed, the longest, slowest months Zach could ever remember. With his share of the profits from the cattle drive he bought land adjoining Charlie Kingman's spread and good starter stock, and built a sturdy barn, a bunkhouse and three corrals. He also started digging the foundation for the ranch house. He wanted it built of stone, with a big fireplace in every bedroom. He guessed he kept imagining Dusty getting up in the morning and putting her bare toes on a cold floor and...

Oh, hell and damn. He tossed the last pitchfork of dry grass into the horse feed bin and stood studying the four prize animals he'd acquired. He'd done well, he acknowledged. He was working his butt off building this place, and his new spread was slowly taking shape.

But if he was honest with himself, he was split right down the middle. Half of him loved his new ranch. Half of him felt his life was over.

He gazed around at the corrals he'd constructed of peeled pine poles and then lifted his gaze to the grassy meadow beyond, still green even though it was almost

November. He had everything he'd ever wanted, his own ranch, plenty of water, good stock, four hundred acres of good grass and a capable crew of ranch hands headed by Juan Tapia, the top hand he'd wooed away from Charlie Kingman.

But he didn't have Dusty. He'd never have Dusty. He gritted his teeth, turned his back on the ranch house foundation he'd been digging and bowed his head over the spade. Dammit, why did it matter so much?

He knew why. He loved her. He loved every freckle on her nose, the way she laughed when she was trying not to, every inch of her skin and her soft, responsive body. The ache in his heart was like a hunger that never went away.

The first Saturday in November he rode into Smoke River and paid a visit to the dressmaker, Verena Forester. Kind of a funny thing to do, he guessed. And it sure raised Verena's thin eyebrows. But he'd been thinking about it every day since the cattle drive.

On Sunday, Alice and Charlie Kingman expected him for dinner, as they had every Sunday since he'd bought his own place. He looked forward to it, not only for the ranch news and Consuelo's cooking, but because the cowhands always brought copies of Dusty's latest *Chicago Times* newspaper columns to the dinner table, and they insisted on reading every one of them out loud.

Today was no different. Curly could hardly wait to brag about being featured in last week's write-up.

"Lissen to this, fellas," he announced. "'One of the most intrepid of cowboys on the cattle drive was the point rider, Curly Garner.' That's me!" he crowed. "Uh... what's 'intrepid' mean?"

"Brave," Alice supplied. "Courageous. Unstoppable."

"Yeah?" Curly puffed out his clean Sunday shirt.

"Read what she says about Roberto," Alice said with a smile.

"Ay," Consuelo remarked from behind a huge platter of fried chicken. "My brother, he gets the big head."

Roberto grinned but said nothing.

"Well, let's hear what she says about Roberto," Zach prompted.

"'On the cattle drive, the chuck wagon cook, Roberto Sandoval, created delicious meals and made the most succulent pies and fruit cobblers from the bounty he gathered along the way. Such a man is a rare find for any cattle crew.'"

A blushing Roberto ducked his head, then shot a sly look at Charlie. "Good for raise, eh, *señor*?" Charlie just grinned.

"Hey, Zach," Curly called. "How come Miss Alex never says anything in her newspaper about you?"

"Yeah," the hands around the dining table clamored. "How come?"

"Guess she didn't like me as much as you fellas," Zach said.

Oh, God, he missed her. No one would ever know how empty his life felt without Dusty. Even with the ranch he'd hankered after all his life, he still wanted… He couldn't stand to think about it.

He shook his thoughts and his longing back into his brain and turned his attention to Consuelo's cherry pie.

Chapter Twenty-Eight

Alex stared at the icy sidewalk ahead of her, concentrating on avoiding the slippery patches. Icy-cold flakes swirled over the streets, the lawns and front porches, even into her hair in spite of her knitted red wool fascinator. If it didn't stop snowing soon, she could build an igloo right in front of the *Chicago Times* office.

She plowed on down the sidewalk, fighting off an ever-present longing for the hot, dry desert of Oregon.

She missed it. Despite everything she'd endured during the cattle drive, the dust and the thirst and the blinding glare of the sun, she still missed it. Never in a million years did she think she ever would, but she did.

Her heart double thudded. Deep down, she knew it wasn't the cattle drive she missed so much. It was the man she had ridden with over the long, arduous miles to Winnemucca. The man who had left her at the railway station with her heart in his pocket. Zachariah Strickland.

She gingerly planted her black leather high-button shoes on the slippery stone stairway of the *Chicago Times* building and marched up the seven steps to the entrance. In the foyer she brushed the snow off her heavy gray coat and shook out her damp fascinator.

Her editor, Nigel Greene, his thick white hair standing on end as if he never combed it, greeted her with his ever-present grin. "Good morning, Alexandra. Do you have another column ready for me today?"

"Good morning, Nigel. Yes, I'm just going to finish it now. Could you wait five minutes? I have a stack of unfinished pages waiting on my desk."

The older man nodded. "I guess I'll have to, Alex. One of your stories is worth waiting for, I assure you. Our circulation is way up."

She hung her wool coat on the carved oak rack in the hallway and headed through the glass door to her desk. It had been freshly polished, she noted, sniffing the air. Apparently the errand boy was still nursing a crush on her. He was only twelve years old, but ever since she had returned from Nevada, Tommy was the only male she could stand to smile at. Except for Nigel, of course. But of course she had to be nice to her editor.

But smiling at Tommy, or even Nigel, wasn't the same as smiling into the fern-colored green eyes of Zachariah Strickland. *Nothing* was like smiling at Zachariah Strickland. Or looking at him. Or talking with him. Or... She sighed. Doing other things with him.

She sank down onto her oak desk chair, surveyed the pile of notebooks and proof pages that faced her and gave herself a good shake. *Concentrate. You have a newspaper column to write.*

She unfolded the proof page with her feature story, the ink scarcely dry, and scanned yesterday's column. In it she had described how the herd of a thousand steers had splashed into a wide river and swum across to the other side.

She closed her eyes and envisioned it all again, the muddy bank, the lazy blue-green river, the whoops and shouts of the mounted cowhands. She remembered every detail as clearly as if it had happened yesterday. The afternoon sun had been scorching, and the smell of grass and willow trees had been sharp in her nostrils. She could still hear a thousand cicadas rasping their song in the hot air.

She would always remember the worried looks Zach had sent her after that first river crossing, when she'd been swept off her horse and had nearly drowned. If not for him and the lasso he'd dropped over her shoulders, she probably *would* have drowned.

She remembered that worried look he sometimes got, his fine mouth pressed into a tense line and his eyes shadowed under his battered gray Stetson.

A knife blade sliced into her chest. She couldn't forget hearing him shout. Or laugh. Or… Well, she just couldn't forget him.

There's no two ways about it, Alex, you miss him.

"'Scuse me, Miss Murray?"

The office boy, Tommy, stood in front of her desk, his face as red as his hair. "I brought you a package," he puffed. "From the mail room. Just arrived by special messenger, an' I thought it might be important, bein' as it's Christmas an' everything."

Christmas! Was it Christmas already? She'd been so busy at the newspaper she had barely noticed. Only at night, in her chaste bedroom at Mrs. Beekin's boarding-house, when she lay awake hour after hour thinking of

Zach, was she aware of the slow turning of the seasons from summer to fall and now to winter.

Last night she had jerked awake in the wee hours of the morning, asking herself question after question. *Is this what I really want? Am I wasting my life?*

"You gonna open it, huh?" Tommy danced from one scuffed shoe to the other and then hung over her shoulder. "It's from some funny-sounding place in Oregon."

Her heart skipped a beat. "Of course I'm going to open it." She stood up, grabbed her scissors and snipped the heavy twine. Tommy helped her peel back the brown wrapping paper and expose the cardboard box underneath.

"What is it, miss?"

Alex slowly unwrapped the package and stared dumbfounded at the contents. Nestled in layers of tissue paper lay a pink gingham apron with a deep ruffle around the edge and two big pockets in front.

"Aw, gosh, miss, how come you're cryin'? Don't you like it?"

Alex blinked rapidly. "I—I'm not crying, Tommy. I'm just…surprised."

"How come? It's kinda pretty, even if it is pink."

"I think it's beautiful," she said in an uneven voice. "It's the most beautiful present I've ever received." Impulsively she snatched the apron up and buried her face in the folds.

Something clunked against her knuckles. She fished in one of the pockets, withdrew a hinged daguerreotype case and unfolded it with fingers that trembled.

Oh, my. Cradled in her palm was the photograph of Zach and herself taken at Henslee's Photography Studio that night in Winnemucca. She studied the sepia image through a wash of tears. Zach was sitting straight and unsmiling and she was standing at his side, one hand resting on his shoulder.

"Oh," she cried. *"Oh."* Her heart was cracking in two.

"Golly, Miss Murray, don't cry! It's a really nice picture."

"Y-yes, it is," she sniffed. "It makes me very…h-happy."

That afternoon she left the *Chicago Times* office early and walked slowly back to the boardinghouse, her mood unusually pensive. She had to admit she loved her career as a newspaper reporter. She had worked diligently for years to get where she was; it was hard work, but learning the many complicated aspects of newspaper publishing was exciting. She knew she was good at what she did. "Exceptional," Nigel often said.

She was an accomplished journalist, and she felt valued. Working at the *Times* was fulfilling, and yet…

And yet, at times another part of her felt a tug of something she was missing. Sometimes she wondered if some part of her was being bypassed. She called it her "pink apron" feeling. A part of her, deep down, felt an odd, nagging hunger.

But, as Nigel assured her, she had the world on a string. She had everything she needed for a fulfilling life.

Didn't she?

On Friday Alex again left the office early and dragged herself up the steps to the porch of Mrs. Beekin's Walnut Avenue boardinghouse. When she walked in, her landlady looked up from the sewing machine she'd set up on the dining table.

"Why, you're home early, Miss Murray. Got another one of your headaches?"

Alex shook her head. "No, Mrs. Beekin, I'm fine. Just…tired, I guess. I'm feeling a bit blue now that winter is here with all this snow."

"How about I make you a nice cup of tea?"

"Oh, thank you, Mrs. Beekin."

"And a slice of my apple cake. You're lookin' a bit peaky lately, if you don't mind me sayin' so. And mighty thin."

Alex nodded. She did, in fact, feel peaky. She felt completely flat inside. *And that is really puzzling, considering my success at the newspaper.*

The boardinghouse owner set a cup of tea at her elbow, followed by a delicate china plate on which rested a thick slice of apple cake. "Now, you just eat some of this, dearie. Put some meat on your bones."

Alex reached for the fork, stared at it a moment and then set it down. "Forgive me, Mrs. Beekin. I guess I'm not very hungry."

The plump woman sank onto the chair next to her. "Didn't eat much of your breakfast, either. Fact is, ever since you got back from that trip you took out to Oregon, you haven't eaten enough to keep a sparrow alive."

Alex hadn't the energy to protest. She admitted she'd paid little attention to her eating habits since the cattle drive; she'd been too busy writing up her experiences to stop for lunch during the day, and she even refused young Tommy's offers to bring her a sandwich from the restaurant next to the *Times* building.

Instead, she spent the long hours at her desk. She did miss Roberto's chili and corn bread and his apple pies, she admitted. No doubt it was all that fresh air that piqued one's appetite.

Mrs. Beekin reached out and smoothed her veined hand over Alex's. "Are things with your Mr. Greene at the newspaper office not going well?"

"Oh, no. Nigel is wonderfully supportive. He's even encouraging me to write longer articles. He says our circulation is increasing and his banker is very pleased."

Her landlady smiled. "I read your newspaper every single morning, you know. I think those articles you write are mighty fine, Miss Murray. Maybe you're working too hard?"

Alex sipped her tea and considered that. "Oh, I don't think so, Mrs. Beekin. The time I spend at my desk just flies by, and I do enjoy it."

Mrs. Beekin nodded, but she didn't say anything.

"True, I am putting in long hours," Alex added, "but I truly love what I'm doing. I love the extra hours I spend proofreading all the typeset galleys and writing and rewriting my stories. I'm striving to be a really good reporter."

The boardinghouse owner gave her a long, thoughtful look. "I see. Well, you're certainly building a fine reputation."

"Yes," Alex agreed. But her voice seemed to lack enthusiasm, and she did wonder at that.

Chapter Twenty-Nine

Sunday afternoon rolled around again, and as usual, Zach and Juan rode over to the Rocking K for dinner. Alice looked particularly pleased to see him, and for some reason Charlie wasn't as short-spoken as usual. Even Curly seemed in good spirits. Guess the cocky cowhand had swallowed his upset when Zach had hired Juan instead of Curly as his top hand. Hiring Juan had made Consuelo so proud she had baked her special cherry pie for Zach every single Sunday since he'd returned from the drive and started his ranch.

Today the hands were gathered around Alice's dining table, exclaiming as usual over Dusty's latest *Chicago Times* article. The newspaper was delivered to the Rocking K regular as clockwork, and Zach knew the hands clipped every one of her columns and pinned them up on the bunkhouse wall.

"Lissen to this, Zach," Jase exclaimed, punching his forefinger at the typeset page. "'The cowboys of the Rocking K are gentlemen of the highest order.'"

"Whooee," Curly exploded. "Ya hear that? The 'highest order.'"

"Well, of course," Alice said with a smile. "Everyone knows that."

Consuelo entered with a huge platter of roast beef, then dashed back to the kitchen for a bowl of steaming baked potatoes. On her return, Curly reached for one and she rapped the serving spoon against his knuckles.

"You behave!" the cook snapped. "First give thanks to God, then eat."

The men dutifully bowed their heads, and Charlie intoned an unusually long-winded blessing, ending with "And God bless even Zach and his damned Z-Bar-S steers."

Zach laughed. "How come they're my 'damned' steers, Charlie? I paid good money for every last one of them."

Charlie focused watery blue eyes on him. "How come? I'll tell you how come, Zach," the ranch owner growled. "'Cuz come next spring you're gonna drive yer own steers to Winnemucca and undercut my price."

"Not if you get there first," Zach replied. "Besides, I'll only have about three hundred head." He nodded for Consuelo to fill his coffee cup.

Skip suddenly slapped the newspaper he'd been reading onto the table. "Hell, she can't do that!"

Charlie sent him a sharp look. "Who can't do what?"

"Miss Alex. Says here she's takin' something called a leave of absence. Her column won't be printed for the next four weeks. What're we gonna do with nuthin' to read for four whole weeks?"

Consuelo sniffed. "You read the Bible, maybe. Many good stories and much wisdom."

"Not as good as Miss Alex's columns," Skip said

with a groan. He shoved his cup toward the coffeepot the cook lifted toward him.

"They can't do that," Curly blurted out. "I'm gonna write a letter to that newspaper."

Skip snorted. "Didn't know you could string that many words together, Curly."

Zach set his coffee down without tasting it. Leave of absence? After all that interviewing and note-taking Dusty did on the drive? Why would she stop writing her columns? Was she tired? Sick?

Across the dining table he met Roberto's puzzled brown eyes. The older man lifted his shoulders in an I-don't-know shrug.

"Jupiter, we been readin' her columns every week," Curly complained. "She can't just stop writin' them. She hasn't gotten to the part where we captured them cattle rustlers yet."

Jase ran his hand over his just-shaved chin. "And remember that night we danced the Virginia Reel at the Double Diamond camp?"

"Or when we taught Señorita Alex to play poker," Juan reminded them.

Alice started. "Poker! Surely not."

"*Ay, señora*, she did play poker. We teach her, and Miss Alex, she won three hundred dollars!"

"How about her drinkin' that whiskey?" Curly added.

Alice's fork clattered onto her plate. "Whiskey!"

"Just a leetle glass of whiskey," José explained. "She no like it very much."

"Well!" Alice huffed. "That is a mercy I'm sure. I am shocked. Shocked! Zach, how could you let my niece be corrupted in this manner?"

Zach bit his lip so hard he tasted blood. He'd done

much more than play cards and drink whiskey with Dusty. Much more. His gut tightened into a knot.

"And the stampede we have one night," Roberto added. "Señorita Alex, she did not cry or nothing. She very brave lady."

"And what about all those suppers of corn bread and beans and rolling out of our bedrolls in the dark for breakfast?" Jase shot. "She hasn't written about any of that yet."

Skip grinned at the hands clustered around the dining table. "And remember when Zach and me tossed Cassidy out of the Rocky Rooster saloon, right on his—"

"Señor Skip," Consuelo warned.

"...uh, his fancy trousers."

The men continued to trade reminiscences back and forth, but Zach tuned them out. Those things weren't what he remembered most. What he remembered was watching Dusty bravely volunteer to ride drag and choking on all that dust. Scribbling in her notebook half the night. And lying next to her under the chuck wagon, listening to her soft breathing. Sure as shootin' he'd better not mention any of that to Alice!

And, God, he'd never forget other things, like seeing her with her hair down and wearing that silky yellow dress at the hotel in Winnemucca and smiling at him across the restaurant table. And later that night...

He clenched his fist under the table. He missed Dusty with every breath he drew.

Consuelo hovered at his elbow. "You like big slice of peach pie, Señor Zach?"

"No, thanks, Consuelo."

She eyed him and frowned. "But is your favorite!"

He shook his head.

"But, *señor*, I make special and…why you not want any? Is not like you."

He was afraid to answer for fear his voice would be unsteady.

At the opposite end of the table Alice cleared her throat. She was looking at him kinda funny and was trying not to smile.

"Zach, since you're not having any of Consuelo's peach pie, perhaps you would step into the kitchen and fetch me a…a clean fork? I seem to have dropped mine."

Glad to escape all the comments about Dusty, Zach shoved his chair back and headed for the kitchen. He went straight to the silverware drawer, scrabbled around inside for a clean fork and closed his fingers around one. He had just turned back toward the dining room when he heard a voice.

"Take two forks, Zach. I want some peach pie, too."

He spun toward the speaker. "Dusty!"

He stared at her, unable to move. She was wearing the pink apron with all those ruffles, the one he'd ordered from Verena Forester weeks ago and mailed to Chicago.

He must be dreaming.

"Dusty, what are you— Where'd you come from?"

"From the train station, of course. That nice Sheriff Rivera drove me out to the ranch this morning."

Zach dropped the fork and closed the distance between them.

"Dusty. Dusty, I—"

"Zach, hush. Just kiss me."

Tears sparkled on her cheeks. His lips found hers and he felt his insides jolt at the sweet taste of her mouth. He was so hungry for her he was shaking, and as he kissed her she began to tremble, as well.

"Oh, honey—"

"Don't talk, Zach. Just keep kissing me."

"Gladly," he murmured against her lips. His brain began to spin, and all at once he wanted to take her to bed. "Dusty," he whispered. "Are you really here, or am I dreaming?"

She gave a soft laugh. "This is no dream," she said quietly. "I'm here and this is real and I want you to keep kissing me."

With pleasure, he thought. *With very great pleasure*.

After a long few minutes, Alex stepped out of Zach's arms and walked into the dining room. Instantly the ranch hands fell silent, and then they all started talking at once, asking questions and then more questions.

Roberto rose, his eyes shiny, and kissed her cheek. She was so close to tears she couldn't even smile at him.

Zach guided her to a chair. It had been his seat, she deduced from the untouched cup of coffee and the uneaten slice of pie on his plate. She didn't want to sit down. She wanted to grab Zach's hand and pull him out to the front porch so he could kiss her some more.

He spilled Curly out of the chair next to hers and settled himself beside her while she nibbled on his peach pie and tried to answer all the questions the men fired at her.

"How come you're here, Miss Alex?"

"You get fired or somethin'?"

"Miss Alex, you sure write good columns. I saved every one of 'em."

"What's a leave of absence, anyway?"

"You miss all them beans 'n' bacon, huh, Miss Alex?"

"You played any more hands of poker lately?" This from Curly.

Consuelo alternately beamed and poured more coffee.

"We keep good secret, no, *señorita*?" she whispered. "I tell not even my José."

Alex reached to squeeze the woman's work-worn hand.

The questions went on and on until they were replaced by tales about their adventures since the cattle drive. She loved that they wanted to tell her everything, about all the horses they'd broken and the miles of fence they'd repaired and the new line shack they'd built on Vinegar Butte, and on and on.

But as much as she enjoyed it, she thought the afternoon would never end.

"You gonna be here for supper, Miss Alex?" Curly asked. "Maybe we could talk some more." He glanced inquiringly at Aunt Alice.

"Sorry," Zach said. "She's comin' out to my ranch for supper. You can see her tomorrow."

That announcement met with groans, but Alex was already impatient to see his new ranch. *Oh, be honest, Alex. All you really want to do is be alone with Zach.* The men could groan all they wanted.

She grabbed his hand, and together they walked out to the front porch. Four horses were tied up at the hitching rail in front.

"Could we ride double?" she asked.

He didn't answer, just untied his bay mare, pulled himself into the saddle and held out his hand. She thought she saw Aunt Alice walk out onto the porch and hide a smile.

He held Alex on his lap all the way over to his ranch. She refused to take off her pink apron, so she hiked up her skirts and didn't care a whit that her petticoats showed.

Zach proudly showed her the barn, the bunkhouse, the corrals and the half-dug foundation for his ranch house, talking nonstop about his plans for stone fireplaces and his herd of cattle and kitchen stoves and indoor sinks.

She was impressed, so pleased for what he had accomplished. "This is everything you wanted, isn't it, Zach?"

He took his time answering. "Yeah, in a way," he said at last. "It's good land and I've got good stock. There's no money owing on it. It's just…"

She waited.

"Dusty, what in hell are you doing out here?"

"Well," she said slowly, "I…came to visit Aunt Alice and Uncle Charlie."

His eyes clouded, but he said nothing.

"And," she continued, "I wanted to show off my beautiful pink apron."

"You like it, do you?"

She nodded. "It's the most wonderful gift I have ever received." Her throat was so tight she had to stop talking.

In the silence he came over, stood in front of her and waited.

"I came for all sorts of reasons, Zach. But mostly, I came to see you."

He drew in a long breath. "Why? Dusty, it won't be any easier to say goodbye now than it was last summer."

"Yes, I know."

He gave her a long look. "Every Sunday the hands read all your newspaper articles out loud at the dinner table. It got so I could hardly stand it."

"I worked hard on those articles, too. I wanted you to like them, Zach. You more than anybody."

"All the hands are plenty upset that you won't be writing any more columns for a while."

"And what about you? Will you miss them?"

He sent her a sharp look. "What's a leave of absence, anyway?"

"Oh, that. Well, it's some time my editor, Nigel Greene, is allowing me to…" Her voice trailed off.

"Allowing you to what? I thought you liked working for your newspaper."

"I do like it. It's exciting and demanding, and Nigel says I am very good at it. He says I am building a fine career in a time-honored profession."

"No surprise there, Dusty. I'm proud of you. If that's what makes you happy, I'm—"

"And then you sent that apron, all pink and ruffly, and…" She swallowed. "I just wanted to be sure there wasn't something else…"

He studied her face as if he'd never seen her before. "Something else like what?" he asked, at last.

"Well, like… Oh, Zach, it's so hard to put it into words."

"Try," he said, his voice dry.

"Um, I needed time to think."

"Think," he echoed, his tone suspicious. "Think about what?"

She took a deep breath. "About who I was. And who I was becoming."

"Yeah? Go on."

"Well, ever since last summer and the cattle drive… and you," she added, "I started to see things differently. I'll always love writing for the newspaper. That will never change."

"I figured that, Dusty. You don't have to explain."

She gave a soft laugh. "Well, I have to admit it's really kind of amusing. I, who have the world on a string, as Nigel puts it, find that I have to ask myself some hard questions." She stopped and swallowed.

Zach frowned. "What kind of questions?"

There was a long pause while she worked up her courage. "The first question was why this pink apron…" she ran one hand over the crisp gingham garment tied around her waist "…touched me so deeply. It meant a lot to me, Zach. And it made me so happy that I had to ask myself why."

He just looked at her with a question in his green eyes. "Okay, I'll bite. Why *did* it make you happy?"

"Because you sent it, and because it touched a part of me I was trying to pay no attention to. And that brings up the second question."

"What's the second question, Dusty? Don't think I can stand here and listen to you much longer without wanting to… Oh, hell, I'm gonna do it anyway." He bent and scooped her up into his arms and held her against his chest. "Never did like long philosophical explanations, so just spit it out."

She tightened her arms around his neck and he pressed her head into the curve of his shoulder. There was no escaping it now; she had to say it.

"The second question was, well, what did I want for the rest of my life? Did I want a career as a newspaper reporter more than I wanted a life that included a…a pink apron?"

He said nothing for a long minute, just held her. Then he started walking toward his unfinished ranch house. "You could wear that pink apron in Chicago, Dusty.

That's why I sent it. You said it was something you'd always wanted."

"Yes." She sighed, tipping her head back to look into his eyes. "But it made me ask the second question. What do I really want for the rest of my life?"

"And? Make it short and simple, Dusty. Like I said, I don't like long phil—"

"I'm not sure I can explain it short and simple."

"Try," he said.

She closed her eyes and took a deep breath. "Well, I decided there might be more to life than writing for the *Chicago Times*. There might be something that I would sorely miss when I am an old lady and I'm looking back on my life."

He stopped walking. "Like?"

"Well, like…maybe helping you, um, build your ranch house?"

"What?"

"I said—"

"Dammit, I heard what you said. I just don't know what you mean." He frowned. "You mean you might stay out here in Oregon?"

"Maybe."

His frown deepened. "On…on my ranch?"

"Well, yes, maybe."

"With me? Dusty, are you saying… Dammit, are you saying you'd be willing to… ?"

"Yes, Zach. That is exactly what I'm saying."

"Hell's bells, now I know for sure that I'm dreaming, honey, but for God's sake, don't wake me up. You mean you'd actually come out to Smoke River and…and…" He took in a gulp of air. "Marry me?"

She laughed with delight. "My stars, Zach, I thought you'd never ask!"

He said something else then, but she paid no attention because he spoke the words against her mouth. Then he set her on her feet, took her hand in his, and guided her over to his unfinished house. He poked his forefinger at the space he'd left for a front window.

"Big kitchen?" he asked.

She kissed him.

He pointed again. "Big bedroom?"

She kissed him again.

"Three bedrooms? Four?"

She kissed him four times, once for each bedroom.

And then he lifted her into his arms, ruffly pink apron and all, and carried her out to the hayloft.

Epilogue

After three days of feverish planning by Alice King-man, frantic hours of sewing and fitting by dressmaker Verena Forester, and long hours spent in the Rocking K kitchen by Consuelo and her brother Roberto, on a beautiful crisp January day, eight ranch hands, four on each side, escorted a smiling Dusty Murray, swathed in yards and yards of ruffled pink challis, down the aisle of the Smoke River community church and handed her into the care of Zachariah Strickland, owner of the Z-Bar-S ranch.

After vows and rings and kisses were exchanged, the eight men gathered in the bright sunlight outside the church and formed an arch of crossed rifles—not loaded, of course—under which Zachariah and Dusty walked to start their new life.

The very first wedding gift was a telegram from *Chicago Times* owner Nigel Greene.

Readers clamoring Stop Please send future columns from Oregon Stop Congratulations Stop

When the wedding guests were all gathered in the Rocking K front parlor, José produced his guitar and sang a song dedicated to Zach and Dusty. The words brought tears to their eyes.

I will lay me down to bleed awhile,
then I will rise and fight for you.

Later, while Alice Kingman and Consuelo sniffled into their handkerchiefs and Charlie Kingman poured double shots of aged whiskey for the guests, Zach and Dusty cut slices of a four-tier wedding cake and toasted each other and everyone else who was assembled in the Rocking K ranch house. Then they climbed into a buggy festooned with strings of popcorn and cranberries and drove off to no one knew where and stayed for an entire week.

Alex continued to write newspaper articles about life on the Western frontier, which she sent by telegraph to Nigel Greene at the *Chicago Times* office.

And in the spring of that year, Alice and Consuelo began to knit tiny garments in shades of pink and blue, and all summer long the ranch hands made bets. As it turned out, *both* colors were needed.

Twins Mariana and Roberto Strickland grew up to be the most unusual and best-respected ranchers in the state of Oregon. Outside of their father and mother, of course.

But that is another story.

* * * * *

If you enjoyed this story, you won't want to miss these other great Western tales from Lynna Banning:

Marianne's Marriage of Convenience
The Hired Man
Baby on the Oregon Trail
Her Sheriff Bodyguard

Read on for a sneak peek at
The Highlander's Dangerous Temptation
by Terri Brisbin.

"Athdar?" Isobel said, caressing his face. When had she touched him? When had she risen from her chair and approached him? "Are you ill?" She crouched down closer before him and stroked his forehead and cheek with the back of her hand. "No fever."

"I am well," he said, though he was trying to convince himself of it more than her. "What happened?" He swallowed, but his mouth and throat were parched. She noticed and held out a cup to him.

"You were telling me of your confrontation with my father and then something happened. You looked as if in pain and then ill. Now?" she asked, taking the cup from him and kneeling next to him.

Strange. He had been thinking about the true humiliation of learning the unintended consequences that Jocelyn suffered, when some other memories or feelings surged forward. Now they were gone and he felt fine.

"'Tis a painful thing—exposing a man's youthful stupidity to a beautiful woman who is the daughter of the man who exposed it in the first place. You now know my sordid past with your father, Isobel."

HHEXP46767

Her hand still caressed his face and, with her kneeling at his side, it would be easy, oh so easy, to lean down and kiss the lips that tempted him so much. When she lifted her head and her mouth opened slightly, he did what he wanted to do.

Her lips were soft and warm against his and he could feel her heated breath against him before he touched her mouth with his. Athdar did not touch her, but she did not let go of his face, stroking it as he deepened the kiss by sliding his tongue along her lips until she opened to him… For him.

God, but she was sweet.

He knew not when it happened, but his hand slid up and he tangled his fingers in her hair. Then he cupped her head and held her against his mouth. His tongue felt the heat deep in her mouth, and he tilted his head, tasting her and kissing her. For a moment, he drew back, but she looked at him with such wonderment in her eyes that he kissed her again and again and again.

Don't miss
The Highlander's Dangerous Temptation
by Terri Brisbin, available now.

www.Harlequin.com

Looking for more satisfying love stories
with community and family at their core?

Check out **Harlequin® Special Edition**
and **Love Inspired®** books!

New books available every month!

CONNECT WITH US AT:

Facebook.com/groups/HarlequinConnection

 Facebook.com/HarlequinBooks

Twitter.com/HarlequinBooks

Instagram.com/HarlequinBooks

Pinterest.com/HarlequinBooks

ReaderService.com

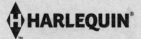

**ROMANCE WHEN
YOU NEED IT**

HFGENRE2018

Love Harlequin romance?

DISCOVER.

Be the first to find out about promotions, news and exclusive content!

 Facebook.com/HarlequinBooks

Twitter.com/HarlequinBooks

 Instagram.com/HarlequinBooks

Pinterest.com/HarlequinBooks

ReaderService.com

EXPLORE.

Sign up for the Harlequin e-newsletter and download a free book from any series at **TryHarlequin.com.**

CONNECT.

Join our Harlequin community to share your thoughts and connect with other romance readers!
Facebook.com/groups/HarlequinConnection

Reward the book lover in you!

Earn points on your purchase of new Harlequin books from participating retailers.

Turn your points into **FREE BOOKS** of your choice!

Join for FREE today at
www.HarlequinMyRewards.com.

Harlequin My Rewards is a free program (no fees) without any commitments or obligations.